Praise for Leslie O'Kane
and her Molly Masters mysteries

"Endearing characters, touching family and friend relationships, and a feisty heroine."
—DIANE MOTT DAVIDSON

"O'Kane delivers a satisfying whodunit."
—*San Francisco Chronicle*

"Molly Masters is a sleuth with an irrepressible sense of humor and a deft artist's pen."
—CAROLYN G. HART

"Molly is a realistic heroine you'll feel you've known for years."
—*Romantic Times*

By Leslie O'Kane

DEATH AND FAXES
JUST THE FAX, MA'AM
THE COLD HARD FAX*
THE FAX OF LIFE*
WHEN THE FAX LADY SINGS*

PLAY DEAD*
RUFF WAY TO GO*

*Published by The Ballantine Publishing Group

WHEN THE FAX LADY SINGS

Leslie O'Kane

FAWCETT BOOKS • NEW YORK

Published by The Ballantine Publishing Group

www.randomhouse.com/BB/

Library of Congress Catalog Card Number: 00-110322

ISBN 0-449-00568-2

Manufactured in the United States of America

First Ballantine Books Edition: April 2001

10   9   8   7   6   5   4   3   2

To my sister, Sally Mitoff,
my brother-in-law, Ken Harmon
(thanks again for the title, Ken),
and (last but never least)
Nathan and Emily

Chapter 1

TAG. You're It.

"Tell me again. Why am I doing this?" I asked Lauren Newton, my best friend. Lauren looked over my shoulder in the mirror as I sighed at the reflection that—thanks to the layers of grease paint—had lost all likeness to my face.

We were at the dress rehearsal for a PTA variety show in which I was to be a clown. Lauren, comfortably dressed in jeans and a T-shirt, had opted out of performing and was in charge of costumes and makeup. "For our children," she answered, before dabbing more ruby-colored lipstick on my painted smile.

Against my personal preferences, all seven of us clowns—five females and two males—were supposed to look exactly alike, from our half-bald, half-redhead-being-electrocuted hairpieces down to our oversized shoes. Our director had felt that the similar appearances made our entrance funnier, as we piled one by one out of a golf cart transformed into a clownmobile.

Stephanie Saunders, pacing behind Lauren and three of us would-be clowns, scoffed. "We're doing this because *you*, Molly, sold everyone on this stupid fund-raising idea of yours."

I glared at her reflection in the mirror above the vanity table that ran the length of the dressing-room wall. Stephanie wore a shimmering black evening gown with a slit up the side that showed off her Tina-Turner-has-nothing-on-me legs. Her long blond hair, nary a strand amiss, was fastened on top of her head with gold clips. At the heart of the skit we were about to rehearse, she would sing a serious love ballad, which we clowns would interrupt.

Giving my reflection a disparaging look, she continued, "Lest you forget, Molly, you were the one who came up with this so-called brilliant campaign. As I recall, your exact words were: 'Let's force our children to watch *us* perform for a change.' "

Though her recollection was accurate, I'd been joking. In as gentle a tone as I could muster, I replied, "Stephanie, you look stunning, whereas—" I held out my hands to indicate my two fellow clowns at the vanity table and Elsbeth Young in the back of the room. "—all of us are made up as Bozos. If you don't want to become a victim of clownicide, be nice to us, okay?"

Lauren laughed. Stephanie shot her a dirty look. Refusing to have her mood dampened, Lauren said with a smile, "This fund-raiser was a great idea, Stephanie, and you know it."

"I agree," Danielle Underwood said, her typically melodious voice now sharp. For some reason, whenever she'd spoken tonight it had been to snap at someone. Perhaps stage fright was turning her into a grouchy clown. She was drawing triangular eyebrows over her snow-white forehead with my eyeliner pencil. This was only the second time that particular makeup implement had been used; I'd purchased it solely for my children's Halloween costumes last fall. "When I think of all those interminable performances and pageants I've been to, just so I could be there when my son said his one and only line. And half the time his face was hidden behind his giant hamburger or tree costume."

I looked again at my reflection, trying to decide if I would feel better dressed up to look like a hamburger, rather than as its spokesperson, Ronald McDonald. I decided it was too close to call.

Seated at the far end of the table, Nadine Dahl, a secretary at the high school within Carlton Central's all-grade-levels school, let out a sharp, "Ha!" She had been attempting, with limited success, to center the red ring of hair on her head, and I was beginning to suspect that her head might be lopsided. "You ladies only have to go to your own child's performance. Try being on the school *staff* sometime. We have to go to damn near every production the school puts on." She winked at Lauren, who worked with her in the high school office. "I'll be seeing school performances in my delirium when I'm old and senile. Which will be next week, at the rate I'm going."

I could appreciate the sentiment, though I suspected that Nadine was only a couple of years older than my own forty. I studied her in profile, amazed at how complete the transformation was. She and I looked like twins—well, provided one of the twins had been dropped on her now-lopsided head—and yet in real life, she was thirty pounds heavier and had a button nose, unlike my very nonbutton one.

"You said it," Lauren added. She donned an impish smile and rubbed her hands together. "So, kiddies, it's payback time. Every one of us jumped at this chance. It's not as though anyone could have predicted . . ." Lauren let her voice fade away and cleared her throat.

She'd been inadvertently about to bring up the subject we were all studiously avoiding—the uproar between Olivia Garrett and Stephanie. Claiming that Olivia only wanted her because of the sizable trust fund left by her late father, Olivia's teenage daughter was "divorcing" Olivia in favor of Stephanie. Stephanie, on the other hand, was already wealthy, and her daughter and Olivia's daughter were best friends. To make matters worse, Stephanie's callous remarks to a local television reporter last night had alienated half of the cast, as well as half of the town of Carlton.

Olivia was also a clown in our skit, but was steering clear of Stephanie by dressing someplace else. So were our two male clowns.

The situation between the two women was unlikely to escalate in the forty-eight hours leading up to Friday night's performance. In the wake of the scathing outburst that had been aired on the eleven o'clock news, Stephanie's lawyer had told her not to say another word about the case. Especially not to television reporters.

"As Molly pointed out, you should be the last one to complain, Stephanie," Elsbeth Young muttered from the back of the room. "You're not made up to look ridiculous." Elsbeth was struggling to get into her suit, pulling the red-checkered shirt and yellow-striped pants over her clothes.

"Not true. *You're* the lucky ones," Stephanie retorted. "*You* get to be anonymous. *I'm* the one who's out there center front, supposedly trying to sing a serious song."

"That reminds me, Stephanie," I said, rotating in my chair to face her. "The entire reason I thought up this skit in the first place was because *I* was supposed to be singing the serious song and *you* were supposed to be a clown. I, for one, would have paid good money just to see you—our forever classy and impeccably attired PTA president—in big floppy shoes and a red putty nose. I'll bet a lot of other parents in this community would have felt the same way."

Stephanie scowled at me, then leaned close to gaze at the mirror and check her perfect hair for the fiftieth time. "Me, a clown, and you, a torch singer? Please, Molly. There's something to be said for not trying too hard to go against type. Besides, I've heard you sing."

Lauren put her hand on my shoulder to keep me seated. Not to be thwarted so easily, I slammed my upper arm against my side and squeezed the rubber bulb hidden there, squirting water out of the flower on my lapel and into Stephanie's face.

Stephanie gasped and stepped back. Her face dripping, she stared in horror at me.

"Oops," I said in a monotone. "Sorry."

Stephanie swiped the water from her face and narrowed her eyes as she scanned the room to stifle the laughter that had erupted. "Well, Molly. Thank you, at least, for merely using water," she said under her breath, then met my eyes with unmasked fury. "Olivia hates me so much that she undoubtedly would have squirted *acid* in my face."

Her words made me wince. This parental divorce was a terrible ordeal for all concerned. Stephanie sincerely believed she was doing the right thing to try to gain custody of her daughter's friend. "I'm sorry," I said quietly. "I should have given you more slack, considering the stress you've been under lately."

She was having none of my attempts to mollify. With a few adept strokes, she freshened her makeup, but now spoiled her lovely features with a sneer. "You always were a sore loser, Molly. Our director, if you remember, explained very clearly that it made the most sense for *me* to sing the solo, since I have to be well-dressed for my role as magician's assistant in the preceding act."

"Where *is* our illustrious director?" Nadine asked, primarily to change subjects, I thought. "I'm not sure that I've seen Corrinne once tonight. Makes you wonder how much she cares about the production."

"Last I saw, she was having a heated discussion with Jack Vance," Stephanie answered, referring to the principal of Carlton Central School. Ironically, he had been our classmate at Carlton Central some twenty years earlier. "She's probably in the rest room, trying to restore her dignity."

"It's far too late for that," Elsbeth murmured.

Surely Corrinne was not in trouble with the principal over the parental divorce case, which couldn't possibly involve her. The last thing any of us needed was a *second* major controversy involving the high school.

Elsbeth continued, "I can't believe that she, of all people, is our show director. Talk about putting the biggest nut of all in charge of the nuthouse."

Everyone was looking at her. To ease the tension, I joked, "Which would make us all, what? Pistachios?"

Elsbeth held her arms out wide and looked down at her outfit, then at me. "Take it from one clown to another. We've both looked more dignified."

"You don't know Molly well, do you?" Stephanie said under her breath. She gave a glance at my squirt-gun flower and wisely stepped back.

Actually, Elsbeth had been my daughter's piano teacher for three years now and knew me quite well. So forcing myself to ignore the remark, I returned the subject matter to our director. "What's wrong with Corrinne Buldock? She seems perfectly nice to me. And I hear she's popular at the school, right?"

"Haven't you heard?" Elsbeth asked. She was smiling, till she caught sight of Danielle's reflection in the mirror. Despite the wide red-painted smile there, Danielle's acute discomfort with this subject matter showed in her eyes. Elsbeth, the only one of us not yet in clown face, averted her gaze and returned her attention to her costume, her cheeks now blazing red.

How could Corrinne's troubles with the principal involve Danielle? Putting two and two together, I decided this must involve Danielle's teenage son, who was in Corrinne's class. I glanced at Lauren, who normally kept me filled in on the major gossip from the high school. She indicated Nadine to me with her eyes, which must have meant that Nadine—senior secretary and Lauren's immediate supervisor—had told her to keep quiet.

For an awkward moment nobody spoke. Meanwhile, Danielle continued to act transfixed by her clown shoes, as if to avoid everyone's eyes.

"Danielle," Stephanie said gently, "if it's any consolation, the latest word is that she's going to be suspended, at the very least. In fact, many of the students in Corrinne's classes are expecting her to be fired by Monday."

Fired? Now I was really curious. All of the parental clowns, except me, had children in Corrinne's senior TAG language arts class; she'd recruited the participants in this skit from the parents of her Talented and Gifted Students, or TAGS, an acronym that always struck me as annoyingly over-the-top. Some assessment official was apparently in charge of saying such things as, "Sorry, ma'am, but we feel that your son is merely gifted. I'm afraid that he has no discernible talent whatsoever."

"I've got to get some fresh air," Danielle murmured. But just at that moment, Corrinne stepped into the room, and Danielle jumped back as if a force field had repelled her.

Corrinne, meanwhile, was perspiring heavily and all but foaming at the mouth. Her red-rimmed eyes suggested she'd been crying. Under normal circumstances she was a pretty woman in her mid-thirties, with kinky, short blond hair. She had lost weight recently, though, and was now so thin that she had an angular appearance.

She let her jaw drop at the sight of us. "What the hell are you people doing? You should be dressed and waiting backstage by now. All of you. And where the hell is—" She turned and spotted Stephanie, leaning back against the wall beside the doorway. "There you are, Stephanie. What are you doing?"

"Preparing myself mentally to be humiliated by a batch of clowns. Why?"

"You're supposed to be on stage right now, as Martin the Marvelous's assistant!"

"And *you* were supposed to tell me when he was ready to begin," Stephanie fired back.

Meanwhile, Danielle quietly and deliberately cut a wide arc around Corrinne and Stephanie, and left the room. Corrinne gestured at the rest of us. "And those of you already in costume should be waiting backstage!" She stomped her foot in frustration. "For God's sake, people! What good does it do us to have a timed dress rehearsal if you won't even try to see how quickly you can go through the costume change?"

I was too surprised by the woman's fury to respond. Corrinne grabbed Stephanie by the wrist and began to pull her out of the room; Stephanie appeared to be stunned into acquiescence. I'd known her since junior high, and she was not the sort to allow others to touch her, let alone drag her by the hand.

As they were leaving, Corrinne said over her shoulder, "I'll have you ladies know that you're reinforcing a terrible stereotype. Both men in the skit got dressed in half the time that you gals need, and are backstage, waiting."

"Men are used to being clowns," I called after her.

A silence settled onto the room in Corrinne's wake. "Them that can, do," Nadine said sourly. "Them that can't, order the rest of us around." She rose, dressed and in full makeup.

Elsbeth claimed Nadine's recently deserted seat, and Lauren began to help her apply makeup. "All I know," Elsbeth whispered, "is putting Corrinne Buldock in charge of the show was a big mistake. For this dress rehearsal to go any worse, somebody'd have to keel over."

"Please don't say that," I moaned. Ever since I'd moved back to my hometown in upstate New York six years ago, some miserable curse had turned me into Soccer Mom cum Angel of Death. That thought evoked an image of myself in a hooded black cape, wearing jogging shorts and cleats and carrying a soccer ball. Perhaps there was some way to turn the concept into a greeting card. On second thought, no way. With my home business—designing faxable greeting cards—in a lull, I must have unconsciously been trolling the bottom of the pickle barrel.

The room returned to silence, the tension still palpable. Lauren had probably considered it a favor not to tell me about whatever new controversy was stirring up the already overstirred staff and parental community, but this had put me in the unenviable position of needing to watch my step. Not one of my fortes, even while *not* sporting enormous clown feet.

"Well," I said, rising, "no sense in delaying this any longer. I'm off to be a clown." I pumped a fist and, as I did so, remembered that my outfit was lacking one item. I glanced at the small table by the doorway on which I'd laid my gloves prior to putting on my makeup. The tabletop was now bare. "Elsbeth? Lauren? Did you see a pair of red gloves on this little table by the door?"

"No," they said simultaneously.

"Huh. I could have sworn that's where I put them. I'd better retrace my steps."

Easier said than done. For one thing, my steps were now as exaggerated as a landlocked scuba diver's. For another, Carlton's high school auditorium was something to behold. The stage and entire backstage area were unbelievably extravagant and, for me with my poor sense of direction, something of a labyrinth.

I found my way to the stage and paused to watch Martin pull a rabbit out of a bouquet that he'd just given Stephanie. With her usual showmanship, she acted completely surprised and then brought the rabbit offstage toward me, as if afraid the furry little guy would bite her.

She ordered, "Open the rabbit's cage for me."

"Right away, m'lady."

She sighed. "Oh, it's you, Molly. In that case, here." She handed me the rabbit to put away myself, then returned her attention to Martin, who was now doing some card tricks that apparently did not require Stephanie's "lovely" assistance.

Trying to make nice, I simply did as demanded and put the rabbit in the cage, then asked, "How's Martin's act going?"

She rolled her eyes and said sarcastically, "Tonight, Carlton High School. Tomorrow, Broadway." She sighed. "It is so difficult working with you amateurs."

I moved my arm, and she immediately stepped back.

"Molly, if you squirt me with that thing one more time I'm going to have to kill you."

". . . and kazaam!" Martin said from the stage. This must have been Stephanie's cue, for she retrieved her glorious smile and strode onto the stage.

Too annoyed to watch Stephanie, I decided I should check the second dressing room for my gloves. One of the men could have inadvertently picked them up earlier and left them there. I found the room, but no gloves. Frustrated, I sat down. My pent-up emotions were pointless. Stephanie was always going to be Stephanie, ever annoying, ever capable of goading her fellow Carltonites into forking over a staggering amount of cash for good causes.

"Still haven't found your gloves, Molly?" Lauren asked, entering the room behind me.

"They were right by the door in the other dressing room. Someone must have grabbed them thinking they were theirs."

"They'll turn up. Let's go 'Send in the Clowns,' shall we?" She wiggled her eyebrows at me. "One of us had to say it, right?"

"And I'm glad it was you." That joke had been parlayed about so often in rehearsals that it had become quite the groaner. We headed toward the stage. Or at least, I *think* that was the direction we were going. "It's too bad you couldn't convince Tommy to be in the show," I said, referring to her husband.

"He said he has no talents." She grinned at me. "At least not G-rated ones."

Ignoring the innuendo, I said, "Too bad. It would have been nice to have a police sergeant on stage with us. Everyone is so on edge. Quite frankly, all this tension has me a bit spooked."

Lauren rubbed her eyes. "Your voice is serious, but it sounds so strange when you're dressed like that."

We passed a full-length mirror in the hallway and I caught sight of myself and saw what she meant. Strangely, I'd never felt less like clowning around than I did right at the moment.

We found ourselves on the stage-right wing. Lauren squeezed my arm and whispered, "Actually, I think I'm going to watch from the front row. I'll let you know what I think of the skit."

"Okay. Thanks." Trouble was, though, it was already well after ten P.M. on Wednesday night. If this skit proved to be a disaster, it was too late to improve much before Friday night's performance. I heard some murmurings behind me and rounded a curtain in search of double-gloved clowns.

I stopped the first person in a clown suit I ran into and asked if she—or he, since there was no telling—had picked up my gloves by mistake.

The clown held up red, fuzzy palms. "Not me. These are mine." She pointed. "You might want to try stage left. Or is that right? I think I saw another clown over there."

"Thanks, Olivia."

"How'd you know it was me?" she said, playing with her already unmistakably high-pitched voice.

I chuckled, glad that she seemed to be in a good mood despite her daughter's "divorce." Spotting another clown at the opposite side of the stage, I moved in that direction and called out, "Are those your gloves?"

"Shush!" both Martin the Mediocre and Stephanie the Stuck-up simultaneously said.

The other clown answered, "Yes, they're mine," and I recognized Nadine's voice.

"Hey! What are you doing back there?" Martin said, interrupting his act to shout at me. "I'm about to do my tour de force! I can't have people wandering around behind me now!"

"Oh, for heaven's sake, Martin," I retorted, not appreciating being treated like an idiot, even if I *did* happen to be dressed like a clown. "I won't be back here during the actual performance. I'm just trying to find my missing gloves for the rehearsal."

I looked at Corrinne, sitting beside Lauren, expecting her to yell at me. She didn't. Except for the two of them, the auditorium was empty. We hadn't wanted any of the students to watch the final rehearsal in lieu of the paid event Friday night, so we'd deliberately scheduled this rehearsal well past any after-school activities. There had been a mass exodus of the show's cast who weren't in the last two acts. I only hoped the same thing didn't occur during the real thing on Friday.

"Use the passageway underneath the stage or behind the back curtains!" Martin snarled. Then changing his demeanor, he rubbed his hands together and once again transformed Martin the grouchy tax attorney into Martin the magician. "Now, ladies and gentlemen, I need a volunteer." He turned to speak to our director. "This is the part where I would normally ask the audience for a volunteer."

To her credit, Corrinne resisted saying "Duh" to Martin's obvious explanation, and he continued, "Corrinne, why don't you stand in? Of course I'd never pick you as a volunteer. You and Stephanie look far too similar."

Corrinne beamed. Stephanie's face fell, and she said under her breath, "In her dreams, maybe."

With Martin too engrossed in his act to yell at me a second time, I crossed the stage and reached the other wing. There I saw another clown, leaning against the back wall. "Danielle?" I asked cautiously, merely guessing; the posture was that of someone who wanted to be left alone.

"Yes. Molly?"

"Could you have accidentally picked up my gloves from the table by the dressing room door?"

"No, I keep mine in my pocket."

I nodded and tried to sort through the voices of clowns I'd spoken to already to see if I'd asked everyone. The only clowns I hadn't asked were the male clowns. Or had I asked Elsbeth? I couldn't recall.

Not having seen this trick of Martin's, and curious as to how it was done, I returned my attention to the stage.

From someplace behind the curtains some woman cried, "Oh, no! The birds! They're getting away!"

Danielle immediately rushed back to help, but this was at least the third time Martin's stupid doves had flown the coop, and I was not about to lend a helping hand. Especially not since discovering that the birds tended to *bite* anyone's hand, except Martin's.

From the stage, Corrinne called, "Forget about the damned birds! You're all supposed to be behind the curtain by now, except for Chester. He should be at the wheel of the golf cart. All of the clowns! Line up behind the back curtain." Corrinne gestured wildly for us all to get into position.

Still wanting to watch the act, I very slowly made my way to my position offstage. Martin closed Corrinne into her black booth on my side of the stage. He had already closed Stephanie into hers. Martin said some magic words, then paused. Nothing happened.

Switching from bad magician into bad ventriloquist, Martin maintained a wide smile, but said out of the corner of his mouth, "Come on, Stephanie! You know what you're supposed to do. What seems to be the holdup?"

"I'm stuck," Stephanie said, banging on the booth. "Someone closed up the back flap."

"That's impossible," Martin snarled. "Let me see what's going on."

A clown suddenly pushed past me, shoving me off balance. "Hey!" I cried, in indignant surprise. The clown, heading toward the stage, was reaching into a black plastic garbage bag. "Watch where you're going. We're supposed to be—"

The clown turned slightly. I stared, unable to believe what I was seeing. A dark cylinder that looked just like the barrel of a gun poked through the plastic bag. I gasped and froze, suddenly unable even to scream out a warning.

The clown marched onto the middle of the stage, where the magician's back was turned as he worked on Stephanie's booth. My brain screamed at me to do something, anything, but my body wouldn't respond.

Shots rang out. The clown fired at the booth that Martin had sealed Corrinne Buldock into only moments before.

Chapter 2

A Confederacy of Clowns

As the shots were fired, I instinctively dropped down flat on the floor. The gun came skittering toward my face across the smooth waxed surface of the stage.

With the noise of the gun's reports still resounding in my ears, I rose and watched the shooter fling the garbage bag away while crossing the stage and then disappearing behind the black-curtain backdrop. In the shooter's wake was the handgun, the garbage bag—and the red cloth gloves, which I now saw had clear plastic over them.

I got up and ran to the wooden booth, an upended coffin-shaped box, where Corrinne Buldock had been trapped as the shooter targeted it.

Praying against logic that magic had transpired and the box would be empty, I reached for the latch. It didn't budge.

"Martin! Help me open this," I cried.

Immobilized with fright, Martin was on the far side of the stage, flat on his stomach with his hands over his head. Beside him stood the second wooden box, where Stephanie was apparently trapped.

"Molly!" Stephanie demanded, pounding on her box. "Get me out of here! What in God's name is going on?"

I ignored her. Opening Corrinne's box was much more important than freeing Stephanie. I pressed harder on the latch.

"Get me out!" Stephanie continued to yell. "What was that noise? It sounded like gunshots!"

After squeezing with all my might, the latch finally clicked. I flung open the panel of the bullet-hole-riddled box. Corrinne's eyes were wide open but unseeing.

Her bloodied, lifeless body toppled out of the box toward me. As I caught and struggled to support her, I saw several clowns, in my peripheral vision, approaching me. A loud noise resounded nearby as Stephanie kicked open her box and emerged, panting from the effort.

All these visual images careened at me, as if seen under a strobe light. The horizon line rapidly shifted positions. Then everything went black.

Lauren's upside-down face loomed in front of mine as I opened my eyes. "What happened?" I asked, feeling groggy, disoriented.

"You fainted. Don't worry. The police are on the way. I reached Tommy's cell phone."

In a rush, the events of the final few seconds came back to me, and I propped myself up on an elbow, hoping this had been a nightmare. But Corrinne's body lay beside me on the stage, close enough to touch. I turned my head. "Oh, my God, Lauren. This can't be happening."

I sat up. The smell of gun smoke lingered in the air. I must have blacked out for only a few seconds. Surrounding Lauren and me on the stage were all the clowns, still in full makeup. I counted. There were six of them. I made number seven, I realized dully; we were all present. One of them was holding Corrinne's hand and caressing her hair. The others were murmuring among themselves about how hideous and heartbreaking this was. "She was so sweet," one woman said. "Such a caring, dedicated teacher," another replied.

Martin and Stephanie also remained on the stage. Martin was as white as the rest of us, while Stephanie's perfect tan apparently prevented her from ever allowing her face to pale.

I looked again at the clown who'd been holding Corrinne's lifeless hand. He now scanned the faces of the other five clowns, who remained on their feet. "Who did this?" he cried. "Someone killed my Corrinne!" His voice broke and he began to sob. "One of you did this! I'm not going to let you get away with it!"

He yanked off his fake nose and wig. I could now tell by the dark curly hair that it was Dave Paxton, an art teacher at the high school. He was a divorced forty-something who had been dating Corrinne, at one point at least, though according to my latest information the two of them had broken up some time ago.

"Oh, my God," one of the female clowns wailed. Olivia Garrett, I thought, judging by the high-pitched, almost childlike voice. "This is my fault."

Dave stiffened and stared at her. She looked to either side as if to verify that, indeed, everyone else was staring at her as well. Olivia wrapped her arms around her midsection. She started crying, the tears running down her grease-painted face. "I . . . I jammed the latches on the doors to the boxes. I just wanted to louse up the trick to embarrass Stephanie. But . . . my God. That might have saved Stephanie's life and cost Corrinne hers." Olivia pulled off her wig and let her long reddish-blond hair tumble free.

Stephanie gave her a long look. "Wouldn't you have just loved that? Getting custody of your daughter back by killing me off? Only Corrinne's the victim instead."

"Don't anyone accuse me," Martin said, holding up his palms. "I'm completely innocent."

"Everyone knows that, Martin," Lauren said. "Molly and I saw the whole thing. You had your back turned, and someone in a clown suit shot her."

He pursed his already thin lips below his handlebar

mustache and raised an eyebrow. "Maybe so, but everyone always points their fingers at the magician."

Stephanie snorted. "Please, Martin. Don't kid yourself. You're not that good. The bunny rabbit is a likelier suspect."

Martin glared at her, hands on his hips. "How dare you! How dare you accuse me of . . . of being inept!" He glanced at poor Corrinne, then looked away. David's face remained scrunched in agony over his loss as he cradled Corrinne's hand in his lap.

This was all too bizarre, surreal, even. Had I possibly smacked my head when I fainted, and was I now hallucinating? Clowns, standing around a murdered woman. A magician, insulted *not* to be a suspect. Meanwhile, someone we had all known lay dead, right beside me.

"How could this have happened?" I said, surprised to discover that I was speaking out loud. "This was supposed to be a silly skit, a school fund-raiser."

Lauren's and my eyes met. She, too, was clearly horrified at this scene. "At least none of the students were here to see this," she said quietly.

I shivered at the image of any child having been here. That was, indeed, something to be grateful for, though despair and humiliation seeped into me. The murderer had brushed right past me. I could have prevented this. Could have screamed. Tackled the would-be killer. My one chance to save someone's life. I'd frozen, and my inaction had cost Corrinne her life. I felt woozy once again and clutched my knees to my chest, closing my eyes.

A security guard rushed in. He eyed Corrinne's body, the gun, then scanned our faces and said, "That *is* ketchup, isn't it? Right?"

No one answered.

He looked again. "Oh, my God! Somebody really did get shot. It wasn't part of the act." His forehead was already damp with perspiration. "I heard the shots, but I thought . . ." He surveyed the group of us on the stage, then held up a palm and said in a half shriek, "Stay where you are and don't anyone touch that gun."

Sergeant Tommy Newton arrived then, and not a moment too soon, in my estimation. Lauren and I were on a stage with a dead body, the murder weapon, and a killer disguised to look identical to half a dozen of us witnesses. Tommy stopped and surveyed the scene, his eyes lingering on me. "That you, Molly?"

I nodded.

He glanced at his wife, still seated beside me. "Were you a witness?"

"Yes. I was seated in the front row. It was one of the six clowns, other than Molly. One of the ones with their gloves on."

There was an immediate reaction on all of the clowns' parts; they simultaneously looked down at their own hands, then at the hands of the other clowns.

"Uh-huh. Typical. Murder follows Molly like a cart behind a horse."

I clenched my teeth but said nothing. The remark was unwarranted, and I had to remind myself that we all make unfair remarks at times. He slowly scanned the stage. As I glared up at him, I spotted one of the doves on the railing that crisscrossed the stage area overhead.

" 'Fraid I'm gonna have to separate y'all 'n' get your statements."

Tommy was not a Southerner; he had lived in this upper New York town all his life, but he lapsed into a folksy drawl as part of his policeman persona. Over the years, I'd come to accept this about him without undue annoyance.

"Sergeant Newton, how long will this take?" I recognized Nadine's authoritative tones. She'd used them on me, more than once, when I'd come to the office to chat with Lauren. "We're all horribly shaken and upset, and

I, for one, would like to get to the comfort of my own home as quickly as possible."

Tommy regarded her coolly, then rocked on his heels. "It'll take as long as it takes. Couple of patrol officers will be here momentarily. We'll get y'all into separate rooms."

"Can we take these costumes off first? Please?" This time it was Danielle, who had an especially melodic voice. She had acted so upset at Corrinne back in the dressing room that Stephanie had reassured her Corrinne was going to be suspended, possibly fired. "I really don't want to wind up on the front page of the *Times Union*, photographed in this outfit."

"Sorry. Y'all have to stay in costume till we can get each one logged as evidence at the station house. Look at it this way," Tommy intoned. "Now even your best friend wouldn't recognize you."

At least two hours later—I'd lost track of time in the auditorium, where there was no clock—one of the officers responded to my request that I be allowed to make a phone call. He escorted me to the principal's office, then waited on the other side of the door to let me call home in privacy. No answer. Jim, my husband, must not have returned from his business trip to Boston. He was supposed to have been back an hour or two earlier.

Having anticipated this possibility, I'd arranged for Nathan and Karen to sleep at my parents' house, which was in our immediate neighborhood. I glanced at the wall clock. It was dreadfully late now, nearly midnight, but my parents always turned the ringer off before they went to bed. By calling now, I could leave them and my children a reassuring message so they wouldn't panic upon hearing the news on the radio or TV in the morning. Before the fourth ring, which was when the machine picked up, I heard the sound of the phone being lifted and my mother's groggy, "Hello?"

I winced. "Mom. I'm sorry to call at this hour. I was hoping you had the ringer turned off so I'd just get the machine."

"What's happened?" She sounded fully awake and alert now. "Are you hurt? Is it Jim?"

I rolled my eyes. I should have assumed that with my children sleeping there, Mom would adjust her habits and leave the ringer active. When, *when,* was I going to learn that my mother was a combination pessimist and alarmist? She would, *of course,* assume that a phone call at midnight meant that a loved one had died. "I'm fine. But there was a shooting at the school and I—"

"Oh, my God! A shooting? Who shot whom?"

In the background I heard my dad, his voice thick with sleepiness, ask my mom, "What's going on?"

"Molly was involved in a shooting!" Mom replied.

I grabbed a handful of hair—my own shoulder-length brown tresses, now that my costume was fully removed to be labeled and stored as possible evidence. "Don't put it that way, Mom!" I protested.

"You mean, somebody shot *at* her, right?" Dad asked. "Give me the phone."

"No! I've got it!"

"Well, hold it out so we can both listen, for God's sake!"

"Go ahead, sweetie. Tell us what happened."

Through the glass in the office door, I spotted one of the officers and the gun in his holster. *Please, just shoot me now.* As calmly as possible I said, "One of the teachers at the school, Corrinne Buldock, was shot by one of the people in the clown skit with me."

"What clown skit? What's she talking about?" my father asked.

"That's hardly the point, Charlie! Who cares about the clowns! I want to know if our daughter was injured!"

"Mom, I'm fine. I just wanted to leave a message for Karen and Nathan and let them know that I love them and that I'll see them first thing tomorrow, okay?"

I hung up the phone and instructed myself to take deep breaths. That entire conversation was my fault, I reminded myself as I tried in vain to stop grinding my teeth. My parents were simply trying to make sure that I was all right. In their inimitable style.

Tommy, looking tired, entered the room. "You okay, Moll?"

"Fine. Just . . . envying orphans."

Seemingly with no curiosity regarding my response, he gestured with a slight motion of his head for me to have a seat. "Let's get your statement and see if we can get you out of here."

I launched into a full description of my search for my red gloves, the woman yelling about the doves having escaped, and Danielle rushing off to help; how the killer in a clown costume had brushed right past me. Tommy did not comment, refraining from asking me why I didn't take some kind of preventive action. His reticence, if anything, made me feel even worse.

Afterward I asked, "Couldn't someone else have sneaked into the building, dressed like a clown? Or still be hiding out here in the school, even as we speak?"

He shook his head. I knew better than to ask a question like that—to make it seem as though I were a professional investigator instead of a civilian witness—but with my awful record of late as a horse pulling the cart of murder, as Tommy had so kindly put it earlier, he had dropped the pretense of treating me as an outsider.

"We were real lucky in that regard. School security knew y'all were s'posed to be the only ones in the building, and so they had their cameras focused on not just the main exits, but on the only entrances to the wing that houses the auditorium. They double-checked all the emergency exits, and all of the alarms on 'em were working."

"And you're certain nobody could have hid themselves and snuck out later?"

"Even if someone could have managed, Lauren picked up those clown suits just this morning, which wiped out the costume store's entire inventory of that particular design. A killer not in the skit couldn't have matched the costume so perfectly. It had to be one of you original seven clowns."

"Please. It's one of the six, not counting me. Remember, Lauren was in the front row. She saw the killer brush right past me." I sighed and pressed my fingertips against my throbbing temples. "I can't understand how the killer managed to just . . . blend in with the others."

Tommy let out a puff of air and shook his head. "You're tellin' me? Started out with every single one of 'em able to attest for one or two other suspects. Then they each backed down when we asked 'em to sign a sworn statement to that effect. Decided then that maybe they weren't so certain which clown they were next to after all."

"Why? How come none of them were certain?"

"The killer must've deliberately opened the cages for the magician's animals as a diversion. They all scattered. Caused a mass of confusion backstage. There's still a white rabbit missing."

"Well, I do know a couple of the clowns had possible motives," I said. "David Paxton had a onetime love affair with Corrinne, and Danielle had some major problem with Corrinne, though I don't know what it was."

Tommy said nothing, but was glaring at me. He hated when I volunteered my opinion of how he should do his job. But I wanted this murder solved, and if there was some clue I possessed about the suspects, he was getting my help whether he wanted it or not. I went on, "Olivia might have thought Stephanie was in that booth. Nadine could have had a big beef with Corrinne. Nadine is always pretty abrupt with people. On the other hand, Elsbeth is my daughter's piano teacher, and as far as I know, she had no problem with Corrinne. I don't know Chester Walker well. I recently hired him to install a sunroom, though."

"So you see most of the suspects on a regular basis. Meanin' you got both your big feet and your nose stuck into my murder investigation, as usual."

The visual image of both my feet and my nose "stuck" into something at the same time gave me pause. "It's not intentional, Tommy. It's a small town. Everybody knows everybody else's business."

"Uh-huh. And occasionally somebody gets killed as a result." He leaned forward on the table to stare directly into my eyes. "One of these days, Molly, you're going to push one of these loose cannons too far. And it's gonna explode right in your face."

Chapter 3

When the Circus Comes to Town

I finished giving my statement to Tommy and left—
though if "my statement" had been entirely of my own
choosing, it would have been: "Catch this murderer
now, before anyone else at my kids' school gets shot!"

Despite the outrageously late hour, Lauren was
waiting for me in the lobby. We had carpooled to the
school that evening, but that now felt so long ago.

"How are you doing?" I asked.

She mustered a smile on her attractive, round face and
tucked her straight, brown, shoulder-length hair behind
her ear. "I'm okay. How about you?"

"Hanging in there." We pushed out the door and
trudged through a chill March breeze to her car. In truth,
I felt so numb that it was hard to believe I was still able to
walk. Yet even though part of me was appalled by my
compulsive need to joke when times were at their worst,
I heard myself reply, "With the police confiscating seven
costumes tonight, I sure hope there isn't a run on clowns
for birthday parties anytime soon."

She unlocked the door to the passenger side and I got
in, grateful to be alone with her, away from clowns and
magicians and Stephanie and policemen. "They kept
your costume as evidence, right?" she asked, sliding behind the wheel. "I don't know what good it'll do,
though."

I fastened my seat belt, though with the weight of the

world on my shoulders, the seat belt seemed redundant. "I'm sure they kept the suits in the hopes that they'll find trace evidence—gunpowder residue."

"Oh, right. Of course." She started the engine.

"I wonder if Jim's home yet. He's supposed to come back from Boston sometime late tonight. The kids are sleeping at my parents' house."

"Joey and Jasper are home with Rachel," she replied. Tommy's sons from his previous marriage served as occasional sitters for Lauren's daughter, though she, like my daughter Karen, was fourteen now and a baby-sitter herself.

We pulled out of the lot. There was no traffic at that hour, and the school was less than three miles from our houses. I tried to shut my eyes, but was instantly unnerved by the memory of Corrinne's body when I first threw open Martin's box.

I jerked upright in my seat, remembering something. "Those gloves. The killer's gloves. They had those clear plastic gloves over them. Like those plastic Baggie gloves they wear in the cafeteria."

"Pardon?"

"The killer wanted to make sure gunpowder residue didn't pass through the fabric of the gloves. Maybe it was someone at the school, the art teacher or Nadine, who pinched a pair of those gloves."

"Molly, anyone could have gotten disposable gloves like those from the school cafeteria. People have been coming and going through the cafeteria kitchen all night. They kept a coffee urn operating tonight for cast members."

I frowned. "Whoever it was thought this through to the letter. If only Corrinne hadn't insisted on us all looking identical."

"Bet the killer put that idea in her head, back when she was first planning the skit."

"Probably," I murmured, leaning back in the passenger seat once again. I felt drained of all energy. "Maybe Tommy will be able to trace the owner of the gun."

"I hope so. But let's face it—if the gun were much of a clue, the killer wouldn't have dropped it in plain sight, after being so careful to hide her . . . his identity in every other respect."

She was right, of course, and I shuddered at the helplessness I felt. "This was so . . . insidious. Why do this in front of witnesses? On the stage like that? It's just crazy. What's happening to our world? Why are people so evil?"

"Molly, it's just one person. There's always been a small percentage of people who choose evil."

"Not at my kids' school, though," I insisted, shaking my head. "This can't happen here. I won't stand for it." I took a deep breath to try to calm myself.

We reached my driveway. The garage door was open. To my relief, both our red Toyota and the Jeep Cherokee were in the garage. Jim had made it home safely. I said good-night to Lauren, then let myself in through the garage, shutting it behind me.

Jim was sound asleep in front of the TV. He woke as I sat down beside him on the couch. "You're back," he murmured sleepily. "Where is it you said you were tonight?"

"Weren't you listening yesterday when I reminded you that I'd be at the school?" I closed my eyes and rubbed my forehead. The horrid vision of what had happened that night passed in slow motion before me. The killer with gun in hand, walking right past me, an arm's length away. An arm's length that, had I closed the gap, could very likely have saved Corrinne's life.

I took a halting breath. Talking to myself, I protested once again, "This is a school! I won't sit back and watch while things like this happen in a place where children go to learn!"

"I'm sorry I forgot, Molly, but I didn't realize you'd get quite this upset. You were rehearsing for that variety show, right?"

Jim had the volume on the television set turned way low, but the image on the screen now caught my eye. They had interrupted normal late night programming to show a live telecast of the investigation. A couple of men in white uniforms were rolling out a human-sized form on a gurney. Obviously this was Corrinne's body. The television reporter was standing in front of the high school, her face reflecting the tension of the scene. Across the bottom of the screen, a banner headline declared that school was closed tomorrow due to the shooting death of a teacher.

"I was playing a clown," I said, tears forming in my eyes.

Jim murmured, "Oh, no," as he stared at the screen. He put his arm around me and said gently, "Tell me all about it."

The next morning at six forty-three sharp my doorbell rang. I bolted upright in bed, but Jim managed to sleep through the sound. A moment later I heard the door open and my mother call, "Molly? It's your mom."

She always identified herself first, as if I couldn't recognize her voice after all these years, not to mention that she and Lauren were the only people we'd entrusted with copies of our house keys.

"Be right down," I yelled, and glanced over at Jim, whose eyes were still closed and his breath, heavy. Yeah, right. He wasn't *that* solid a sleeper. Come to think of it, if he wasn't going to get up, neither was I. Surely my mother was only there to drop my children off and would let herself out, now that she knew I was home. I lay back down and pulled the covers up to my face.

Downstairs Karen and Nathan were arguing about whose turn it was to get the dog out; we lock her inside her crate in the kitchen at night. "MOM!" hollered Karen, who'd taken to speaking in capital letters now that she was a teenager. "School's canceled today!"

She threw open Jim's and my bedroom door. Our cocker spaniel, Betty Cocker, BC for short, dashed in, so excited to see her family after a night's sleep that her entire back half was wagging along with her tail. She thrust her cold, wet nose into mine, but I merely rolled over. The trouble was, unlike the rest of the family, I'd been unable to sleep and had only gotten two or three hours of shut-eye.

To Karen, I muttered, "I know. There was an incident at the high school last night."

"Mom?" Nathan, my twelve-year-old, asked. "Are you getting up?"

I shifted my position in bed and opened my eyes a crack. He was leaning in the doorway behind his sister. He was taller than she was, and had a string-bean frame, wavy brown hair, freckles, and dark-brown eyes. Karen was so pretty and petite that those who didn't know her well assumed she was immature and fragile. In actuality, she was as headstrong as her mother, but had a solid, positive self-image that my husband and I could only envy.

My head throbbed from lack of sleep. "Let's all just go back to sleep, okay?"

"But we're already awake!" Nathan said. He had inherited the tendency to point out the obvious from his father. "We walked over here from Grandma's. She's downstairs. She says she wants to talk to you, right away."

I shuddered at the thought of an inquisition from my

mother this early in the morning. "Has she had her coffee yet?" I asked cautiously.

"Yes," Mom called from below. She must have been planted at the bottom of the stairs listening to all of this.

"Okay. I'll come down. Right away." Accepting the inevitable, I rose. I stepped into my pseudosheepskin slippers. Meanwhile, the kids and dog scattered for parts unknown. Now that Karen and Nathan were older, they wandered farther more frequently, and unlike our cocker spaniel, they didn't come running to me when called. After a few rudimentary morning routines, during which I verified in the mirror that I was indeed a sight to cause sore eyes, I made it down the stairs without incident.

Mom, her tall, thin frame in its usual ramrod-straight posture, awaited me at the bottom of the steps with hands on her hips. "I just wanted to make sure you were really all right. I heard about the shooting on the early morning news."

I had a horrid image of the morning newscasters chuckling about the killer being disguised as a clown. "Did they say anything about the suspects?"

"Only that the police were in the process of interviewing witnesses and possible suspects." She looked me up and down, but at her almost six feet of height to my five-six, it was mostly down. She smoothed her short, salt-and-pepper hair. "Well, now that I can see for myself that you're all right, I'd better get going. Is there anything you need?"

"Just some sleep."

She raised an eyebrow. "Join the club."

"Sorry I woke you last night."

"I'm glad you did. I'd have panicked when I listened to the news this morning, otherwise."

I brightened a little at this. "That's what I figured."

"See you later," she said, letting herself back out again.

"Someone got shot?" Nathan asked. His voice was emanating from the stairway. Evidently, he had been eavesdropping on the conversation.

I peered around the corner and saw that both Karen and Nathan were sitting on the stairs.

"Yes. Nobody you know. She was a—" I hesitated, not wanting to use the word "teacher" and make him afraid in his classroom, and searched for another term. "—curriculum coordinator at the high school."

"Did you know her?" Karen asked gently, restoring my faith that she hadn't changed all that drastically from the sweet little angel girl I'd known.

"Not well. She was the director of that variety show the PTA was putting on."

She leaped to her feet. "Hey, Mom. Since school's out, I'm gonna invite Rachel over." Karen was, alas, fourteen once again.

"That's no fair!" Nathan immediately chimed in. "I want a friend over, too."

"No friends over this morning. Your friends are too young to be traumatized by the sight of me operating on this little sleep."

"Thanks a lot, Nathan! Mom just doesn't want any boys to see her in her ratty old bathrobe! And now I don't get to have Rachel over!"

While the two of them continued to argue, I, in my ratty old bathrobe, staggered into the kitchen in search of Jim's caffeine cache. My lone "delicate" feature—my stomach—had caused me to have to give up caffeine, except in emergencies such as now.

The morning progressed. Jim grabbed a breakfast bar, yogurt, and his briefcase and, after receiving my reassurances that I intended to stay home all day, left for work. Karen watched some stupid game show on television, while I diverted questions from Nathan. He tended to stew about things and was certain that it was no longer safe for him to return to the Carlton Central School campus. Not an avid student, he eagerly jumped on any excuse to stay home. Meanwhile, I was in a daze. Witnessing someone's murder was the most horrific thing that had happened to me, and I'd meant it when I said that I intended to stay safe at home.

The doorbell rang. "I'll get it!" Karen hollered over the sounds of our ferocious, barking little dog, who raced her to the door. "I hope this is Rachel."

She looked out the front window and turned to me, crestfallen, while I trudged toward the door. "It's some lady," she grumbled. "So you get to traumatize *your* friends with your appearance but *I* don't get to traumatize mine." She opened the door and said, "My mom's coming," then spun on a heel and marched back to the family room.

At the door was Olivia Garrett. Unlike me, she was fully dressed in khakis and a navy-blue V-neck pullover, but she, too, looked haggard. Her long, strawberry-blond tresses were pulled up in a haphazard ponytail, and her eyes looked puffy.

I quieted our barking dog, then swung open the screen door. "Good morning," I said, feeling disconcerted. At one-out-of-six odds that Olivia was last night's gunman, I really didn't care to welcome her with open arms. Besides, she'd never been to my house before. She must have found my address in the phone book, which raised the question of why she hadn't called first.

" 'Morning, Molly," she said, her high-pitched voice hard to listen to in my current state. "I'm sorry to barge in on you, but I didn't know where else to turn. I have to talk to someone. I can't talk to my friends about this." She stepped inside, ignoring BC sniffing at her ankles.

"That's quite all right," I said, always a softie whenever the opportunity to feel needed arose. "Would you like some coffee?"

"That'd be great. Thank you."

"Can someone call for the dog?" I hollered, annoyed on Olivia's behalf at BC's ankle sniffing.

From the other room Nathan called, "Betty, come," and she raced off, ever in hopeful expectation of a treat.

With the opposite demeanor, Olivia followed me to the kitchen and dropped down in a chair as I poured coffee for both of us. I knew almost nothing about her background, but she had a dancer's body and gracefulness.

After she'd taken a couple of sips, she finally spoke again. "Molly, I know you're good friends with Sergeant Newton. Things are . . . looking really bad for me right now."

Her hands were shaking so badly that she sloshed a bit of coffee out as she set down her mug. She dropped her hands to her lap to hide them from view beneath the table. "I know I'm not perfect. I've made a lot of mistakes in my life. But I don't deserve this. My own daughter honestly seems to believe that I just want to be her mother so that I can get my hands on her trust fund."

I had read almost that exact quote from Olivia's daughter, Jenny, in the newspapers. As a mother of one teenager and a second almost-teenager, I could imagine few things more painful than Olivia's plight, and barely knew what to say to her. "How did all of this start, anyway?"

She met my eyes briefly, then diverted her gaze. "I was trying to protect her. I didn't want her to know that her father had committed suicide. So, eight years ago when it happened, I simply told her that he'd died in a car accident. I never told her that the 'accident' involved carbon monoxide, which he'd inhaled in our own garage. I kept the newspapers with articles about his death out of sight. I should've known that she'd learn the truth eventually. When she did, she got so upset, there was no reasoning with her. She got it into her head that I'd kept the cause of death secret because I had something to do with it."

"She thinks you killed her father?" I asked, horrified.

Olivia absentmindedly fidgeted with one of her strawberry-blond tresses, trying to stuff it back into her ponytail. "Oh, I don't think she really believes that. She just says it now to hurt me." She let out a heavy sigh. "So, last year, when I finally told her that much of our money was coming from a sizable trust fund her dad left for her, everything blew up on me. She said I was an unfit mother because I don't clean the house, which is a big exaggeration. The place is cluttered, yes, but it's not a 'roach trap' the way Jenny describes it." She gestured angrily in the air with fisted hands. Her vocal tones had lowered, and she no longer sounded like a child. "Then, that damned Stephanie Saunders has to come along, with her nose in the air, thinking she's just oh so cultured and oh so superior to the likes of me. *I'm* the one who owns an art gallery, for heaven sakes! I can't believe that she actually found a judge who agreed with her!"

Disconcerted by her suddenly fierce mannerisms, I said mildly, "It's not all over, though. You have some sort of appeal hearing coming up, right?"

"Yes." She searched my face, her eyes wide with worry. "Which is why I can't have this hanging over my head now, Molly. You have to help me. You have to help me convince Sergeant Newton that I'm innocent." Both hands were still fisted, and she practically pounded on my table as she spoke.

"I don't know how much influence my word will carry with him, Olivia. Probably next to none."

"But it will if you tell him you spoke to me right before the shooting. That I wasn't in the back where the shooter came from so it couldn't have been me. And I *didn't* kill her. I had no reason to kill Corrinne. I liked her. She even testified on my behalf at the first hearing."

"Olivia, I am not going to lie to the police and provide you with an alibi."

"You *wouldn't* be lying. We did speak, right when we were on the one wing of the stage, right before the shooting. Don't you remember?"

"Yes, but that was at least a minute or two before the shooting."

"No, I was standing next to someone when the shots were fired. I was sure it was you."

I shook my head. "I was with Danielle, and she rushed backstage to help capture the birds. I was alone at the time of the shooting."

She sank her face into her hands. "My God. This is every parent's worst nightmare. My only child has turned against me and is joining forces with that bitch, Stephanie Saunders. Now Stephanie's trying to convince everyone that I did it, mistakenly thinking that she was in that box."

I remained quiet, but it did seem that Stephanie had been making that point quite clear to all concerned last night. Because she had been the quintessential the-world-revolves-around-me Stephanie, her words hadn't really registered with me, until now when Olivia repeated them.

"Like I told everyone last night," Olivia continued, "I closed up the fake panel so Stephanie couldn't get out. That only proves that I didn't do it. I knew full well she was in the other box. And I would never, ever murder anyone. Especially not if I knew that it would cost me my daughter." She started to cry, but quickly regained her self-control.

"Maybe you can talk to the other clowns," I suggested. "Figure out who was with you at the time of the shooting."

"I can't." She rose and took a couple of steps as if too nervous to remain seated, then returned to the chair.

"Everyone knows *you're* innocent. But if I tell the other clowns about this, and one of them claims to have been with me, well, that person might be lying. I'd risk giving the murderer a phony alibi. It's not worth it. I want this lunatic behind bars. Just not at the expense of getting mistakenly convicted myself." She placed her hand on top of mine. "Molly, are you absolutely certain you didn't know I wasn't backstage just before the shooter appeared?"

"I don't know where anyone was but me. I'm sorry."

She nodded and frowned, then picked up her coffee cup and took a sip, avoiding my eyes.

"Tommy Newton may be a bit unorthodox in his methods and his people skills, but he's an excellent cop. He'll find the person who did this." And, though I wasn't about to say this aloud, he would have my help, whether he wanted it or not. The "or not" was actually a given. But if anything warranted risking my own life, it was the protection of children and schools from violence. I'd failed to meet that standard when I'd frozen last night, unable to prevent the shooting. I was not going to let anyone down a second time.

My assurances appeared to have a negative impact on Olivia, who once again was crying softly. "Jenny never got along well with that Jasper, Tommy's son. I don't think Tommy likes me at all."

"That's not going to affect him either way. Tommy's not like that. Like I say, he's—"

The doorbell rang. A second later I heard the sound of the latch opening, followed by an unmistakable, "Yoo-hoo. Molly? Are you home?"

I gritted my teeth, instantly incensed. How dare she open my door, uninvited! "Stephanie, I'm busy. Go away."

BC, meanwhile, launched again into her vociferous barking and resumed her duties as watchdog. For once I actually hoped she might frighten the houseguest off, but unfortunately, Stephanie was more than eighteen inches tall, which is how short one would have to be actually to find my dog intimidating.

Olivia rose. "Stephanie Saunders?" she said to me accusingly. "You're friends with Stephanie Saunders? Why didn't you just tell me that right off? I never would have . . ." She stepped back from the table as if just discovering that she'd consorted with the enemy.

Stephanie waltzed into the room, saying, "Molly, I didn't mean to intrude, and I'll only stay a minute. I simply—" She froze at the sight of Olivia, and both women stared aghast at each other. "Olivia. What are you doing here?"

"How is that any of your business?" Olivia asked, tossing her head.

"Don't flatter yourself, Olivia. I assure you, it isn't. In fact, your reason for coming here isn't of the slightest interest to me. It's just one of those things people say when they're surprised."

"I was just leaving." She marched out the front door without another word, shutting the door firmly behind her.

BC, meanwhile, was sniffing at Stephanie as if she'd been near another small animal lately, though to the best of my knowledge, the only small animals Stephanie ever came in contact with had been skinned and made into mink stoles.

"Betty, come," I called. To my surprise, the dog obeyed. Must have been the result of that repelling force field surrounding my intruder.

Stephanie put her hands on her hips and regarded me. "Molly, are you and Olivia in cahoots? Are you honestly taking her side against me? After all the time we've known each other?"

Too angry to quell my natural sarcasm, I paused and pretended to consider her statement. "Granted, we've known each other for eons. But how exactly is that an argument in your favor? For one thing, *Olivia* allowed me to open my own door!"

"Is that Rachel?" Karen called from the family room. Her television show must have ended.

"No, but you can come get BC again."

"Another friend of *yours*?" Karen said, clicking her tongue as she entered the room. She then recognized Stephanie and grinned, but didn't say anything. Karen, too, knew Stephanie's status as one of my least favorite human beings.

Stephanie smiled at my daughter. "Hi, sweetie pie."

"Hi." She gave me a sympathetic smile and said, "Sorry, Mom," as she grabbed Betty's collar and brought the dog upstairs with her.

"I apologize for letting myself in, but which of us is worse? Me, for opening your door, or Olivia, for murdering Corrinne?"

"You don't know that."

"True. But I do know that she hated Corrinne almost as much as she hated me. I'm just fortunate she didn't fire into both of Marvin's boxes."

"Not according to what Olivia told me. She said that Corrinne even testified on her behalf at the trial."

Stephanie stared at me wide-eyed. "Olivia lied to you, Molly. Corrinne testified on *my* behalf, not hers."

"Why would she lie like that?"

"She wants everyone to take her side. She wants to cover her tracks."

I didn't know Olivia, but this portion of what Stephanie was saying made sense. "She seemed so nice," I murmured.

"She's every bit as calculating as I am. She just hides it better." Stephanie scanned me at length, then chuckled. "I must say, Molly, you look terrible. All of this is getting to you. You need to stay home today and get some rest."

The obvious audacity of her saying that to me when

she'd let herself into my house uninvited angered me so much that I could only growl.

Stephanie held up her palms. "I'll let you go. I've still got Mikey in the car. His Montessori kindergarten class is still holding classes today."

"Why did you come here in the first place?"

She whirled on her heel in a Ginger Rogers move. "Oh, I'm glad you reminded me. I know what a personal interest you take in these—" She flicked her wrist. "—murders and things, so I thought you might want to know the latest."

"What?"

"Jack Vance was indeed about to fire Corrinne."

"Why?"

She studied my face. "You really haven't heard?"

I shook my head.

She chuckled and waltzed to the front door, murmuring, "Well, *that's* a first. Lauren must have actually kept her mouth shut."

"About what?" I asked, so angry now with the implied insult of my best friend that I shouted the question at her.

"Corrinne was having sexual relations with one of her students." She gave me one of her patented cover-girl smiles. "Take care, Molly."

She let herself out.

Chapter 4

Goldilocks and the Troll

The moment Stephanie closed the door behind her, Nathan and Karen trotted into the kitchen to join me, led by the ever-enthusiastic BC. The two-footed participants of that particular trio tended to avoid Stephanie themselves, but enjoyed observing my agitated emotional state that invariably resulted from her visits.

"Hi, Mom," Nathan said. Already apparently fresh out of small talk, he glanced back at his sister.

"What did Stephanie want?" Karen asked with a big smile, unable to mask her glee at my obvious agitation.

Her usual pound of flesh, I thought. Stephanie should be an employee of Weight Watchers. "Just to chat," I replied.

"If you're going over to Lauren's now, can I come with you and see Rachel? Nathan's going to go to Robert's house."

Nathan chimed in, "His mom says it's okay. I already called."

"Why do you assume I'm going to Lauren's house?" I asked Karen, deeply annoyed that I was this predictable. "I haven't even had the chance to read the paper. And I have work to do. Cartoons to draw. Greeting cards to design. Faxes to . . . fax."

Nathan grabbed a jar of Skippy peanut butter, then headed toward the garage. "I'm bringing this for lunch.

His mom is into that yucky organic stuff. I'm riding my bike."

"Don't forget to wear your helmet."

"I always wear my helmet. Why do you say that to me every time I ride my bike?"

"Because bikes don't have seat belts, so it would be silly of me to remind you to fasten your seat belt, now wouldn't it? Have a good time and tell Robert's mom that—"

"I will. 'Bye, Mom." He closed the door behind him before I could finish the sentence. I'd have to call her later.

Karen grabbed an apple out of the refrigerator. "Did you get a new customer?" she asked, then took a noisy bite.

"No, but I still have to troll."

"Troll?" she said with her mouth full. "You mean you're going to make like Rumpelstiltskin?"

"Exactly. I'm turning myself into a short, ugly, gnome-like creature so I can scare new clients into hiring me," I said over my shoulder as I went upstairs to change my clothes.

"So can I come with you to Lauren's?" Karen called after me.

"Sure."

Lauren and I sat in her kitchen as she nursed her cup of coffee and I sipped blackberry tea. We were in reflective moods, neither of us having slept well, both deeply disturbed by the murder we'd so unwillingly witnessed. In the background were the occasional vibrations of bass guitar that blared from the boom box in Rachel's room, where Rachel and Karen had set up camp.

"Our daughters are going to be attending high school next fall," Lauren said quietly. "They'll be using that very same auditorium."

"I know. The sooner the killer gets arrested, the

sooner we can put this behind us. Does Tommy have any strong leads?"

She shook her head, then fought off a shudder. "It could have been *me* in that trunk, or booth, or whatever you want to call it. I almost volunteered so that Corrinne would be free to watch the performance. But she was being so unpleasant all evening, I decided not to do her the favor."

"I've been thinking about that. About the timing, I mean. I think that the killer was gunning for Corrinne, not for just whoever happened to be inside Martin's box. At one point Stephanie suggested the killer was really aiming for her. Did it seem that way to you from where you sat?"

"No, it was obvious that Stephanie was stuck in the other box, so there's no way."

"Which reminds me," I said, proud of myself for holding off on this particular subject for several minutes now. "Stephanie told me that Corrinne was having sex with one of her students. I take it she means Danielle's son, right?"

Lauren grimaced. "She means Danielle's son, all right. But there's room for doubt regarding what exactly had been going on. The two of them were spotted from the restaurant of an inn north of Saratoga a couple of days ago, coming out of a room. Corrinne, of course, had said it was all perfectly innocent—that she was simply counseling him in school matters and had checked into the room because her house was being painted. In any case, he's eighteen, so technically he was of age."

"Why would she 'counsel' him in her hotel room?"

Lauren tilted her head slightly in her personal version of a shrug. "It did strain credibility, though of course she claimed he wasn't sharing the room, that they'd merely met there to talk in private. Rumor around school has it that even though they *had* been 'dating,' they'd broken up a couple of months ago."

"Who was it who spotted them at this inn?"

"Elsbeth and her daughter."

Karen's piano teacher? I let this sink in for a moment. "No wonder Elsbeth had been so ready to share the news with me when we were in the dressing room last night, though she didn't get the chance."

"Furthermore, lately Danielle's son and Jenny, Olivia's daughter, are arm-in-arm nearly every time the two of them pass by the office."

"And Jenny's soon to be considered Stephanie's adopted daughter."

"Right."

"Well, that's quite the extended family, then. Yuck. Makes me so glad I've got such an ordinary, simple life. My kids are too young to date, and I—"

"Wait till next year."

"What do you mean?"

"Karen and Rachel will be in high school. That's when the dating starts."

"No way. They're way too young. They'll still only be fourteen."

"Don't you remember ninth-grade couples back when we were at Carlton High School?"

"Yeah, but that's . . . different."

"How? Because now you're a mother, talking about your daughter?"

"Exactly. And I'm old enough now to know how young fourteen really is."

"Sure, but try pointing that out to a fourteen-year-old."

My stomach was doing flip-flops, and my tea had suddenly lost its flavor. I couldn't face the thought of my one and only little girl riding in the car of some boy who'd just gotten his license and felt immortal. There had to be some way to delay this. Maybe I could start feeding her chocolate and greasy foods and hope for an outbreak of acne. Ninth grade was still six months away, at least, and this murder case had better be solved long before then.

Tommy's sons were in high school, now that I thought about it. They might know exactly what was going on between Corrinne and Danielle Underwood's son. "Are Joey and Jasper here?"

Lauren scoffed. "With school out? Of course not. They're hanging out at the mall."

Which was probably where most of the high-schoolers were. I knew Tiffany Saunders well, and she'd be easy to broach the subject with. Getting to my feet, I asked, "Want to come shopping with me?"

"Shopping? You're asking me to go shopping?" She narrowed her eyes and studied me. "Okay, who are you really, and what have you done with my friend Molly?"

"I want to locate Tiffany Saunders and see what I can find out about some of these messy relationships that have been affecting our clown suspects."

I easily found Tiffany at a table in the food court at the mall. Featurewise, Tiffany and her mother were dead ringers, but Tiffany always did interesting things to her hair. Currently she was going for the wet look, wearing her raven-dyed hair slicked back against her scalp. Surrounded by four other teenagers, she looked less than thrilled to see me. I greeted her by name, and she said, "Hey." When I didn't move on, she said to her companions, "This is Molly Masters, guys. I used to baby-sit for her kids."

"Hey," a couple of them mumbled, or at least gave a grunt that sounded close enough.

"Nice to meet you." I looked at the pretty girl next to Tiffany. Her hair had the same strawberry-blond hue as Olivia Garrett's, along with similar attractive features and a slim, dancer's body. "You must be Jenny Garrett, right? You look a little like your mom."

"Please. I look like my dad. Everyone knows that."

"I stand corrected," I replied, though I was thinking that her late father had to have been her mother's look-alike for this to be true.

A solidly built young man with bleached-blond hair had his arm around her, and I suspected that he must be Danielle Underwood's son. His overall bearing was tense and unhappy, and he wore a deep frown. Such could often be said of teenagers in general, however. Returning my gaze to Tiffany, I asked, "Can I talk to you for just a minute, please?"

She looked around at her friends as if this were a horrid imposition and said, "Sheesh. We were, like, just in the middle of an important conversation. But I guess if you guys don't mind . . ."

No one objected, no doubt to Tiffany's chagrin. She scooted out of her chair and walked away from the table with me, which was no easy feat, for she was wearing clogs and a tight-fitting, floor-length black skirt with slits up the side that reached almost to her panty line. Why not just pin a pair of black towels to a belt?

When she decided we were at a suitable distance so as not to be overheard, she mumbled, "So what's up?"

"I'm sure your mother told you about the shooting last night."

"Well, duh."

"I feel . . . partly responsible, and I'd like to see if there's anything I can do to help get this person behind bars." She was already looking over her shoulder at her friends' table, so I got right to the point. "Would you and your friends be willing to discuss what you know about Corrinne Buldock with me?"

She shrugged and fidgeted with a plastered-down lock of black hair. "What's in it for us?"

A small table emptied beside us, so I sat down and gestured for Tiffany to do the same. Once she did so, I said, "I could take you and your four friends out to lunch, anyplace you'd like."

She studied my face for a moment, then let out a guffaw. "You're serious, aren't you? I meant something *good* for us, not punishment. I mean, no offense, but like, jeez, you're older than my mom."

"Actually, she's almost a full year older than I am."

"Really? She told me you had two years on her."

"Not to contradict your mother, but we were in the same graduating class, Tiffany."

"Yeah, but . . . didn't you get held back a couple times? That's what my mom said."

In spite of myself, I found myself having to resist a smile. I'd been a good student, which Stephanie knew. "No. A lot of women have trouble being honest about their age, once they hit forty." My own fortieth birthday had only recently come and gone, and Jim had failed to pick up on my frequent hints that I wouldn't be depressed, so long as I was in Bermuda at the time. The experience had taught me to dispense with subtlety in the future. For my fiftieth, I was booking the trip myself.

Tiffany managed to nod her youthful and greasy-looking head sagely. "Yeah, come to think of it, the big four-oh is prob'ly a killer for Mom to face up to."

"So what can I offer that would be appealing? I could give you tips to use when interviewing with college admissions officers."

Tiffany not only grimaced but looked as though she might be physically ill. An obvious no.

"I could draw a caricature of the five of you."

"Hmm. I can toss that out to the others, but like, somebody else might see the drawing, and we'd die. What else you got? Could we, like, borrow your Jeep and take it off-road?"

"No. Whatever it is has to be something I wouldn't be ashamed or embarrassed to admit to your parents."

She scoffed. "I'll see what I can do. I wouldn't hold my breath if I were you."

"I'll just sit here and breathe normally, in that case. But remember, my entire agenda here is to help catch the person who killed your teacher."

She hesitated. "Yeah," she said quietly. "Ms. Buldock deserved better than what she got." Tiffany went back to her group. They had a small powwow, glancing over at me from time to time to make sure I wasn't listening, but from my vantage point their conversation entailed a lot of shrugging and general indifference. Finally, the boy who'd had his arm slung around Jenny Garrett's shoulder came over to my table.

"Molly, right?" He turned his chair around and straddled its back as he sat down across from me at my small chrome-topped table.

"Yes. Are you Brian Underwood?"

"Yeah. Uh, I already, like, talked to the police first thing this morning. Tiff says you once helped get her dad's killer put away, and I'd sure like Corrie's killer to get what's coming to him."

"Corrie?"

"Corrinne Buldock."

"Can I get you a cup of coffee or anything?"

"Nah. To tell you the truth, we're really too old to hang here at the mall. It's just for the kids without wheels. We were all set to Audi five-thousand when you showed up. I've only got a minute. What did you want to know?"

"I was concerned because I heard a rumor about you and Corrinne—"

"That Corrie and I were doin' the big nasty?"

"I guess that's one way of putting it." Though certainly not *my* way. "I've got an eighth-grader who's just about to start high school next fall. I'd kind of like to know how . . . common this fraternizing between students and teachers is at the high school."

He couldn't help but give me a cocky smile. "Not at all common." He was obviously well-aware of how handsome he was, though his bleached-blond hair was a bit distracting overall.

"That's nice to hear."

He crossed his arms on top of his backward-facing seat and leaned closer to me. "Look, Molly. Corrie was the one who went after me. You know? I had my eye on Jenny and, you know, she's more fun. I had to cool it with Corrie. That's why I was there at the inn when we got busted. I was trying to let her down easy, you know?"

"I see. And you and Jenny Garrett have been going out for a while now, right?"

"Yeah. So that's why I called it off with Corrie. 'Sides, I had to do *something* to get Dave off my case."

"Dave?"

"Paxton. An art teacher at the high school. He 'n' Corrie were hot 'n' heavy for quite a while. And he was, like, threatening to flunk me in art history."

"You're certain that was because of your relationship with Corrinne?" I kept the cynicism from my voice, but my thought was that, because of his physical maturity, I might have assigned too high an intellectual and emotional maturity to him; it was typical behavior to blame the teachers and external causes for poor grades.

He spread his hands. "What else? I mean, I go to class every day, and it's just, you know, an art class. Who flunks art? Give me a break! I'm working on a four point six and—"

"Four point six?" I repeated, wondering if he'd misspoken. "Isn't a straight A average equal to a four point oh?"

"Nah. They got everything weighted. And double-honors classes like Corrie's were worth another half point each."

The cynical side of me couldn't help but wonder what Brian was doing to earn his extra half point. Corrinne had always struck me as competent and sensible. But maybe she hadn't been with regard to her love life.

"She was a nice lady, you know?" He paused, fisting his hands. "My mom hated her, though."

"How did she find out about you and Ms. Buldock?"

He shrugged. "The buzz got around pretty fast this week. Tamara Young must have blabbed."

Or her mother did, I thought, remembering how eager Elsbeth had been to discuss it in the dressing room last night. "Huh," I murmured noncommittally. He was certainly turning Danielle Underwood into a viable suspect.

He seemed to realize this, for he scowled. "Mom didn't kill her, though. That's for sure. She freaks at loud noises. Couldn't possibly fire a gun." He rose, flipped the chair back around, and waggled his thumb in the direction of his friends' table. "Listen, we gotta jam. I'm sorry that I can't be more help, but like, none of us saw this coming. Far as we know, everyone liked her. Thing is, though, I think it was Dave, 'cause Corrie left him. It's not like anybody's mom would be gunning people down, you know?"

If only it were true that being a mother prevented one from committing murder, we would have fewer suspects. "Thanks for talking with me, Brian. It was nice meeting you."

"Yeah. Likewise. I really hope they nail whoever did this."

"So do I."

He nodded, then returned to his table. I left the food court and headed toward the exit, then decided to stop at the public phone and call my machine, because both kids were at friends' houses and couldn't reach me otherwise.

There was a message from Jim, mentioning in accusatory tones that he "couldn't help but notice you're not home, despite what you said this morning about not leaving the house." Great. The man almost never listens to me and yet had committed every word to memory this morning, now that I'd gone back on those particular words.

A second message was from Jack Vance, principal at Carlton High. He said he'd "like to talk" as soon as I had a few minutes and asked if I "could stop by" that afternoon. Now was as good a time as any, and I made the short drive to Carlton Central School.

The front door to the high school was unlocked. The instant I entered, Nadine called, "Can I help you?" She was sitting sentry in the office. The big sliding-glass windows of the office gave her an unimpeded view of the door.

Even with school not in session, she was wearing a dress, a simple blue-nylon shift. The only time I'd ever seen her in anything other than a dress was when she was in her clown costume. She had close-cropped curly hair, was plump, and wore reading glasses halfway down her little nose. The glasses, I believed, were only a prop, so that she could officiously peer over them.

"Hello, Nadine. I didn't think there'd be anybody here today."

"Just me. I'm the security guard for the front entrance." Neither her tones nor her face bore even a hint of a smile. "What can I help you with?"

"I'm here to speak to Jack. He called me a few—"

Just then Jack Vance emerged from his office behind Nadine. He had once been considered the hunk of our graduating class, but he hadn't aged well. His once-muscular frame was now pudgy, and his former glorious hair was mostly gone, though he wore the vestiges in a silly-looking ponytail. "Molly, good to see you." He gave me a wan smile. "How are you handling things? I know we're all reeling from what happened last night."

"Yes."

He ushered me into his office, closed the door behind us, and had me take a seat in front of his desk. Then he sat down, laced his fingers, and said, "From what I understand, you had the best chance to identify the killer. You were closest to him, or her, at the time."

"That's true, but I don't know who it was, even so. I just couldn't tell anything to set that one clown apart from all the others."

"For all I know, then, it could be one of my employees—Dave Paxton or my secretary."

"I know. It's awful." The thought of an employee at my children's school being a murderer was harrowing, but not much worse than its being one of the more active parents of the PTA.

Jack's eyes were bloodshot, his face pale. "I wish I could suspend them with pay till this thing gets solved, but that makes it look bad for them, and at least one of them is innocent. I'd like to think they both are."

"I wish I could have seen something, some telling detail that differentiated the killer's costume from the others, but I just didn't." I paused, and decided I had to ask about the rumor Stephanie had passed to me. "When we were in the dressing room last night, someone said they'd overheard you and Corrinne in an argument."

"It's true. She was a good teacher, but her personal judgment wasn't always as solid as her classroom skills."

"So I gather. I heard about her and Brian Underwood."

He nodded, grim-faced. "What a mess. This is something the district trains us principals to handle. You have to expect the occasional teacher dating another teacher. You dread the teachers dating students." He dragged his hand across his thinning hair. "I keep thinking I should have stayed in the building last night till everyone was gone. The school's such a powder keg these days, what with who's dating whom and a student suing for divorce from her parents."

"Don't blame yourself for going home. It must have been ten P.M. by then. If either of us can feel bad for not preventing the murder, it's me. I never even screamed in warning or did anything when the killer brushed right past me."

"If you had, the killer might have shot you first." He forced a smile. He placed his palms on the surface of his desk. "Tell you what, you don't blame yourself for not taking out an armed gunman single-handedly, and I won't blame myself for not personally supervising after hours, despite knowing I had a ticking time bomb on my hands. Deal?"

"Deal," I replied, but I felt no better and could tell that Jack didn't either. For just a moment the thought crossed my mind that maybe Jack had done it, that he could have gotten a clown costume someplace, despite Tommy's assurances last night. "When did you hear about the shooting?"

"Almost immediately afterward. An officer came to my house. Even made me feel like a suspect, for a while there. If I hadn't happened to stop at an ATM on my way home and then bumped into a neighbor, I wouldn't have had an alibi and might still be under suspicion."

I blushed a little. "Tommy told me there was no way it could have been anyone other than the seven of us in clown suits. And I was cleared only because the killer swiped my gloves." I studied his features, once again barely able to see the handsome boy I'd known when we were students at Carlton.

"Like most high schools, we've tightened security, and the guards put the place in lockdown the instant they heard the gunshots. Everything was bolted shut. Nobody left the building till after the police checked every inch of the place."

"I guess that's reassuring," I muttered.

He smiled sadly. "Remember when we held that boy-cott because they were serving us banana-and-peanut-butter sandwiches for lunch?"

I nodded. "We called the local television stations, and they came and did a segment on us."

"The world's changed. I listened to the national news this morning. They're reporting this as 'another school shooting,' saying we were lucky that only one teacher was killed." He met my eyes. "Molly, please think hard about everything you saw last night. I can't have a killer walking the same halls as me and these kids."

"I couldn't agree with you more, Jack. I'll do whatever I can." I added sadly, "I just don't see how I can make much of a difference." I left his office.

Nadine had deserted her sentry post. The front door was now propped open. From the doorway, I heard someone whispering around the corner. This had to be some lookie-loos, titillated by surveying the scene of the crime. Irritated, I decided to embarrass them, and tip-toed around the corner.

I had to stifle a gasp. It was Chester Walker, my erst-while sunroom contractor, in some sort of clandestine meeting with Nadine Dahl. Nadine was accepting cash from him. He straightened in surprise at my sudden ap-pearance. "Molly. What are you . . . I was just—"

"Purchasing some tickets for the show," Nadine com-pleted on his behalf.

"For the variety show?"

"Yes," Nadine said. "We're postponing it, but when it takes place, we're going to set up a memorial fund in Corrinne's honor." She smiled at Chester. "Thank you for being so generous."

"It was the least I could do." The color had risen so high in Chester's face that his bald scalp had pinkened.

"If you'll excuse me, I need to get back to work," Nadine said.

"Me, too," Chester said. "Molly, I'll be over first thing Monday, to get the workers started on your addition."

Monday? During our last conversation on the subject, he had said it would be today, at the very latest. "Uh, that's great, Chester. Thanks."

He gave me a sheepish smile, then left, heading for the west parking lot, rolling some sheets of paper into a tube shape as he walked.

Those sheets looked vaguely familiar, but I couldn't quite place them. I was halfway back to my house before it hit me what those forms were—school transcripts.

Chapter 5

The Sun Will Come Out, Tamara

"Are you *sure* there's school today?" Nathan asked me, even though at the time I was standing in the doorway, waving to Karen as her bus for junior high pulled away from our cul-de-sac. Karen had long since decided it was "uncool" to wave goodbye to one's mother, which was why I made a special point of waving. If I'd learned anything from my teenage years, it was that at no time is it as important for parents to show how much they love us than when we are acting our most unlovable and the least in need of parental love.

I pointed out the window. "You see that? It's a school bus."

"Yeah, but that doesn't mean *I'll* have school today. Maybe they won't open the elementary schools today. It's a Friday. Nobody learns anything on Fridays anyway."

"Well, maybe you can be the first." I glanced over at him. He was currently wiping down the kitchen counters. Betty Cocker was at his feet, attempting to sniff out the inevitable spillage. "Nathan, quit cleaning and go to school."

"But the house is a mess."

"It's barely in the beginning stages of disarray. Meanwhile, your bus is coming."

"Fine!" Nathan set a bowl containing milk and some dregs of his sugar-coated Cheerios on the floor and swept up his backpack. BC was, of course, delighted and ran over to lap up the milk while Nathan stormed out of the house.

Well-aware of the diminishing point of return from reacting to this type of behavior, I called cheerfully, "Have a great day. And be sure and buck the system and learn a lot, even though it's a Friday."

He let the glass outer door slam behind him.

" 'Bye, Nathan," Jim called after him as he came down the stairs. Nathan said nothing, merely continued his trudge toward the bus, doing the slouch-shouldered forward lean he takes on whenever he's especially unhappy. Jim looked at me. "What's the matter with him?"

"He's mad at me, as usual." I hugged myself with feigned delight. "Ah, the rewards of motherhood! It hardly seems fair. All of this adoration, bestowed on one mere mortal."

Jim chuckled, grabbed a cereal bar and a yogurt to eat on the drive, then rubbed the dog's tummy, gave me a quick peck on the cheek, and left for work. So long as he remembered which of us received which display of affection, things were all right by me.

The phone rang. I answered and was greeted with a particularly melodious, "Good morning, Molly. This is Nadine Dahl."

" 'Morning," I replied, confused. The woman had never called me before, plus her vocal tones were so different in person. She seemed to have a phone voice and a regular speaking voice.

Nadine said, "Under the circumstances, I thought that I had best call first to verify that you're still coming in this morning."

" 'Coming in'?"

"You're supposed to give a demonstration and talk at the high school about cartooning."

"Oh, my gosh. That's right. I'd forgotten."

"Can you still come?"

"Yes, though I'm not sure that it's appropriate. I can't imagine any of the high school students caring about cartooning on the first day back after what happened to one of their teachers."

"True, but it's not as though you have to keep them enraptured. I think it's best that we give the assurance to the students that life goes on as usual, don't you?"

"I'm not sure. Life *doesn't* 'go on as usual' for Corrinne. Plus it's a Friday, so nobody will be paying attention," I said, effortlessly employing my son's logic, even if it hadn't worked on me. "Maybe it'd be better to let the teachers have open discussions in their classes. Encourage the kids to talk about their feelings."

She made a noise that sounded like a puff of derision, but maybe I was being overly sensitive. "You're scheduled for Dave Paxton's second- and fourth-period art classes. What you and he decide to do during that time period is up to the two of you."

"Right. I'll be there." Her statement, too, was surprising. Dave Paxton had been so distraught Wednesday night that it seemed odd he was even planning on coming in today. "Nadine, does Lauren happen to be nearby?"

A clattering noise resounded, as though the phone had been dropped. Without another word from Nadine, Lauren was on the line and said, "Hello?" as if confused.

"Lauren, is everything all right there? Business as usual?"

"Sure. Everyone's a bit more subdued. Some teachers are wearing black ribbons or armbands."

"Such as Dave Paxton?"

"Yes. He's really dragging today, but he's here."

"I forgot to tell you about something strange I witnessed yesterday. Is Nadine nearby?"

"Yes. Maybe we can talk about it later today."

"Sounds good." We said our goodbyes, then I rushed

upstairs and started to change my clothes. While scanning my choices of apparel, I realized that I might as well stay in my casual, no-great-loss-if-ink-is-spilled-on-them clothing. I fed the dog and then drove to the school.

Originally, today had been planned as a career day at school. Though I'd felt that high school students were far too old and cynical to want to hear presentations on what some of us parents did in our jobs, the staff apparently disagreed. I suspected that this had more to do with their wanting to give themselves a day away from teaching while they prepared the second-trimester report cards, but perhaps the "old and cynical" onus was only applicable to yours truly.

A half-dozen or so parents stood in the school lobby, waiting to sign in and get visitor badges. I recognized two of them: Chester Walker, my sunroom contractor, and Elsbeth Young, my daughter's piano teacher. Chester was perhaps here to demonstrate something in the shop class—if they still had such classes in high school—and Elsbeth for music.

She and I greeted each other. "Seems almost disrespectful of us to be here," Elsbeth immediately said.

"I agree."

Though I liked her well enough, she always struck me as someone who had taken the thought of "artist's temperament" too literally. She dyed her hair an unnatural shade of red and rarely combed it, and wore brightly colored Indian blouses, often with beaded necklaces—a youthful look for someone who appeared to have successfully pushed past fifty a couple of years ago. The March weather had brought its normal upstate New York chill, so that today she was also wearing a black cape, felt tam, and gloves.

"They have the auditorium locked shut. That's originally where I was scheduled to perform today."

"Are you just using the upright piano in one of the music rooms now?"

She nodded, looking past my shoulder. She clenched her jaw as Chester approached us.

"Glad to run into you this morning, Molly," he said. "Shall we count on getting the construction into gear at your house Monday afternoon?"

Hadn't he said "first thing Monday" the last time we spoke? "Sure. And it's just three days from start to finish, right?"

"That's what I said, all right."

"Yes, but is it true? It's hard to believe."

"As well it should be," Elsbeth said under her breath.

He turned his attention to Elsbeth and glared at her. "Ah, Elsbeth. Good morning. I got the chance to scan the top students' class schedules the other day. I see you padded your daughter's stats with some automatic A classes this last semester."

I was already appalled at Chester for announcing that he'd done such a thing. What right did any parent have to scan other students' class schedules?

"Tamara chooses her own course work, Chester," Elsbeth retorted, "which she's entitled to do." She narrowed her eyes at him, her hands fisted. "She'll have to do that next fall at *Stanford* anyway."

I was next in line for signing in and getting my visitor's badge and did so. Both Lauren and Nadine were staring past my shoulder at Chester as he teased, "Yeah. Sure she does. You expect me to believe it's just a coincidence that she's got the easiest graders in the entire school this year?"

"I don't expect or want you to believe anything of the kind, Chester. Tamara has done an excellent job in school. That's earned her my trust. She certainly doesn't have to answer to you."

"Yeah? I heard about those great grades of hers. Word

has it that that was quite a paper you wrote for music theory."

"Tamara wrote that herself! Honestly, Chester! Are you really so bloodthirsty that you think I would stoop to *your* level and turn in papers for my child?"

Although first period was currently in session, some students had this as their free period and were only now entering the building. A pair of them conspicuously listened in to Elsbeth and Chester's discussion.

"I don't turn in papers for my son!" Chester snapped. "He has always—"

"Excuse me for interrupting," I said. "Did you notice that there are other people around, listening to you?"

Chester looked at me, his face clouded with anger. He yanked the pen from me, signed the register, then returned his focus to Elsbeth and pointed a finger at her. "Don't act holier than thou. Everyone's parents help their children when they get to this level. I'm not about to let some artificial sense of ethics destroy my son's future." He snatched the visitor's tag from Lauren and stormed off.

The moment I glanced at Nadine, she averted her eyes. My thoughts returned to the secretive rendezvous I'd stumbled into yesterday. This little interaction verified to me that Chester had indeed been bribing Nadine into supplying him with student transcripts.

Elsbeth quietly signed in. "Jeez. I'm sorry anyone overheard that. It's so embarrassing to see a grown man treat his son as though he were his own personal puppet."

"Yes, it is," I said firmly, so Nadine would hear this as well.

Elsbeth suddenly smiled and searched my eyes. "Speaking of prize pupils, you know that I've progressed Karen into Chopin and she's doing just beautifully. She's quite a gifted pianist."

"Thanks. She's not always great at practicing, though. I sometimes have a hard time dragging her away from the phone or the TV."

She laughed. "Sometimes I'd throw the circuit breakers in my house and insist that the power wasn't going back on until my daughter got her practicing in and completed her homework."

"I imagine that would get quick results. So long as she could still see the piano music and her homework." In fact, I was surprised that I'd never thought of this myself. Whoever coined the expression "necessity is the mother of invention" didn't opt for the word "mother" for nothing.

"Good luck with your presentation," Elsbeth said. "Cartooning, right? I believe my Tamara mentioned that this morning."

"Yes. Hardly an appropriate subject, though." I excused myself and made my way down the hallway. In my nervousness, and despite my apprehension about the timing of my presence in the school, I found myself singing, "The sun will come out, Tamara . . ." Fortunately, there were no immediate witnesses.

I hoped I wouldn't have to sing that song all the way home to cheer myself up after my fiasco of a presentation. Never have I had so many bored faces aimed, more or less, in my direction. In fact, when I picked out Tamara's face in that sea of placidity, I was tempted to sing a reprise just to get a reaction, knowing full well that she must get this joke all the time.

I moved away from my discussion of what makes something funny, having proven beyond a shadow of a doubt that the answer was: nothing that I had to say on the subject. Instead, I talked about caricatures—how to select one characteristic feature and exaggerate it to comic effect.

Not wanting to subject a child to possible ridicule, I

asked the teacher to be a model. This was, after all, the person who had originally subjected me to *my* current unease by selecting me to give this presentation in the first place.

He obliged by having a seat on the stool beside me in the middle of the art room. "Now Mr. Paxton here has what appears to be unusually widely spaced eyes."

"That comes from having to keep watch in all directions on my students," he said with a smile.

A couple of snickers indicated that I had made a good decision; Dave was clearly game, and the class needed this opportunity to relax by having fun with the teacher. Now, if only by some minor miracle I were instantly granted the ability to produce good caricatures on the spot.

"We'll just give Mr. Paxton a big head and a little body," I said as I drew.

"So it's an exact likeness, then?" somebody wisecracked from the back.

"One more remark and you're Mrs. Masters's next model," Mr. Paxton said amiably.

"Notice that I'm making his curly hair look wild to augment the basic comic effect, and that I'm putting him at an easel himself, to show that he's an artist. By putting the subject in their natural element within the cartoon, you make it easier to identify the person." A technique for masking basic lack of artistic ability, I silently added.

I chattered throughout the drawing process and finished the sketch, which portrayed Dave Paxton as a wideeyed wild man. I pulled the sheet off its pad and held it up for everyone to see. The students laughed and applauded. Afterward, I let Dave see, and he grinned and shook his head. "You flatter me, Mrs. Masters."

"Now you know why caricature drawing is just a sideline for me." I sneaked a surreptitious glance at the clock and saw that I still had twenty minutes to fill. "Are there any questions?" I asked. No raised hands. Drat! Was I going to have to do *more* drawings?

"Turnabout, as we know, is fair play." Dave started handing out sheets of drawing paper. "This being an art history class, you rarely get the chance to do your own compositions, but let's all draw a caricature of Mrs. Masters, shall we?"

Being a model was easier than being an artist—I can do nothing with the best of them—so I switched places with Dave eagerly. "Draw away," I said.

"Ten minutes, then we'll hand them in and let our guest artist comment."

During those ten minutes, I obsessed about my posture and my state of exhaustion, not having slept well for two nights in a row. The student drawings would likely feature bags under my bloodshot eyes. I also pondered the bad will between Chester and Elsbeth. Could one of them have been so angry over a bad grade that they'd killed Corrinne? Surely not. Besides, I truly didn't want to consider Elsbeth as a viable suspect. Karen spent too much time in the woman's company for me to acknowledge any possibility that she could be a murderer.

The students were getting such a big kick out of the awful drawings of me that I was only halfway through the stack of thirty or so when the bell rang. The classroom began to empty out immediately, no one pausing long enough to get their pictures back. When I asked about this, one student called out, "Keep the drawings as our present to you."

I breathed a sigh of relief, glad that I'd survived. "One more presentation and you're done," Dave said, nipping my sense of relief in the bud.

"Oh, that's right. I keep managing to forget that I said I'd do this twice today." I massaged my neck a little. "I'm already exhausted. I can't tell you how impressed I am that you do this every day, all day long."

"It does get a bit trying at times. Especially today."

"I'm surprised they didn't keep school closed for another day; start fresh on Monday."

He shrugged and said bitterly, "Typical of the way things work around here. Lose a close friend and a peer, but we're supposed to carry on as if it never happened."

"I'm sorry for your loss, Dave."

He frowned. "We'd recently agreed to see other people, but all that was doing for me was showing me how special Corrinne was." Under his breath he added, "Not that I knew that her definition of 'other people' was going to include a student."

"That must have made you pretty angry," I prompted, thinking about how Brian Underwood had named Dave as the person he most suspected.

He gave me a lopsided smile. "Actually, Corrinne was the one who was angry. It was my decision to see other people for a while. I'd gotten out of one bad marriage and wanted to be absolutely sure. She chose Brian Underwood as a means to rub my nose in my mistake." His expression became almost unbearably sad. "It worked, too. Once the hubbub around the variety show settled down, I'd planned to propose to her."

"I'm sorry."

"Not one-tenth as sorry as I am to lose her."

Feeling awkward at seeing someone I barely knew in such obvious pain, I averted my eyes and searched for a distraction. I started flipping through the students' remaining drawings, until one froze me in place: a drawing of a clown, dangling from a hangman's noose.

Chapter 6

Not Good Enough
for My Daughter

"What's that you've got there?" Dave Paxton asked, stepping toward me as if to peer over my shoulder. "An insulting caricature?"

"No, just different," I replied as casually as possible, quickly flipping the drawing onto the bottom of my stack. The student artist was clearly venting some raw emotions. There was no chance that I'd let anyone who'd been dressed like a clown see the drawing and risk stirring up reactive emotions.

Come to think of it, the students were unlikely to know that *I* wasn't a suspect. Furthermore, whoever drew the hanged clown had to assume that Dave *would* see it. Was it intended as some sort of accusation or dare, to him or to me? That thought sent a chill up my spine.

Olivia Garrett stepped into the room, looking very classy in a peach-colored business suit that brought out the red highlights in her hair. Her expression fell at the sight of me. Apparently she still resented me for the way Stephanie had barged into my house yesterday—guilt by association, I suppose. She nodded slightly to me, then turned to Dave. "Good morning. Have you got the painting for me?"

"I forgot all about that. Good thing one of us is still thinking clearly." He attempted to tamp down his hair—which did resemble my wild-man drawing—as he led Olivia toward a door at the back of the art room. "It's still in my office." He unlocked the door, then glanced at me. "Now that you've shared one of your drawings with my class, want to see one of mine?"

"I'd love to," I replied, rolling up the stack of student drawings as I spoke. I grabbed a rubber band en route and slipped it over the tube-shaped papers.

"Olivia has a gallery in Ballston Spa, and she sometimes exhibits my work," Dave explained.

"He's one of my best-selling artists," she said in a haughty tone, though with her high-pitched voice, it wasn't especially effective.

"That's wonderful, Dave."

He gave me a friendly wink. "And it pays so well that it allows me to hold down a second full-time job here at the school."

His office was packed with file cabinets, most of which featured thin, oversized drawers, which allow artists to store their work flat. One drawer was open a couple of inches, and I caught sight of a portion of the sketch on top. "Mind if I flip through some drawings?"

He glanced over from his task of removing a protective carrying case. "Go ahead. Those are my handiwork, too. Just don't judge my ability too harshly. They're preliminary sketches I was doing for my oils."

I pulled out the stack of papers and leafed through them. They were all competently drawn, mostly of objects or what appeared to be sections of compositions he'd been studying. As he'd warned, the sketches failed to indicate how good his final work might be.

Two-thirds through the stack one drawing stopped me. It was a portrait of Corrinne, in a much later stage of completion than the preceding drawings. "Corrinne," I murmured appreciatively and studied the sketch. The drawing had an Andrew Wyeth quality to it, with Corrinne shown in full-body profile on the left side of the page. Her hands rested in her jean pockets, and the wind blew her hair back as she stared across the otherwise barren field. Though beautifully rendered, the drawing was visually out of balance. Something was needed on either the right side or the center of the work to draw the viewer's eye.

"Let me see," Olivia said, and I turned so she could look over my shoulder.

She took it from me. "Ah, yes. That was the first painting I ever sold. I like the composition of the final piece much better. Remember, Dave?" She held the drawing up for him to see.

He looked at the drawing. "Of course. That was *my* first big sale, too. Though I like to think I've improved since then. Who'd you sell it to, anyway? Do you remember?"

"That German couple, visiting from Frankfurt."

"Right. How could I forget? The sale made me an internationally selling artist," he said to me, wiggling his eyebrows. Though his facial expressions had been playful ever since Olivia arrived, there was an underlying sadness to his bearing, as if he were playacting for her benefit. He held a picture frame, which was roughly three feet across and four feet high. Taking a nervous breath, he turned it around so we could see. "I hope you agree that my newest work is much better."

It was a full-body self-portrait done in oils, in which he sat against the trunk of a tree. Dressed in jeans and a navy-blue T-shirt, he was barefoot and was seated crosslegged with his elbows on his knees, his face slightly turned. His work, almost too lifelike for my personal tastes, reflected an incredible skill that I greatly envied. And the rendering of light and shadow as sunlight filtered through the leaves of the tree was exceptional.

"It's . . . astonishing," I said. "I had no idea you were this good, Dave. I can't believe you brought me in to do a demonstration to your class."

"Thanks," he said, beaming. He turned his hopeful eyes to Olivia. "And you?"

"Astonishing, indeed," Olivia said. "But that frame! Did you pick out that matte work yourself?"

"You don't like it?"

She shook her head. "Not at all. Should have been darker. A deep forest-green would have accentuated the colors. Don't you agree, Molly?"

"I . . . yes, now that you mention it, but I don't think that the sandstone matte detracts from the work."

"It doesn't detract, just doesn't accentuate." She sighed. "What do you want to do, Dave? Shall I hang it as is for a while and see if we get any action?"

She'd dampened his enthusiasm. "Yeah. I guess."

Taking much less care with the rewrapping than Dave had used in its unveiling, Olivia continued to chastise him for having mounted his painting without consulting her. As she left with his painting, I recognized remorse on his features. It was akin to that of parents as their kindergartners disappear into the classroom. In this case, his "child" was being admonished for wearing an ugly dress.

The second bell had already rung, signaling the start of the next school period. "I'd better get back to work," he said.

No one had come into the art room in the meantime. "Where are your students?" I asked. "I was hoping to just watch you do all the work for this next class, since I'm not supposed to do my demo again for another hour."

"Unfortunately, I'm on study hall duty now." He gestured at the couch along one wall of his small office. "You're welcome to stay and make yourself at home."

"That'd be great. Thanks."

"There's just one catch. Art supplies being what they are—i.e., often poisonous—I have to either know that a responsible adult is in here throughout or lock this room."

"I'm not sure that I consider myself a responsible adult, but I can probably find one to stay with me."

He chuckled. "What I meant was, if you think you might want to come and go, I'd better give you my key."

"If you don't mind, that'd be great. I'd like to go say hello to Lauren for a minute."

He gave me his keys—one for the art room and one for his office—then left, chastising himself for already being late.

I looped the strap of my purse around the tube-shaped collection of students' caricatures so I wouldn't forget them when I left. After perusing Dave's sketches a second time, I returned them to the drawer and decided to visit Lauren. The building was mostly quiet, with only a few students in the halls.

"Lauren will be back in a minute," Nadine immediately told me when I entered the office.

"Thanks. Mind if I wait for her in here?"

She smiled a little. "Not at all. How did your presentation go?"

I took a seat in Lauren's chair. Sizing Nadine up as a possible killer at worst and an unethical, bribe-accepting creep at best, I studied her features—her piercing gray eyes, downturned lips, button nose. Interestingly, she seemed to be studying me just as carefully. "The kids sat there like lumps of clay. I'm fairly certain I bored them to tears."

She peered at me over the top of her reading glasses, as was her habit. "Kids this age are so conscious of their peers that they don't always want to take the risk of giving you a whole lot of feedback."

"In that case, they succeeded."

She pursed her lips and made no comment. "Lauren

tells me you're about to embark on a home construction project. Have to say, I don't envy you in the least."

"I'm not looking forward to it either, but it's really nothing major, just putting on a sunroom. The room itself has already been made for us at the factory—it's a prefab aluminum-and-glass structure. They just have to come out, remove the ten-by-twelve upper-deck section, put in the footings and flooring, anchor it, and cut a door where we now have a window. Chester says the whole process only takes three days."

"Ah, yes. My husband and I had a simple remodeling job done on our house a few years ago. We had to sell the house at a loss as a result. And he's now my ex." She smiled ruefully. "Overall, it was worth every penny."

I, however, having no desire to lose my husband in the process, asked nervously, "Chester Walker wasn't your general contractor, was he?"

"No. I know nothing about Chester as a contractor."

Just as a cohort in crime, I thought sourly. "He seems to have quite the pulse on the top students at Carlton. What classes they're taking, their grade-point averages . . ."

I let my voice fade. She had no reaction whatsoever to my thinly veiled accusation, merely continued to watch me, so I upped the ante. "I saw him carrying school transcripts as he was leaving the grounds yesterday."

"Yes," she said, as if she hadn't a care in the world, or, more likely, had been prepared for me to bring up the subject. "They were his son's, which he'd asked me to provide for him, as he's entitled to request." She forced her downturned lips into something of a smile. "It may have looked suspicious yesterday, the timing of how you stumbled onto us right as he was making a school donation and where we happened to be standing at the time. I had been sneaking a cigarette, to tell you the truth."

"I didn't realize you smoked."

"I don't. Except when I'm seriously stressed. Old habits die hard, as they say."

So does suspicion, I thought, but kept this to myself. I have a keen sense of smell and could not believe that I would fail to detect the odor of recent cigarette smoke on a person's clothing and hair. Nadine had walked right past me as she returned to the building yesterday and bore no traces of smoke.

Lauren returned just then, and I sprang to my feet, still dying to tell her about my very strong suspicions regarding her de facto boss, Nadine. "Hi, Lauren. I've got thirty minutes free till I have to give my last presentation. Can you grab a cup of coffee with me in the teachers' lounge?"

She glanced at Nadine, who nodded, then said, "Let's go."

We headed down the hall. "I've got to tell you something in private, about Nadine," I whispered. "If there's anyone else in the lounge, let's just head outside, okay?"

"Sounds like a plan."

We entered the empty lounge and headed straight for the coffeemaker. "I think Nadine is accepting bribes from Chester Walker to keep him apprised of the top students' grades," I told her quickly as she was pouring herself a cup. "Yesterday, I saw—"

"Molly, there you are." Elsbeth Young entered the room and joined us. " 'Morning, Lauren. How's everything going?"

She directed the question mostly at me, so I replied, "Fine. Though I hope your presentation went better than mine."

"Not much chance of that," she replied. "I was hoping to drum up some new students, but I've played at wakes that were more receptive. I'm so glad this is Tamara's final year here, and we'll be done with Carlton Central School forever."

Because neither Lauren's nor my children would be done with Carlton Central School for a number of years yet, and Lauren *worked* there, I was not of a mind to congratulate her.

She shifted her vision to Lauren. "My daughter doesn't stand a chance of being valedictorian with all the adult interference that's taking place. I just overheard some kids talking in the hall. Olivia Garrett, Jenny's mother, sells Dave Paxton's paintings. So you can bet that Jenny gets nothing but A's from him. Jenny is one of the three or four strongest candidates for valedictorian, along with my Tamara."

"That's nothing to worry about," Lauren replied. "Dave would never let a personal relationship influence his grades. Besides, I don't think Jenny is even in his class."

Elsbeth furrowed her brow, her normally pretty features now in a scowl, which, matched with her ratty-looking red hair, made her frightening to look at. "Trust me. She is. And so is Danielle's son and Chester's son. All three students are neck and neck on their GPAs. Like it or not, one B is going to determine the valedictorian, even if that B is only in an art class."

Good thing she didn't show this side of herself during her lessons, I thought, or we'd be looking for a new piano teacher. I said, "Technically, Jenny isn't Olivia's daughter now. Stephanie is her legal guardian. And anyway, surely a teacher's business relationship with one student's estranged mother isn't something to fret about."

Elsbeth sighed, then said, "I guess you're right. Besides, it really doesn't matter to *me* what happens. Whether or not Tamara gives a speech at graduation, she's going to Stanford next year. It's the other parents who've made it into such a big deal. Personally, just so long as Chester's son doesn't finish number one, and I won't have to watch

Chester gloat, I'll be happy." She started for the door. "I'd better get home. Piano lesson next hour."

We waited in silence as the click of Elsbeth's heels faded. "That cements it," I said. "I don't want my children in high school. Not at this one, at any rate. All of this acrimony over valedictorian. What is wrong with these people?"

"Happens every year around this time, Moll. Generally, the students are gracious no matter what, but a parent or two goes bonkers." Lauren took a quick sip of coffee, made a face, and poured the rest of her cup down the drain. "Listen, I've got to get back to work. Don't forget to tell me the details about our earlier conversation, all right?"

I nodded and glanced at my watch. "I still have twenty minutes to decide what to do for my next presentation."

"Hope it all goes well," Lauren said as we went our separate ways at the intersection of hallways.

I returned to the art room and let myself into Dave's office, retrieved the paperback in my purse, which I'd been toting around with me of late for just such an occasion, and plopped down on the love seat. As is fairly typical of me, though, the minute I'm left alone some silly cartoon idea occurs to me. I quickly deserted my book, grabbed the small sketch pad from my purse instead, and began to draw.

All of those clowns dressed identically the other night had struck me as absurd, despite the tragic conclusion. I drew three identical clowns with those same rings of stiff hair from an otherwise bald cap. Two of the clowns were holding hands and a third was glaring at one of them. With his arms crossed, he says to the nearest one of the perplexed-looking clown couple, "So, tell me something, young man. What makes you think you and my daughter have anything in common?"

An instant later I heard the door creak open. "You're

sure Paxton's still in study hall? The door's unlocked," a deep voice said.

"Positive," a girl replied. "I just saw him a minute ago."

"It's not like him to leave the room open like this. Let's do this quickly and get out of here."

I heard what sounded like the jingling of keys. Whoever this was would bolt the instant they spotted the open door to Dave's office. I sprang to my feet and headed to the doorway. Jenny Garrett and Brian Underwood froze at the sight of me, both giving audible gasps of surprise.

"Mrs. Masters?" Jenny asked. "What are you doing here?"

"I might ask the same of you two. I have Mr. Paxton's permission to be here."

"Uh, so do we," Brian replied. "We were just trying to get some work done."

"By doing whatever you had to do 'quickly' so you could 'get out of here'?"

"We . . . were making out on his couch a couple of days ago when he was in study hall, and I lost an earring," Jenny said, her cheeks now beet-red. "I wanted to retrieve it before we got busted."

That, unfortunately, was a plausible explanation. "How did you get his keys?"

"He gave 'em to me," Brian said. "I'm his student advisor. I get to come in here and work whenever I want."

"I'm sure your privileges don't extend to making out on his couch." With an unsolved murder having recently occurred in this very building, it struck me as an especially precarious time to allow a set of keys to be in the possession of students. I held out my hand. "Give me the keys. Mr. Paxton can return them to you if he so chooses."

Brian shouted, "But he *gave* them to me! You have no right to take them!"

"Be that as it may, I insist. If you're supposed to have them, you'll get them right back."

He scoffed and took on the classic nonchalant teenager air. He tossed me the keys. "Here you go, lady. Knock yourself out."

"Thanks."

"Sure. No problem. Come on, Jen. Paxton will understand about your earring."

She nodded, but she seemed to be looking at something against the far wall. I followed her gaze and noticed the kiln in the room for the first time, but saw no telltale earrings. "I'm sorry, Mrs. Masters," she said quietly as they left.

Curious, I thoroughly checked the love seat—which was apparently appropriately named—but found no earring there or anywhere else in Dave's office, just some sort of rubber bulb under the love seat that was probably part of a handheld aerator of some sort. I decided to check the art room, too. There was nothing revealing here. It seemed so odd that Jenny would sneak into a teacher's office for an earring that she hadn't actually lost there.

The bell rang and Dave returned a moment later, prior to any students arriving. I handed him both sets of keys. "I had an unexpected visitor while you were gone. Brian Underwood. He had your keys. He told me that he got them from you."

Dave's eyes widened in surprise. "That's interesting. It's a lie, of course. I never gave him my keys."

"He and Jenny said they were trying to retrieve an earring that she said she lost during a makeout session on your office couch."

He was turning a brighter shade of red by the moment. "Listen, Molly, Brian and Jenny are both good kids and

are about to graduate. They could get in a lot of trouble
with Jack over this, and I'd really appreciate if we could
keep this between us. All right?" He looked to be almost
in physical pain.

I'd had no intention of running to Jack Vance with any
of this, but his unexpected request for me *not* to made
me reconsider. "Now that you mention it, don't you
think it's important that Jack be told, even if it does get
Brian and Jenny into hot water? I don't think we can be
too cautious, considering what happened two days ago."

That's when it hit me. Having Brian Underwood, of all
people, with a copy of keys had to be incredibly painful
for Dave, because of Corrinne's rumored relationship
with Brian. "You know where Brian got them from,
don't you?"

He hesitated but made no reply. Some students were
starting to come into the room. He gestured for me to
follow him into his office, and I did so. He closed the
door behind us and said under his breath, "You're right,
Molly. Jack has to be told about this. There's all sorts of
liability issues."

"Brian got the keys from Corrinne?"

"He must have. Because he never got them from me."
He stole a glance at the love seat. I knew what he was
thinking, that his own office had been used for illicit
meetings between Corrinne and her young lover. He
shifted his vision and gestured with his chin toward the
corner of the room. "That's her filing cabinet over there.
Her students' records. Like a lot of schools, we're cramped
for space. Corrinne had a floating classroom. So we
shared office space."

I thought about my conversation with Brian yesterday,
and what Lauren had told me about Corrinne's explanation for their being at a hotel together. "You know, Dave,
Brian strikes me as being full of bravado. I think Cor-

rinne was telling the truth when she said that the two of them were just friends."

Dave rubbed his face. He looked so tired and defeated now that it hurt me to witness his pain. "Do you? You're the only one who will, once this last bit of news about the keys gets out." He sighed heavily and grabbed the doorknob to return to his classroom. "Everyone's going to think I killed her to get even."

Chapter 7

Reserved for
Employee of the Month

After the bell rang and class was dismissed, Dave looked at me and forced a smile. "Thanks for doing this for me. I really appreciate it."

"You're welcome," I replied, but had no idea what he meant. Exactly what had I been "doing"? That is, aside from retrieving a contraband set of his keys, which rubbed his nose in his late girlfriend's illicit relationship.

"You were great once again. You've got a real knack for teaching."

Oh, right. My career-day presentation. I'd been on autopilot. "Thanks."

He rocked on his heels and, once again, attempted to smooth down his hair, which I now realized was a nervous habit. "I hate to ask, but do you think you could hang around for a few more minutes? Come with me to see Jack and tell him what Brian told you about how he got my keys?"

"Of course." My stomach was beginning to rumble. My digestive system never wakes up in time for me to want breakfast and it was now lunchtime, but I figured that this shouldn't take long.

Brian Underwood was meeting Jack Vance's stony glare. Brian projected the very picture of innocence, albeit while sporting a bleached white-blond buzz cut—or whatever the current hairstyle is called these days—and ripped-up flair-leg jeans and an ugly RAP RULES! T-shirt.

"I know I told Mrs. Masters that I got the keys from Mr. Paxton, but I made a mistake. I should have admitted right away that I got 'em from Ms. Buldock."

A full minute of silence followed, marred only by my rumbling stomach. Jack had asked me to stay, thinking that with the three of us adults outnumbering the two students, we'd get to the truth faster. If we'd heard the truth yet, we must have missed it, for this was the third explanation from Brian. The previous two were: "I misunderstood Mr. Paxton's instructions and kept his keys by mistake," and, "I wanted to show everyone I wasn't just a geeky brain, so I swiped them, but I didn't do anything except let myself into the room a couple times." When Jack countered by asking which teacher he'd swiped the keys from, it apparently dawned on Brian that he could attribute this to Corrinne Buldock.

Jack finally gave up on trying to stare him down and now turned toward Jenny. She'd remained silent, except for two instances, when she'd stated, "I didn't ask Brian how he got the keys, and he didn't tell me."

"Do you have anything to add, Miss Garrett?" Jack asked.

She shook her head. Another silence ensued. Dave hung his head and said nothing. Neither of us had spoken a word since the teens had entered Jack's office. It was clear to me, as it no doubt was to everyone else present, that Brian was determined not to budge from his current story. He was also unshakable with the search-for-the-nonexistent-earring explanation, to which Jenny would merely nod her assent.

Jack frowned and tented his fingertips, his arms resting on top of his desk. "I must say, I'm very disappointed in both of you. You're two of our top students, candidates for valedictorian. Now I'll have to consider disqualifying you."

"Whatever you think is fair, sir," Brian said evenly. "I'm sorry I didn't come right out and say that Cor—that Ms. Buldock gave me her keys. But Jenny is telling the truth."

She gave him a pleading look and cried, "Bri—"

He froze her with a glare.

She winced and said, "I knew we shouldn't have broken into the art room. It was my idea, not Brian's. I'd like to withdraw my name. I don't deserve to be valedictorian."

"It was your idea, Jenny?" Dave asked. "Why?"

She clenched her jaw, but answered quietly, "I wanted to be alone with Brian."

One of them was trying to shield the other, but it was hard to tell which party was which. Maybe I should have just said to them in the first place, By all means, keep your keys and make out on Dave's couch whenever you like.

"Can we please go?" Brian asked. "Lunchtime is almost over, and I'm hungry. So's Mrs. Masters."

My cheeks grew warm. Jack nodded. "Go."

Brian and Jenny left. Dave and I lingered, to see if Jack had any parting words. He did. While staring wistfully out the window, he said, "I should've gone with my first instincts when I was four years old and become a fireman."

At home I grabbed a quick, late lunch and decided I had time to make a grocery run before the kids showed up. BC was standing at the garage door by the time I'd located my ever-misplaced keys. I looked at her, her little tail already wagging as she stared with all of her might at the door, lest it should open without her getting the opportunity to join me on the other side.

"You're not going to enjoy this, you know, Betty. I'm

only going to the grocery store, and you'll have to wait for me in the car."

She risked one quick pleading glance up at me—gambling that the door wouldn't open and shut in the interim—then returned her concentration to the door itself. "All right. Betty gets to come." She darted ahead of me through the door and leaped into the Jeep. She scrambled into the backseat and we headed to the store.

In the produce section, I was studying some peas, trying to decide if I was gung-ho enough to shell them as opposed to defrosting some preshelled ones, when a very harsh sounding, "Molly Masters!" resounded from someplace behind me. I turned. Danielle Underwood was glaring at me, hands on her hips. Could she already know about my meeting with the principal regarding her son, less than an hour after it had ended?

"Hi, Danielle," I said. "I see we're grocery shopping at the same time."

Danielle's ready smile was absent from her attractive face. In the fluorescent lighting of the store, her skin looked leathery, as if she'd spent too much time in the sun in her younger days. "Brian says you talked to him yesterday about Corrinne's murder. How dare you do such a thing?"

I tried to rapidly assess how I'd feel if she'd been the one to ask my eighteen-year-old about a murder victim. It honestly hadn't occurred to me that she'd object. "I'm sorry. I asked him because I'm trying to come to grips with the murder, and I hoped that learning more about the victim might help me do so."

She lifted her chin in defiance and flicked her long, light brown hair back from her shoulders. "You're not a police officer. You have no right to interrogate my son."

"I wasn't interrogating him. I did talk to him about the shooting, but I merely asked him if he had any theories as to who the killer might be."

"What business is that of yours?"

"It's *everyone's* business. The woman was a high school teacher, shot dead in our school. And it happened right in front of both of us. I would think you'd feel every bit as horrified as I do."

Though her eyes were focused directly into mine, I had the impression that she wasn't listening. She had the glazed and frazzled look of an insomniac, which I'd seen in my own reflection often enough to recognize. "Stay away from Brian. He's been through too much already in this godforsaken town."

"What do you mean by that?"

"Don't play naive. This whole town knows about what that horrible woman was up to. Getting her claws in my son, for God's sake!"

"I can only guess how hard all of that must be for you. But all *I* did was to chat with your son for a couple of minutes. He struck me as a fine young man, Danielle," I added. "You've obviously done a fine job raising him."

She eyed me for a moment. "You're just saying that to butter me up. You're starting to sound like Stephanie Saunders."

My jaw dropped in my offense at the comparison. Nothing raised my ire faster than to be compared to someone I detested. Especially when there was an element of truth involved. "I meant every word of what I said." Even if I *had* thrown in a few words of flattery to appease her.

She started to walk away, pushing her shopping cart, but then stopped and turned back toward me. Her tight features and her red cheeks made her look as if she were about to explode. "We're going to get out of this place just as soon as we can. It's people like you who make Carlton such a dreadful place to live."

"How—" I cut myself off from crying, How dare you say that! There was already more than enough acrimony in this community, and we were starting to turn the heads of fellow shoppers. "What do you mean by that?"

"Everybody insists on knowing everybody else's business, but nobody raises a hand to help."

"That's just not true."

"Leave me alone, Molly. Leave my son alone."

Saturday morning I awoke to find that we were in the midst of what could well prove to be the beginnings of a blizzard. In the muted lighting caused by thick gray clouds, the colors had been dimmed several notches. The ground hog's shadow was irrelevant in upstate New York.

While Jim slept—he's a camel when it comes to sleep, and spreads out the twelve hours he gets on Friday nights for use on the other six days—ever-brewing confrontations emanated below us from the main floor of the house. Karen had a piano recital in the afternoon and was practicing Beethoven's Waltz in D minor. On the lowest octave, "Twinkle, Twinkle Little Star" rumbled in disharmony, punctuated by Nathan's laughter.

I gritted my teeth and clenched my fists in anticipation of what was to come. Before I could get dressed and down the stairs, Karen's pleas had gone from "Nathan, quit it!" to that ever-predictable "Mo-om!" in her nails-on-blackboard pitch, "Nathan won't let me practice!"

By the time I'd reached the landing, I was already my own version of one of those cartoon panel characters with a furrowed brow and huge mouthful of gritted teeth spouting asterisks, exclamation points, and lightning bolts. I snarled, "Nathan! Get away from that piano now! Karen has a recital this afternoon! Your father's trying to sleep!"

I had thrown in the bit about his father, knowing that one angry word from Jim carried more weight than a dozen of mine. Indeed, Nathan backed away from the keys.

"Never mind, Nathan!" Karen cried. "Just keep playing 'Twinkle, Twinkle'! It's too late now!" She rose and hurled her piano book onto the floor with all her might. "I'm going to do lousy at my concert, all because of my stupid brother!"

"Karen—"

"He's ruining my life!" she shrieked, and then stormed up the stairs to her room and slammed the door.

The pitter patter of little feet had been replaced by the thump thump thump slam! of teenage feet. Surely Jim was not going to pretend to be able to sleep through this morning's reveille call. A minute later he called out, "Honey? Is everything all right?"

"Yes. Everything's freaking perfect," I called back.

Nathan was slowly sidling out of the room. He seemed to believe that I had the observation skills of a canary, that as long as he didn't make any sudden movements he would be invisible to me.

I had been through enough of Karen's prerecital jitters to know that she would have gotten upset at missed notes and flown out of the room in hysteria—the moment I was there to witness her distress, that is—regardless of Nathan's actions. "Nathan, did you have any breakfast yet?"

"No," he said in a voice almost as low as the last piano key he'd played.

"We'll let Karen simmer down while you get yourself some cereal. And don't get anywhere near your sister for the rest of the morning. She's just as nervous as you would be if you had to play a soccer game all by yourself in front of a hundred people."

"How could I do that? I'd have to be the goalie and the forward and eight people at once."

"Right. It'd be difficult and you'd be nervous."

"But would I have to play against an entire team? Because all they'd have to do is pass the ball and I'd get scored on. And I couldn't score myself because—"

"It's an analogy, Nathan!" I had lost the last vestiges of my patience, and my voice reflected it. "The point is: Stay away from your sister, or else I'll make you come to Karen's piano recital instead of letting you go to Michael's house to play."

At that foulest of threats, Nathan widened his eyes but, wisely, stopped talking. This was out of character. He normally milked an argument till it was not only dry but was begging for a mercy killing.

There was no coaxing Karen into having breakfast. Once I'd completed my token attempts to do so, I sat down and started doodling, which, as usual, resulted in a cartoon.

In my cartoon, I showed a woman with her hands clasped in delight as she gazes at the sign inside her one-car garage, which reads: Reserved for Employee of the Month. She says to herself, "Me? Again?" The caption reads: "Sharon Gooley takes particular delight in a unique advantage of self-employment."

I studied my cartoon after its completion, trying to decide how to market it. I decided that the inside of the card could be some message along the lines of: Congratulations for getting such a wonderful new boss.

Remarkably, the family managed to survive the next couple of hours, despite the fact that Karen was going through emotional states quicker than Meryl Streep on fast-forward. Jim had, of course, forgotten all about Karen's recital, then didn't hear my reminders while he read the sports section. Rather than get upset or be late ourselves, I told him we'd meet him there, and then I accepted a ride for Karen and myself from Lauren, whose daughter, Rachel, was also one of Elsbeth's students.

"Isn't Tommy coming?" I asked Lauren as we got into her car.

She shook her head. "He's wrapped up in the investigation."

I nodded and waited until the girls were too absorbed in their own conversation to tune into ours. "Did he have any luck tracing the gun?" I asked quietly.

"No. It was purchased at a trade show three years ago. The previous owner died of natural causes last year and left no record of who wound up with his guns."

"So there might be more unregistered guns floating around the neighborhood?"

"That's always a given in this country, Molly," Lauren said quietly, giving a sad glance into the rearview mirror at our beloved daughters.

We didn't know until now that there was a local murderer on the loose to hook up with those firearms, I thought.

Upon our arrival, Elsbeth greeted us as we all claimed folding chairs in her living room. She was deep into her performer's personality, her gestures exaggerated and her booming voice full of pride while she had us all applaud for ourselves for raising such "wonderful pianists." She was wearing a full-length muumuu, elbow-length white evening gloves, and two butterfly clips in her tomato-red hair.

Jim managed to arrive only ten minutes after the recital had begun. This meant that he missed hearing Rachel, Elsbeth's newest student, who therefore played first. She and all the students played well. Karen was wonderful and performed better than anyone, although there were some who hit fewer wrong notes and played with slightly better dynamics and meter. After all, mothers were not put on this earth to be impartial. She was the cutest, in any case.

We all milled around Elsbeth's house afterward for her usual postrecital party. The female students were clustered in one gaggle of gigglers, while the male students, in a second group, eagerly helped themselves to the refreshments.

Lauren and Jim were in one of the larger gatherings of adults. This was when I, too, should have been socializing with the parents and telling everyone how wonderful their children played, which was easily said as it was the truth, but I never had anything additional to say afterward. Therefore, I was stalling, studying a picture on Elsbeth's wall that I particularly liked. It was a landscape in pastels done by a local artist whose work I greatly admired.

From behind me, Elsbeth said, "Karen played exceptionally well, as always."

I turned with a smile. "She's really blossomed under your tutelage," I heard myself say, then wondered just where that had come from—"blossomed under your tutelage"? Who *said* things like that?

"Thank you," Elsbeth said.

"Your daughter didn't play for us today. She's still taking lessons, isn't she?"

"Of course. Tamara's just no longer taking them from me. She's so brilliant that I felt she needed to be with someone even better than her dear old mom. Her instructor is one of the top pianists in the country."

"Does she plan to major in piano?"

"At Stanford? No, but she'll continue her studies."

Despite my own private admission that mothers weren't impartial, Elsbeth had just surpassed my tolerance for mentions of the impressive fact that her daughter was going to Stanford University. Before I could stop myself, I blurted out, "It's too bad she has to go to school so far away. Couldn't she get into SUNY at Albany?"

Elsbeth wasn't listening to me anyway. Stealing a glance over her shoulder as if to see whether we were being watched, she then grabbed my elbow and whispered, "Could I talk to you privately for a moment, Molly?"

"Of course."

She ushered me into her bedroom. My attention was immediately drawn to a splendid photographic display of all stages of development of her daughter, Tamara, and one wedding picture of herself and her husband, whom I'd seen at these functions but had never formally met. An entire wall was covered by the photos.

"These are great pictures of Tamara." I focused on one that appeared to be the most recent. She was sitting at the piano. Her expression was one of such obvious displeasure that it was surprising to me that Elsbeth kept it, let alone framed it and hung it on her bedroom wall.

Elsbeth began pacing in front of the door, which she'd closed behind us. "Molly, I don't really know who else to talk to about this. The more I think about it, the more I realize I'm right. But Tommy's not here, and I don't want to go to the police station, just in case that's the wrong thing to do."

"What's this about? Corrinne's murder?"

She nodded, her expression grim. "I think I might know who killed her."

"Who?"

"Nadine Dahl."

The school secretary. "Did you recognize her somehow as the gunman?"

"No. But she was the one who deliberately let the doves out of the cage right before all hell broke loose. I saw her do it."

"She would have been in full costume. Are you positive it was her?"

"Yes. I saw one of the clowns coaxing the bird onto her finger, so I went over there and said, 'What are you doing?' She gasped, and the bird flew off. It was Nadine, and she told me I'd startled her and cried, 'Now look what you made me do!' But I've gone over it in my head, and I realize that the bird escaping wasn't an accident at all. She waved her arms and scared it even more. I walked away, and only a few seconds later the shooter emerged from that same direction."

The story made little sense to me. I asked hesitantly, "Was Nadine the one who called out that the doves were escaping, just before the shooting?"

"It must have been."

"Didn't you tell Tommy about Nadine when he was interviewing us at the school?"

"Of course, but he didn't seem to take anything I had to say very seriously. He just kept saying 'uh-huh' while writing in his notepad."

"That means he was taking it very seriously, believe me. I've known Tommy for years. That uh-huh of his is a total giveaway. Don't worry. If Nadine did this, Tommy will be onto her in no time."

"I'd like to think so, but Nadine was in the office at school yesterday as if nothing had happened."

"That might only mean that there isn't sufficient evidence against her, not that Tommy is dismissing your reason for suspecting her."

"Just the same, though. It scares me to no end to think that somebody who could do that . . . could pick up a gun and . . . and kill another human being, is in the same building with my daughter all day long. And I can't do anything to protect her."

"I know what you mean. My own children are on the same campus, just different buildings."

"And to think. That damned Chester Walker's been paying her to keep him apprised of all the ins and outs of the teachers' grades."

"How do you know about—"

Someone threw open her bedroom door. The mom of one of Elsbeth's male students leaned into the room. I knew her only as the mother of a young boy who played quite well. "Elsbeth? Oh, there you are. We just wanted to thank you again for doing such a wonderful job."

Elsbeth wandered back into the living room then to join the others. Wanting to think for a minute in peace, I lingered in the hall, but soon heard a distinctive, "Psst." I turned and searched for the source, then saw Tamara standing in her doorway and gesturing for me. She opened the door and pulled me inside. This was nothing like any of my previous experiences at piano recitals. Apparently *this* one was destined to include whispered conversations in bedrooms.

"Tamara? What's going on?"

"I can't let my mom know that I'm here; otherwise she's going to force me to play for everyone. I snuck back inside through my window."

In less than six months she was going to be attending college on the opposite side of the country, and she couldn't tell her mother that she didn't want to play the piano? "What can I do for you?"

"Brian Underwood's a friend of mine. He asked me to give you this."

She offered me a sealed envelope, identified only by the initials MM on the front. "Do you know what this is about?"

"Nah. He didn't say." She flopped down on her bed.

I needed to get back to the party before my husband and daughter started to wonder about me, but I was too curious to let this wait. I opened the envelope. Inside was a short note that read:

Molly—
   Thanks to you, Dave's pissed at me for having his keys. Thought you'd like to know something. They were Jenny's keys. She got them from her mom, who probably got them from Corrie. I was just trying to

take responsibility so Jenny wouldn't get in trouble, but now both of us are in hot water. This is what I get for trying to do the right thing, huh?

Brian

P.S. Did Dave Paxdumb like my drawing?

The postscript must have meant that Brian had drawn the hanged clown. But why would Corrinne have given Olivia a copy of the keys to Corrinne and Dave's shared office at the high school? And when could Jenny have gotten the keys, since she was no longer living with her mother?

"When did you get this from him?" I asked, slipping it into my pocket.

"This morning. He takes piano lessons from the same guy I used to take lessons from."

"A former teacher of yours, you mean?"

"Yeah, former as of today. I quit an hour ago. Mom doesn't know yet, so don't say anything. She thinks I'm still at today's lesson, but it was just a waste of her money and my time. I've hated piano for years now, but she just won't listen to me."

She lifted her window, then turned back to face me. "I've got to get going so I can make an entrance again. Soon as the audience leaves, that is. How much longer do you think this stupid party of hers is going to last?"

"Not much longer," I said sadly as I watched Elsbeth's pride and joy climb out her bedroom window.

Chapter 8

Hello, Dolly

Sunday passed without incident, which was something of a triumph, though I couldn't get Brian's letter and his mother's behavior out of my mind. Did Danielle really think I was a threat to her son or to her? If she was Corrinne's killer, perhaps she thought I knew more than I actually did. And why was Brian telling me now that he got Dave's keys from Jenny?

I couldn't answer those questions, but I finally realized that I could, at least, alert the school principal to my suspicions about his secretary. I called Jack Vance at home and told him exactly what I'd seen transpire between Nadine and Chester, as well as the lame explanations she'd given me. Jack said only, "I'll look into this. Thank you, Molly."

Monday morning I spent a sizable portion of my time complaining on the phone to Chester. His workers had brought the materials as promised, but trusting that nothing could go wrong with what was, after all, only a delivery, I'd worked on my cartoons and simply pointed out where they could stack everything.

Apparently I should have been more specific. They set a heavy box on our window-well covering, which cracked before my eyes. Chester assured me that he'd have his men install a new covering, but no one should have been so stupid in the first place. He also assured me that actual construction would "start tomorrow," six days after the very latest start date he "could possibly foresee" a mere two weeks ago.

That night I left Jim home with the kids and arrived on time for our regularly scheduled PTA meeting. Originally, the meeting was to concern the announcement of proceeds from Friday night's fund-raiser. Tonight there would be no back-patting about the revenue.

Attendance in the cafeteria was unusually high, with nearly all of the folding chairs taken. Because the elementary school parents tended to be the most active PTA members—the ones who weren't yet suffering from total burnout, that is—we met in their building on the campus. Many years ago, when I attended that school, the building housed the entire student body, but it was now the smallest of the five buildings.

Stephanie was in her usual luminous mood whenever there was an audience and a microphone in front of her. She started the meeting and, in contrast to her smile, said, "We all know of the tragic circumstances that caused our fund-raiser to be postponed. I've decided that the PTA should, of course, provide a bouquet for Corrinne Buldock's funeral. I've selected a wonderful floral arrangement from the—"

A shrill voice called out, "Excuse me, Ms. Saunders." Olivia Garrett waved her hand. "Before you write a check with our collective funds, you'd better hear what I have to say."

"Yes, Olivia?" Though Stephanie continued smiling, she was obviously speaking through a clenched jaw. "You wish to interrupt?"

Olivia got to her feet. "I think it's about time we got some new leadership in this school. When I say that, I'm referring to the principal and to you, Stephanie." She paused to let this register. "We need someone to take over as president of the Carlton PTA, and I am hereby throwing my own name into the hat."

Stephanie's face clouded over into an expressionless mask that hid deep anger. "Olivia, in my seven years as PTA president, this is the first meeting I can recall seeing you in attendance. You are clearly just grandstanding because of our personal differences, which my lawyer has advised me not to discuss."

"No, Stephanie, this is officially a coup." The voice was that of Danielle Underwood, who stood up from the back of the room. "Several of us were talking before the meeting started. We realized that there has never been an official election of the president of the PTA, and we want to have one tonight."

"Of *course* there hasn't been an election," Stephanie said. "It's a volunteer position with no benefits and countless disadvantages. Nobody other than me has ever said that they were willing to do the job." She gave Olivia a smoldering look. "So, Olivia, by all means. I officially step down and announce that Olivia Garrett is now PTA president." As she spoke, Stephanie marched off of the small podium in front of the cafeteria and took one of the few seats available, in the front row.

The audience, meanwhile, was stunned into silence. I glanced around the room. Drat! No sign of the secretary/treasurer, currently our only other PTA officer besides Stephanie. Danielle sat back down again, but her cheeks were blazing. I looked over at Olivia Garrett, whose face was also red. With her usual graceful movements, she made her way to the podium, took a seat, and adjusted the microphone. She looked at Stephanie and asked, "Where's the written agenda for tonight's meeting?"

Stephanie held up a sheet of paper in one hand and several three-by-five cards in the other. "I wrote the agenda when I was president. That's one of your new duties."

Olivia pursed her lips and blinked a few times. I squirmed on her behalf. In spite of our considerable differences, this coup was unfair to Stephanie, who had done a fine job in all respects as PTA president. However, Olivia was now horribly on the spot, and I wouldn't want to be in her shoes, either.

"Does anyone have anything they want to discuss?" Olivia asked.

Stephanie raised her hand. For a moment Olivia scanned the audience, her eyes falling pleadingly on Danielle, who merely shrugged. Reluctantly, Olivia returned her vision to the front row. "Stephanie?"

"We need to discuss the status of the fund-raiser from last Friday and decide whether to reschedule or to scrap the whole thing. If we scrap it, we need to come up with an alternative fund-raiser."

"Good suggestion. Thank you, Stephanie."

"No need to thank me. I'm only doing this because I'm a parent, and I'm willing to make whatever sacrifices I can to ensure that my children get a good education." She came forward and placed her agenda and note cards back onto the podium. "Maybe these will be of some use to you."

Olivia flipped through the cards, a pained expression on her face. She sighed and ran trembling fingers through her reddish-blond hair. She started to speak, then shut her eyes for a moment. She looked out at the audience. "It's occurred to me that I no longer have a child at Carlton Central School, whereas Stephanie now has two, plus a son who's about to enter first grade. I was wrong to volunteer to serve in the parent-teacher association when I'm no longer considered a parent in the eyes of the law." She started to cry. "By all means, Ms. Saunders," she continued, her voice breaking, "this is your meeting. I'll leave you to it."

Olivia rose and made her way down the aisle. She

stopped at her seat long enough to retrieve her jacket and purse, then continued past the rows of folding chairs. There was a considerable racket as many of the people whom she passed rose and told her not to leave. She ignored them and continued walking at a steady pace, though she was clearly upset.

Stephanie returned to the podium. Her face conveyed a picture of self-control, though I knew her well enough to know that she was masking her emotions. What those emotions were, however, was not within my ability to grasp. She waited until everyone had quieted, but a quick scan of the faces behind me made it clear that she was confronting a hostile crowd. The woman sitting beside me grumbled to her companion, "This is all Stephanie's fault! She never should have taken that poor woman's daughter from her!"

"That was the judge's decision," I heard myself reply, amazed at the realization that I was squarely on Stephanie's—of all people's—side. "Blame him, not Stephanie." I straightened and returned my attention to her.

"Danielle," Stephanie said into the mike while picking out Danielle's face in the crowd. I could see from my angle that she'd shrunk down in her seat. "You wanted to hold an election. Are you willing to step in as PTA president, at least for the next three months, through the end of the school year?"

She shook her head.

"Any other volunteers?" Stephanie waited, but no one spoke up or raised their hands.

"How about Molly Masters?" some woman behind me said. I looked back, but couldn't spot the person. If I'd located her, I would have been tempted to kick her in the shins. Had I wanted to be PTA president, I'd have volunteered for the position.

A young-looking woman I didn't recognize grumbled,

"Well, *anyone* would be better than—" She stopped when she realized her voice was carrying.

"You're right, Susan," Stephanie said to the young woman. "This is not the time for me to attempt to represent the parents in this town. Clearly, many of you have drawn your own conclusions regarding my being granted custody of Jenny Garrett." She rose and once again gathered her notes. "In a court of law, the judge listens to both sides and tries to make a just decision before condemning one of the parties." She returned to her seat in the front row.

"Molly, you go take over," said some woman a couple of rows back. "You're opinionated and like to talk." I looked back at her, but didn't even recognize her.

"A criterion which fits you, too, obviously," I replied. "Want to thumb-wrestle me for the honors?"

She smirked and crossed her arms. Meanwhile the people seated to either side of me generously moved back to clear an aisle for me to make my way to the front. Grudgingly, I stood up and proceeded to the podium.

I pulled the microphone from its stand and remained on my feet. "Under the circumstances, I'm sure the majority of you will agree that we need to postpone this meeting until emotions are not running quite so high. I move that we adjourn this meeting."

"I second," Stephanie promptly said.

"Agree?" Nearly everyone raised their hands. "Disagree?" No hands. "Meeting adjourned," I said, hoping that these would be my final words as acting PTA president.

Stephanie immediately leaped to her feet and headed for a table along the front wall, where she'd left her coat and belongings. As she made her way to the doors in the back of the room, no one would look directly at her, and yet all conversation ceased as she passed.

I couldn't bear to watch another moment of this. Into

the microphone, I said, "Stephanie, as temporary spokesperson for the Carlton PTA, I hope you'll return to your position as president."

Now two-thirds of the way across the room, she whirled on a heel and faced me, her jaw slightly agape.

"In any case, this entire community owes you a tremendous debt of gratitude for the outstanding job you've done for us, for many years now." I led the room in a round of applause, which started slowly, but was thunderous by the time Stephanie left.

The next day, I was back at Carlton Central as scheduled, volunteering in my son's sixth-grade class. It was the grade school's career day, and this time I spent the time drawing cartoon animals upon demand and dressing them in whatever garments the students suggested. This audience was far more receptive than the audience at the high school, and the time passed quickly.

Afterward, Martin, whose daughter was in Nathan's class, bumped into me in the hall. I'd gotten so used to seeing him in his magician's black pseudotuxedo that I barely recognized him. He was now wearing his accountant's clothes: a brown suit and a light blue, button-down collar shirt with a diagonally striped tie. His thinning black hair was no longer plastered back on his head, nor was his mustache waxed to dramatic Snidely Whiplash tips. He greeted me pleasantly.

"You're here for career day?" I asked.

He nodded and rolled his eyes. "My daughter's home, pretending to be sick today. She didn't want to sit through another of my attempts to make being an accountant sound exciting to a group of children."

"You could always pull a rabbit out of your pocket to liven things up a bit."

"Funny you should mention that," he said, his thin lips spreading into a wide grin. He snapped his fingers, and produced a stuffed toy in his other hand, which he held out to me by its long ears. "I couldn't bring the real thing with me, since I'm coming directly from my office."

"He's very cute, Martin. I'm sure the kids will get a kick out of him."

"Unless he gets hopping mad," Martin said, making the stuffed toy bounce in the air.

I forced a smile. I had to admit that if I were twelve and my father were the sort to bounce a stuffed rabbit at the phrase "hopping mad," I might just want to feign sickness, too. "It was nice seeing you again. I hope your talk goes well."

He frowned and pushed his stuffed rabbit inside one of his sleeves. "It's days like this, when my own daughter is acting ashamed of what I do for a living, that I really regret having such a dull job."

"Martin, all adolescents are embarrassed by their parents. It's part of the growth process. You've got a wonderful home and lifestyle—" I hesitated, realizing that I was merely making a reasonable assumption, but continued. "—and deep down your daughter knows that. Or at least she will years from now when she's an adult herself. Think of how rough it would be if you really were a full-time professional magician. You'd be on the road all the time, doing warm-up acts for low pay."

"Yes, but there's a thrill to being in show business that's without parallel. You'll see what I mean tomorrow."

"Tomorrow?"

His jaw dropped a little and he searched my eyes. "You haven't forgotten about my show at the children's wing of the hospital, have you?"

Yikes! Two weeks ago I'd agreed to fill in for Stephanie for the show he'd mentioned. It had completely slipped my mind. "That *is* tomorrow. I'd forgotten the date." Along with everything else.

"Can you still make it?"

"Um, sure. I don't have anything suitable to wear, though, and I haven't—"

"Maybe you could borrow Stephanie's gown."

I smiled at the thought of my ever borrowing an item of clothing that belonged to Stephanie. "I can't fit into Stephanie's gown, even if she'd lend it to me, which she never would." Not even stuffing my husband's fluffiest wool socks into my bra would compensate for a pair of differences in our anatomy.

He gestured at my clothing. "You can be an assistant in exactly what you're wearing now—khakis and a sexy-looking blouse."

"You think this blouse is sexy?" I asked, smiling in spite of myself.

"Absolutely. Well, I'm late for my talk. I'll pick you up tomorrow night at six, and we'll go over your routine verbally."

I was so flattered that I merely said, "Okay. Great." I could count on one hand the number of times anyone but Jim had termed anything about me sexy, and still have four fingers left.

"Don't worry. There's nothing to it, and you've already seen the whole act several times. You'll be great." He paused, one hand on the doorknob, and gave me a thumbs-up.

"Have fun, Martin."

I decided to walk across campus from my son's elementary school to the high school and have a word with Jack Vance about last night's fiasco of a PTA meeting. All the while, I wondered where my brain had been when I'd first agreed to be Martin's assistant. He'd gotten me so focused on the fact that this was to bring joy to ill children that I overlooked my complete distaste for my would-be role. And he'd just now done it again by calling my blouse "sexy." The man might be an inept magician, but he certainly had mastered the art of distracting his audience.

Jack Vance's door was open, and he was clearly not there. Nadine raised her eyebrows at me, her personal version of: Yes? Can I help you?

Feeling awkward after having gone behind her back to her boss, I said, "Hi. Lauren's not here today, is she?"

"Not on Tuesdays. I'm surprised you don't know your friend's schedule better."

Her voice was so snide that I immediately retorted, "Oh, I do know her schedule. I'm just not very intelligent."

She met my eyes in surprise. "I didn't mean to be rude. I'm sorry. Things are too tense here. In my eleven years in this job, this is the testiest it's ever been around this place."

"I'm sure this is the only time someone's been shot in the building."

"That's true, thank God, but it's more than that." She shook her head and said scornfully, "That woman. She brought this on."

"What woman?"

"Just thinking out loud. Don't mind me. This whole business has totally gotten to me. Even brought one of my dolls in just to calm myself."

She gestured at the doll that was leaning against her in-basket. It was one of those porcelain dolls that I'd seen advertised so often in women's magazines, I knew a lot of women must collect them. I just didn't happen to be one of them. "How sweet. Where did you get her?"

"I made her myself. I have a little part-time business. Dahl's Dolls is its name. At one point I was planning on going into this full-time."

"You've since changed your mind?"

She frowned. "My future business plans have run into some setbacks, thanks to my former . . ." She let her voice fade, but the rife bitterness tainted the air. She forced a thin smile. "Business and friendships don't always mix, as they say."

Nadine was such an enigma, and this might be my chance to get to know her better—and trap her. Whether or not she was guilty of murdering Corrinne, she appeared to be accepting bribes. I knew about the innocent-until-proven-guilty concept, but frankly, I wanted her out of my children's school. "I'd love to see how you do these. Back when I was a Girl Scout leader in Boulder, I took my daughter's troop to a doll manufacturer. It was quite a process."

"Yes, it really is fascinating, isn't it?"

"I couldn't believe how expensive the materials are, though. I sure couldn't afford the hobby myself."

If Nadine picked up on my implication that she perhaps needed an alternative source of revenue, she ignored it. "I've been at it for a long time. I have quite a collection of antique dolls, in addition to the ones I make myself."

"Would you show them to me? Maybe I could get you to custom-make one for my daughter."

Nadine brightened immeasurably. I realized that it was the first sincere-looking smile I'd ever seen cross the woman's face. "I'd be delighted to. When would you be able to come over to my place?"

"You make them at your home?"

"Right in my living room."

"Don't you need to fire them in a kiln?" The moment I asked the question, a possible answer occurred to me. "You can just use the kiln in Mr. Paxton's class room, though, right?"

She shook her head vigorously. "We're not allowed to make personal use of school property. There's a company in Albany that I rent kiln space from."

"I see."

"I'm not doing anything after school, if you'd like to come over then."

"I'd love to. Can you jot down your address for me?"

She did so and handed it to me, but I didn't recognize the street name at all. She began to give me instructions, but I have no sense of direction. We finally settled on my meeting her at the end of the day and following her home.

I glanced at my watch and wandered to my car. It was an hour and a half till school would let out, and I had plenty of time to go home. But if I stayed at the school, I might be able to watch Dave Paxton at work and get a feel for what teaching an art class would really be like. My business, Friendly Fax, was making me no money whatsoever. It was time for me to think about finding a new career. I wasn't about to go back to college to get my teaching certificate, but I might be able to start some night classes for adults in cartooning or drawing.

Resolved, I headed back to the high school. Nadine was now being friendly to me and handed over a visitor's badge after only the briefest of explanations as to where I'd be. With a bounce in my step, I headed to the art room.

Dave looked up at me and smiled. "Back so soon?" He then said, "For those of you who are unaware, this is a fellow resident artist, Molly Masters."

"Thanks. Would you mind if I listened in on your class?"

"Not at all. You can drop in any time, in fact." He gestured at the bowl of fruit in the center of the room. "As you can see, we're doing a still life. I was just making the rounds, commenting on the students' work. Why don't you do the same? Start on the opposite side?"

"Okay." The students were working with oils. I loved the medium myself, but had given it up when my children were babies, always telling myself I'd get back to it someday. Though I now occasionally painted, I never really got involved full-force again; life had taken me in other directions, as it has a way of doing for us all.

Partway around the circle, I recognized the shock of red hair of one of the students and battled a case of déjà vu. Jasper Newton looked so much like his father at this age that it was almost eerie. "Jasper. Hi."

He nodded to me.

"Hey, Molly," Tiffany Saunders said. She stopped her work to come over to me as I stood next to Jasper.

"Hi, Tiffany. I'd forgotten you two were the same age. It's such a coincidence, really. Your father, Jasper, and your mother, Tiff, were once in an art class with me."

"Yeah," Jasper grumbled, "and I'm sure she never noticed my father was even alive, the same way Tiff—" He stopped abruptly and blushed as if shocked that he'd spoken his thoughts aloud.

"Jasper, that's not true. I've always liked you. *You're* the one who never talks to *me*."

He gave me a glance that was clearly meant to signify, Leave us alone for a minute. I turned my back on them and suggested to the student at the easel I'd just passed that he add more yellow to his now lime-green rendition of "white" grapes. Using a talent that I've picked up over the years of being a mother, I nevertheless overheard Jasper reply to Tiffany, "Yeah, but that's 'cause you're beautiful and smart and funny, the hottest girl in Carlton. I always figured: What would she want to talk to me for?"

I glanced over at them. Clearly flattered, Tiffany gave Jasper an appraising visual once-over. In flirtatious tones she said, "Try me sometime and find out, Jas." Now blushing herself, she returned to her easel.

I felt my own cheeks warming and was touched to think that maybe I'd just inadvertently brought the two of them together. If my memory and the rumors were accurate, they'd both ended relationships within the past year.

Now that I looked at them in that way, they would

make a truly cute couple. Instead of blurting out something stupid like, "Aw, shucks," I looked at Jasper's painting. "Nice work, Jasper." Actually, two of the pears suggested certain female anatomy, but I suppose that was predictable.

Having listened to my compliment, Tiffany returned to look at his painting herself. "You're pretty good."

Their eyes met. Looking positively daffy, he said, "Thanks. So are you."

Dave Paxton, who was already rounding the circle of student easels from the opposite direction, said, "Time to get back to work, Tiffany."

He smiled at me and whispered into my ear, "I'd get a whole lot more finished portfolios out of my classes if I could divide them into all girls and all boys."

A couple of hours later I was at Nadine's town house as scheduled. It was a nice enough place, if somewhat cluttered. There was barely a flat surface not occupied by a porcelain doll. I picked up a doll that was propped up against a table lamp. The doll was no bigger than my hand.

Through what was perhaps only some trick my memory was playing on me, I remembered handling a nearly identical doll when I'd first spoken to Corrinne Buldock about the variety show. "Am I imagining things, or didn't Corrinne used to have a doll just like this one?" I asked.

"Yes, she did. She considered it a lucky charm, and often brought it to school with her. We used the same cast to make both of them."

"She used to make dolls, too?"

Nadine pursed her lips. Even here in her home she had an old-school-marm aura about her with her tight, short curls and the ever-present reading glasses perched on the end of her button nose. "She was my business partner. For a short period of time."

"Why just for a short time?"

"She just decided she was too busy. I bought her out. There were no hard feelings."

Despite her words, her clenched jaw and averted eyes indicated otherwise. I studied the doll in my hand, wishing it could provide a clue about Corrinne's murder. "This one's so little." I couldn't resist saying, "Hello, Dolly."

Nadine shot me a withering look. I started to pick up a second doll that was on the top shelf of the cabinet. "Don't touch that!"

I stopped and looked back at her in surprise.

"That's an antique. Worth a small fortune. I already had one antique doll disappear on me."

"Disappear?"

"Unfortunately. Neither Corrinne nor I were very good at keeping track of inventory. As best we could decipher after the fact, she shipped it to some girl in Minnesota by mistake. We sold it at less than a tenth of its estimated value."

She then showed me her work area. She described the step-by-step process of making dolls in such exacting detail that I remained standing throughout, afraid that if I sat down, I would immediately nod out. Noble to my cause, I feigned interest while letting my thoughts wander toward how well she fit the image of the killer. Nadine's wig had been uncentered that night. Would I have noticed that on the killer? No. From the moment that person pushed by me, my vision had been riveted to the gun.

When Nadine's lecture reached the part where the doll was finally shipped out, I thanked her profusely and gave my apologies, saying that I needed to ship out myself and get home to my kids. Her presentation had caused me to lose sight of my objectives for being there. My visit had not been a total waste, though. At least I'd learned that

Nadine had what hinted at a motive, if she thought that Corrinne had damaged her business enterprise.

I drove around in circles trying to get out of her neighborhood, till I decided to pull over and follow the next car that passed, hoping its driver was on the way out of the development. The technique worked, and I soon found my way onto the main road that led home.

Suddenly, my backseat seemed to explode. I could see a flash of light reflected in the rearview mirror. The boom was so loud it felt as though the reverberations were traveling up my spine.

I screamed in fright and pain. My ears were ringing. My neck and shoulder felt as if they were on fire.

Chapter 9

Congratulations! You're My 20,000th Caller!

I slammed on the brakes and pulled on the steering wheel to veer off the road. Stupid reaction. A signpost was now looming in front of me. I managed to swerve and miss the sign, but almost crashed into a telephone pole. The back tires spun on the icy vestiges of that weekend's snowfall. My Jeep went into a full skid and spun into the oncoming lane.

My ears were buzzing so badly that I could feel but not hear myself scream as a pickup nearly hit me front on. I managed then to calm down enough to regain control of my car. I pulled onto the curb and to a stop.

I flung open my door and got out, breathing deeply and attempting to reassure myself that I was all right—just deaf and in considerable pain. A car pulled over behind me, and its driver, a young man in a dark business suit and tie, rushed toward me.

Too scared and disoriented to pay much attention to him, I steadied myself by gripping the top of the door. It was only when the man touched my arm that I realized he'd been talking to me.

"Are you all right, lady?" I could tell by his mannerisms that he was shouting at me. His voice sounded a hundred miles away.

I looked into the backseat and saw little charred pieces of debris embedded everywhere. Amazingly, all of the windows were still intact. "A bomb. Someone put a car bomb in my backseat." I couldn't hear my own words.

Had my eardrums burst? The pain in my ears was intense, as was a roaring noise. It sounded as though my head were inches away from Niagara Falls.

My God! How was I going to mother my children if I couldn't hear their complaints and arguments? I wasn't smart enough to figure out how to live in a silent world at this point in my life!

Aided by the driver's emphatic gestures, I lip-read his words: "I'll call nine-one-one."

"No, I'll just drive myself to the hospital." I started to get back into my car.

The man grabbed my arm. I looked him straight in the eye and he immediately released his grip on me. He shook his head and, as best as I could lip-read, said, "No, you shouldn't do that." Then he said something along the lines of "Baa baaa baa baa," but I doubted that was accurate.

"What? I can't hear."

"No," he said again, shaking his head, though this was one word I could lip-read easily enough. He reached out and touched my back, just past my shoulder, then brought his hand back to show me.

His fingertips were covered in blood.

My good Samaritan, using a small first-aid kit in his car, devised a makeshift compress for my worst injury, a cut just behind my right shoulder. He then waited with me until the ambulance arrived. In the meantime he also called Jim for me on his cell phone. I hoped that he conveyed the message that I was mostly fine—just a bit more daft than usual.

The young man's first name was either Brendon or Brandon or something of the kind. I thanked him profusely and asked for his last name, but I couldn't understand him, and he ignored my request for him to write it down. I wanted to send him a written thank-you. It was so difficult to monitor the volume of my own voice that I kept my talking to a bare minimum.

It hit me on the ride to the hospital that I'd ruined my sexy blouse, just after learning I actually owned one. The emergency room physicians examined me and told me that only the one wound in the back of my right shoulder required stitches; the cuts to the back of my neck were cleaned up and covered with butterfly bandages. Fortunately, the headrest and the back of my seat had taken the brunt of the shrapnel.

Jim got to the hospital just a few minutes after my arrival and joined me in the examining room. He listened to my tale as I told it to the police officer whom someone had dispatched to meet me. Possibly, the hospital didn't get all that many car bombings and had contacted the police. My statement to him was straightforward—that my Jeep had been in a school parking lot most of the day, then parked in front of Nadine Dahl's house for just over an hour. The officer told me that they were towing my car to the police station so it could be examined for evidence.

The doctor assured me my hearing would return to a hundred percent within the next day or two. For now it was at least fifty percent restored. Just in time for a lecture from my spouse as he drove me home. He felt that I had been irresponsible by having gone to Nadine's house. I feigned more hearing loss than I was still experiencing, but he wasn't fooled.

My mother was at my house fixing dinner for Karen and Nathan when we arrived. Noting that I appeared to be completely unharmed—I'd left a sweater and T-shirt in Jim's trunk, and so was even wearing clean clothes—the kids gave me halfhearted hugs. Their indifference wasn't personal, I realized. They were glad I was all right; it's just that they were hoping for more compelling visuals to share with their friends at school the next day.

I took a seat at the stool alongside the kitchen counter so I wouldn't be tempted to lean back. Jim and the kids went into the family room. The moment they'd left the immediate vicinity, Mom gave me one of her patented glares that always makes me feel five years old. "Jim called me and told me what you did. Honestly, Molly. Just who do you think you are, the Lone Ranger?"

"No. He rode Silver as his main source of transportation and never experienced a single car bomb."

"Why must you always get involved in these murder investigations? Can't you just let Tommy do his job and stay out of it yourself?"

"Mom, I went through this with Jim already. I had no intention of getting myself blown up. From now on I fully intend to use more caution and never get into the car again without first checking for pipe bombs."

She furrowed her brow but said nothing. It occurred to me then that the idea of my being a magician's assistant so soon might not sit too well with my family.

Jim came into the kitchen as we were dishing up Mom's tuna casserole. Figuring I might as well get the matter resolved immediately, I said, "Today Martin Henderson reminded me that I'd agreed to be his assistant tomorrow night."

"Can you get out of it?"

"Not without guilt. It's at the children's wing of the hospital."

Jim frowned and said, "Maybe I can go in your place."

"I think you'll look even worse in Stephanie's gown than I would."

"Fine. I'll just come with the two of you." Jim had a determined look that warned me there was no sense in arguing the point. Besides, as I sat there clutching my Tylenol-with-codeine prescription, it struck me as a good idea to have my husband serve as my constant body-guard from then on.

"Your father and I have bridge club tomorrow night," Mom piped up, sensing an imminent baby-sitting job.

"Since when do you play bridge, Mom?"

"Since nineteen fifty-eight. I just took a forty-plus-year hiatus, is all."

"Weren't you rusty?"

"Not compared to your father."

I returned my attention to Jim. "Who's going to watch the kids?"

"We'll bring them along. They like magic shows."

"True, but they've only seen professional magicians on TV. Martin is not exactly David Copperfield. More like . . . David Plug-nickel-field."

"Who's that?" Mom asked, then called, "Dinner's ready," for the sake of the children.

"I was trying to make a joke. Plug nickel instead of copper."

She looked at me blankly. Explaining a joke was about as effective as explaining the sensations of a kiss. She said to Jim, "Karen and Nathan could always come watch us play bridge. They'd probably find that more entertaining than this David person."

"Martin person," I interjected.

"What's bridge?" Nathan asked as he and Karen joined us and grabbed their plates to carry to the table.

"It's a card game," I replied. "So tomorrow night you can choose between watching your grandmother play cards or watching Martin Henderson do magic tricks."

"Is he Brittany Henderson's dad?" Nathan asked.

"Yes. He's the man who came to your class right after me this afternoon."

"That guy? He's terrible. He was making this stuffed rabbit appear, and you could see the lump in his sleeve the whole time. And he tells these stupid jokes where he's the only one laughing." He looked at his sister. "Let's go to Gramma's. She's always got the good kind of cookies."

Just after dinner the doorbell rang, as heard by the dog and my other family members. Jim got the door. I'd assumed it would be my father, but it was Tommy whom Jim led to me in the living room.

"Got one of the guys to follow me over here with your car," Tommy said to me. "We already finished collectin' evidence."

"Can I get you a cup of coffee or anything?"

"Glass of water is all. Lauren sends her regards."

Tommy and Jim followed me into the kitchen. Apparently Jim was taking his vow to keep an eye on me seriously. I poured Tommy his water and jazzed it up a little by adding ice cubes.

"What did you find out?" Jim asked.

"It was a small pipe bomb. Fortunately, it was designed to have almost no explosive force."

"Tell that to the shrapnel that was embedded in my shoulder."

Ignoring me, Tommy continued. "Pretty basic construction, 'cept for the timer. Most home jobs don't use timers like that."

"Were there any fingerprints?" Jim asked.

"Nope. Wiped clean."

"Oh, great," I said under my breath. "So we still have no idea who did this?"

"Could've been much worse. Like I said, the thing was constructed to make noise and leave a mess, more'n anything else. I think it was meant more to scare you than to kill you."

"It went off when I was in traffic, Tommy. I nearly had a head-on collision with a pickup truck. *That* sure could have killed me."

"Wouldn't've done much for the pickup truck, either. What kind was it? I sure like the looks of those Chevy king cabs."

"Tommy, this isn't funny. What if my kids had been with me?"

"Thing that I find int'resting is, what if you hadn't been in the car at all? How'd whoever put it there know you were gonna be drivin' then? 'Course, that's what I mean. Prob'ly figured odds were you *wouldn't* be in the car. Whole thing was prob'ly just meant to put a scare in you." He shifted his gaze toward Jim. "Really made a mess of your upholstery, by the way."

Jim paled a little. "I'd better go take a look," he muttered, and left the kitchen.

Tommy gulped down his water, then said to me, "The shrapnel was also interesting. Not that I'm a bomb expert, but I have seen more than one or two. Never seen shards of porcelain used before."

"Porcelain?" I repeated. "Such as in porcelain dolls?"

"Uh-huh. As a matter of fact, that's exactly what the pieces seemed to be." He rose and recentered his cap into the band it had left in his red hair. "It was smashed-up doll faces."

Jim took the next morning off. He reminded me that the emergency room doctor had instructed me to make an appointment with my own doctor to get everything rechecked, just in case. Jim drove me to the doctor, but they'd gotten backed up and we spent an inordinate amount of time in the waiting room.

As a result of the doctor visit, we learned that there were no random pieces of porcelain embedded in my skin. Except for my shoulder, which was sore to the touch or when I made a sudden movement, I felt fine.

I convinced Jim that there were better uses of his precious free time than keeping me under surveillance, and gave my promise that I would not so much as leave the house without calling him first. He dropped me off, changed clothes, then went back to work.

When I got home, I spent a suitable amount of time greeting Betty Cocker, then listened to my phone messages. The messages consisted only of hang-ups, which always indicated sales calls. I'd once calculated that, because I worked at home and was almost always the one to answer the phone, I was nearing twenty thousand calls from telemarketers that I'd declined.

The thought gave me an idea for a cartoon: A woman answers her phone and says, "Congratulations! You're about to be the twenty-thousandth telephone solicitor I say no to! Hang on while I get my firecrackers and referee's whistle." The caption reads: "Mildred Krumwalker has mastered the only technique known to cause telemarketers to hang up first."

The phone rang in earnest, shaking me from my reverie. I said hello, and was greeted in return with, "It's about time you got home. Oh, Molly, we are in the worst possible predicament."

I braced myself. "What's wrong, Stephanie?"

"It's that Olivia Garrett, *that's* what's wrong. Believe me, Molly, that old saying is so true, 'No good deed goes unpunished in this world.' "

"What good deed have you done lately?" Or ever, for that matter.

"Adopting Jenny, of course. I need you to come over here right away. Though I sorely hate to do this, we have no choice."

"Much as you flatter me, Steph, I've got work to do."

She clicked her tongue. "As I already stated, the problem is Olivia. It's been mandated that Olivia have supervised visits only, and that I am not to be the supervisor. Understandably, Jenny wants the visits to take place within her new home. I'd thought that maybe Tiffany could be supervisor, but she can't come home right after school, and Olivia's going to arrive at three.

She wants to talk to Jenny for an hour at the most, she says. Therefore, you need to do it."

"You want me to be your supervisor?"

"If you insist, fine. You're my supervisor."

"Aren't there any next door neighbors you could ask to—"

"No. It's you or nothing. This is a big enough imposition on me as it is. I have some rights, after all, to say whom I want in my house and whom I don't."

"Boy, Steph, you really know how to charm the warm 'n' fuzzies right out of me, don't you?"

She let out a puff of air. "Molly, please. You'd be doing me a big favor. Besides, this is right up your alley. Olivia is clearly going to try to convince Jenny to move back home, and you're such a do-gooder, you're going to want to help convince Jenny to do what's best. For all your faults, you're a devoted mother and you try to be impartial. You'd be the best person I can think of to advise Jenny."

I was stunned into momentary silence. "That was almost complimentary, Stephanie. Did you mean what you said?"

"Clearly if my words just now have convinced you to do what I want, I'd be an idiot to say anything but yes, now wouldn't I?"

I was tempted to retort, That's never stopped you before, but held my tongue.

"The truth, though, is that Olivia and I already discussed our dilemma with regards to supervised visits. You were the only person we could both agree we would tolerate."

"I'm touched. It's such an honor to discover that I'm so universally tolerated." More to the point, though, Stephanie was right. I did want to see that Jenny was making the right decision for herself, and the more I'd seen of Olivia lately, the more inclined I was to support the judge's decision to remove her daughter from her custody. "All right. I'll be there at three-thirty. I need to spend some time with my children, and I've got plans this evening, too. Which reminds me . . . I'm filling in for you tonight at a magic show."

"I remember. All the more reason for you and me to get together this afternoon. I can help you prepare to be my understudy."

I preferred to think of myself as her supervisor, but a bit of rehearsal could only help. "Okay. Thanks."

"You're going to need all the help you can get." She chuckled. "Martin called me yesterday evening to ask if I could lend you my evening gown. I hope you didn't plant that silly notion in his head."

"No, in fact I already told him that your dress would never fit."

"Not unless you've gotten breast implants since I last saw you. I'll see you at three-thirty." She hung up.

I slammed down the phone and let out a little roar of frustration and anger that energized BC immediately. She rushed up to me and put her front paws on my thighs as if to ask what this new game entailed and whether she could play with me.

I ignored her and dialed my husband's office. He wasn't there, so I left the message, "Jim, we must move immediately. Anyplace where Stephanie Saunders doesn't live would be fine." I took a calming breath, then said, "By the way, I've got to go over to Stephanie's after school. Don't worry, though. She's not a suspect. And there will be too many witnesses for any violent acts to occur. And remember that I've got to be a magician's assistant at six-thirty tonight."

I hung up, cheering myself at the thought that whatever else could be said about me, I seldom left dull or predictable messages on my husband's voice mail.

* * *

Olivia Garrett pulled into Stephanie's circular driveway right after me. She greeted me cordially, thanked me for agreeing to do this, then rang the doorbell.

"Have you gotten any interest on that self-portrait of Dave's?" I asked by way of small talk.

"It's turned a few heads already," she replied. "Of course, I have to keep apologizing for the frame and asking people to envision it with a forest-green matte."

I murmured in what I hoped was a sympathetic tone, but was thinking how similar Olivia's and Stephanie's narcissistic personalities were. No wonder they despised each other.

Olivia rang the doorbell a second time. Stephanie answered the door and led us to the "sitting room," where Jenny was already doing her part—seated in a fancy wing-back chair.

"Well, I'll leave you alone now," Stephanie said. She glanced nervously in Jenny's direction before doing so. "I'll be upstairs if anyone needs me."

Olivia's eyes fell immediately on her daughter. "Oh," Olivia said, clasping her hands over her heart. "How are you, sweetie?"

"Fine," Jenny answered, avoiding her mother's eyes.

Olivia turned her head slightly and listened to Stephanie's footsteps as she climbed the stairs. I took a seat. The instant she could hear an upstairs door shut, Olivia dropped onto her knees, sobbing. "I can't take this, Jenny. You're my whole life. You can't do this to me."

Horrified, I sat there, wondering how—if her emotions were genuine—Olivia could have managed to remain so perfectly under control until the precise moment that her rival was no longer able to overhear.

"I gave birth to you, met your every need, sacrificed everything for you. And it was worth it. I'd do it all again. A thousand times over, just to see you turn out so wonderfully. But I don't deserve to be shoved out in the cold this way. Come home to me, baby. Please. This is killing me."

"You lied to me, Mother!" Jenny retorted. "You said that my father died in a car accident!"

Olivia got to her feet and dabbed at her eyes. "I didn't consider that a lie. He died of carbon monoxide poisoning in our garage. It very well could have been an accident."

"According to the papers, he left a note."

"I was trying to protect you from a painful truth."

"You were a suspect, Mother! The police finally ruled suicide only after investigating whether he could even have been conscious with that much alcohol in his system!"

Olivia's face turned as stony-looking as it had in my house the day after the shooting. "I did not harm your father. The police were wrong to suspect me. They cleared my name." She started to cry once again. "I didn't want you to know that you . . . have that link of suicidal tendencies from both sides of your family."

Jenny's jaw dropped. In her expression of helpless surprise, she looked much younger to me now—Karen's age instead of a near adult. "*Both* sides?"

"Olivia," I interrupted, "this is getting out of hand. I think you—"

She shot me a withering glare, then returned her focus to Jenny. "Don't you realize that the only reason I'm keeping myself alive now is the possibility that you'll stop this? That you'll come home to me?"

"That's emotional blackmail," I cried, too enraged at Olivia's behavior to remain silent. "And of the worst possible kind!"

"Is loving my own daughter enough to be willing to die for her wrong?" Olivia countered. She sobbed into her hands.

"All right, Mom, all right!" Jenny cried. "I'll withdraw

everything legally. I'll return home. Okay? Just quit crying!"

In as calm tones as I could manage, I said, "Jenny, please, let things simmer down before you agree to anything you might regret later." I was livid at Olivia's behavior. How dare she threaten to kill herself if her daughter didn't return to her! "It isn't *any* teen's responsibility to take care of her fully functional parent."

"This isn't your place to interfere!" Olivia said to me.

At the raised voices, Stephanie trotted back down the stairs. "Is everything all right?"

"Not really," I called back, knowing Stephanie would blame me for Jenny's reversal. Perhaps with good reason. As supervisor was it my responsibility to make sure that the conversation not concern ignoring the judge's decision that Jenny was to live with Stephanie?

Stephanie rushed into the room.

Jenny rose and said, "It's *my* right to decide where I live, if I choose to live elsewhere. The judge said so. I've made my decision." She looked down at the floor and with total resignation said, "I'm going to move back home."

Chapter 10

A Fine Mess, Ollie

"What on earth just happened here?" Stephanie cried. "Olivia, this is your very first visit with Jenny, and you've already manipulated her into doing things your way, haven't you!"

"I merely convinced my daughter how much I love her," Olivia shot back.

Stephanie was clearly on the verge of tears. Jenny was deliberately avoiding Stephanie's attempts to make eye contact. "Jenny, are you absolutely certain this is what you want to do? Move back home?"

"Yes," Jenny said in a near whisper.

A look of anguish passed across Stephanie's features. She looked at me. "Molly, do something!"

If only I could! What was there for me to do? Call time out and put everyone in separate rooms? "As the supposed mediator here, no matter what happens, Jenny, I think you absolutely *must* wait at least until the murder case is solved before you consider moving anyplace."

"That might never happen!" Olivia protested.

"Molly's right," Stephanie replied, though she was making no attempt to hide the venom in her eyes, and much of that anger was currently directed toward me. "This is not a good time to make hasty decisions."

"That's easy for you to say," Olivia retorted. "You've got my daughter. I want her home with me right now."

"No," Jenny said, looking in her mother's direction

but backing out of the room. "I think I do need at least a day or two. To explain this to Tiffany." She started to leave, then hesitated, gave her mother a tentative hug, and fled from the room.

Olivia's smile struck me as one more of triumph than anything else. Stephanie was clearly so incensed that I began to rethink my earlier assurances to my husband that no violence would occur. "Olivia, can I walk you to your car?" I offered.

Stephanie glowered at me for a moment, then, with her hands on her hips, regarded Olivia. "I do not profess to be Mother Superior. All I know is that Jenny is a wonderful young woman, and you obviously deserve some credit for that; however, I've also witnessed crocodile tears shed from your eyes often enough to surmise exactly what went on in my house just now."

Olivia's face assumed that stony quality I'd witnessed a few times in the last few days. "All I care about is my daughter."

"I wish I could believe you," Stephanie said, "but I don't. Jenny's felt that you've been neglectful and wanted to get your hands on her trust fund, and the judge agreed with her." She strode toward Olivia and shoved a finger in her face. "If you harm one hair on her head, if you betray her in any way to get at the money that is rightfully hers, you'll have me to answer to, and I promise you, I will make your life miserable. Have I made myself clear?"

Olivia's eyes flashed in anger. "Don't threaten me. You might be the one with all the money and the power, but you're not going to have my daughter for much longer."

"Ultimately, that's Jenny's decision, not yours or mine or even the judge's. I will gladly let her go before I'll see her get pulled apart by us fighting over her. If you want to attack me at a PTA meeting, that's one thing. Just don't sacrifice Jenny's future simply to make yourself victorious over me."

"She's my daughter, damn you! She belongs with her mother! And soon, that's exactly where she'll be, you rich bitch."

I'd instantly lost my desire to accompany Olivia to her car, and she marched out of the house with her nose in the air. I turned back to Stephanie. "Stephanie, I am so sorry about all of this. You should have seen her. She practically fell on the floor at Jenny's feet, threatening to kill herself if Jenny didn't come home. I didn't know what to do to stop her. I don't think I've ever seen anyone totally change colors that fast."

Stephanie paused from massaging her temples. "What did you think, Molly? That I was adopting Jenny because of some ego trip? That the judge sided with me only because I'd bought him off?"

That pretty much summed up the suspicions I'd once held. My cheeks were warming, so Stephanie knew the answer.

"There are easier and infinitely better ways to glorify myself than to gain custody of a second teenager, believe me, Molly."

"I'm sorry, Stephanie. Maybe I should go talk to Jenny on your behalf and—"

"No. I meant what I said to her so-called mother. I will not treat Jenny like a wishbone. She's decided to return to her mother, even though the woman cares more about her silly art gallery than her own daughter. As long as Olivia knows that she's going to experience the wrath of God if she tries to cheat that poor girl of her inheritance, we're going to support Jenny's decision."

Feeling numb and mildly nauseated, I nodded and got to my feet. "How could I ever have misread Olivia so badly?" I murmured, thinking out loud.

"Oh, don't beat yourself up over this. Self-pity doesn't

become you. You were working from the disadvantage of being such a totally decent person. As I tried to tell you earlier, it takes one to know one."

We ate an early dinner that night so that I'd be on time to be a magician's assistant. Remarkably, Jim was home by six and we were finished eating and ready to go by six-thirty, when Martin rang the doorbell. By then the kids had decided they'd have a better time making fun of Martin than of Grandma—a wise choice—and so we all met him at the door and grabbed our coats. I introduced everyone.

"It's nice to meet you," he said with a small bow, tipping his top hat in the process.

"Is there a rabbit in there?" Nathan asked, trying to peer inside the top hat during its return trip to Martin's head.

"Why, I'm not sure," he replied, and stared at Nathan. "But there does seem to be something in your ear."

"Yeah, I'll bet." Nathan rolled his eyes just as Martin started to reach for Nathan's ear. "And if it's a quarter, can I keep it?"

Martin indeed revealed the quarter he'd "found" in Nathan's ear and gave it to him. Forcing a smile, Martin said to me, "Clever boy. We'd better get going, Molly. Show starts at seven, and we'll have some prep work to do as well."

"We're all going. They'd like to see the act."

"Ah. Wunnerful. Wunnerful." He rubbed his hands together and smiled. "The only thing is, I have a shortage of passenger seats. Have to haul my own equipment in the pickup, you see."

"We'll just follow in our car," Jim said. "Are you coming with me, Moll?"

Martin immediately said, "I thought we would verbally run through the routine during the drive. I'd hate to have my assistant louse up and make me pull a turtle out of my hat, hey, Carol?" he said with a smile, looking at my daughter.

"Karen," she corrected. "Actually, a turtle would be great. No one would expect it."

"That's stupid," Nathan told his sister. "Rabbits are cute. A turtle would just go into its shell. He might as well pull a rock out of his hat."

The two continued to bicker as we went to our respective vehicles. I considered apologizing to Martin for having subjected him to this, but was distracted when I saw what was in the back of his pickup. "They look just like the booths from your finale at the variety show."

"Not exactly. Only the one that Stephanie was in is the same. Chester built me a new one to replace the one that Corrinne was in. He built the original ones, too."

"Martin, I'm sorry, but there's no way I'm doing that trick. I cannot and *will* not step into that box after watching Corrinne get shot to death."

He opened the passenger door for me. "I can see your point." There was a rabbit in a small travel cage on the front seat. Jammed into the small space behind the seats, a pair of doves cooed in greeting. "There's not much room. You'll have to hold Bun Bun on your lap."

Fine fine, I thought, but silently followed his instructions.

As he slid behind the wheel he said, "We won't do that trick if you feel squeamish about it. I have a better finale now, anyway. I'm putting a couple of swords through your head."

"Pardon?"

"Don't worry. It's foolproof."

"Before or after the swords are in place?"

Ignoring me, he started the engine and we headed off. "It's this box that sits on a stand that I fasten around your neck, and it has the slots for the swords. Only it's deceptively large."

"So's my head."

"Trust me. For the sake of building drama, you need to scream like you're in agony, but you won't feel a thing. The swords will actually go behind your head."

"If I'm supposed to *pretend* to be in agony, how will you know the difference if your trick isn't working and I really *am* in agony?" I stopped him midchuckle with a glare and went on, "And don't you dare say that the blood will be a dead giveaway."

"I had Chester Walker help me build it just today, and I tested it on him."

"He's bald, and even if you miss my scalp, I don't want chunks of my hair getting cut off. More importantly, I truly think that my head is a lot larger than Chester's."

"I have to have a big finale, Molly. Trust me."

I managed a feeble smile and nodded. Surely it couldn't be easy to poke a sword through someone's skull. If anything went seriously wrong, at least we would already be in a hospital. Chances are I'd only need a few stitches. As would Martin, by the time I was through with him.

"You know," I grumbled, "Chester recently promised me up one side and down the other that he was going to be at my house today, if not yesterday, building my sunroom. Now it turns out that he's been busy building boxes so you could get a sword through my head."

Through the plastic of the travel cage, I could feel Bun Bun trembling. "Your rabbit seems frightened." I opened the cage and reached toward him to stroke his fur.

All of a sudden I felt a sharp pain in my finger. "Ow!" I yanked my hand back. "He bit me!"

"He does that if you're not careful. Don't worry. He's not rabid or anything." He chuckled. "A rabid rabbit. Get it?"

"Pardon me for not laughing. It's just that I'm in a

considerable amount of pain at the moment." I looked again at my finger. "I think Bun Bun bit me clear down to the Bone Bone."

"Sorry about that, Chief."

Now he was doing Maxwell Smart? Last seen on TV in, what? The late nineteen sixties? "Are you sure your rabbit doesn't have rabies?"

"Quite sure. He's bit me more than once in the past couple of years, and yet I'm nerfectly pormal." He laughed heartily.

What were the odds that the word "rabies" was derived from the word "rabbit"? Wrong spelling of the double b. That would be rabbis, not rabies. I spent the rest of the trip trying to distract myself from my throbbing finger to come up with a cartoon idea related to Jewish rabbits, then tried not to take my failure as a sign that my humor was permanently on the wane. After all, had Mel Brooks ever tried to write a joke while traveling in a pickup truck with an accountant cum magician and his vicious bunny? I think not.

The show was held in the small auditorium at the hospital. To my great relief, because I'm hopelessly emotional when it comes to sick children, the auditorium was open to anyone who wished to attend, and the show was casually handled, such that families dropped in for a few minutes to watch and then left.

I had told Martin that I really didn't want to know how he did his tricks. Yet this was something like passing the scene of an accident; I couldn't help but watch out of the corner of my eye.

In truth, though, this was much more like being *in* the accident. Martin's performance was a disaster. The doves kept cooing and popping out of his pockets, and during my feeble attempts to help, the stupid things bit me twice. Then Bun Bun bit Martin, which, though this was poetic justice, really reduced his sleight-of-hand tricks, for he kept shaking his hand in pain and dropping or mishandling various props.

Martin then had an unfortunate mishap when he was supposed to be levitating me. To my mind, the incident was more than overshadowed when, during the finale, a certain twelve-year-old boy in the audience cried, "The slots are at an angle and the swords are going behind Mom's head!" Although there were only a few folks still watching the show by then, those screams of agony that Martin had instructed me to make turned into wails of embarrassment.

Afterward, Jim and I helped Martin carry his equipment back to the truck. I'm sure that Martin was disappointed by the reception our pedestrian performance had received. My thoughts, however, were centered on the flashback experience of having been in the very act that led to such hideous events a couple of nights before.

When he and Jim carried out the last of his things, I asked, "Martin, do you have any solid idea of who the killer is?"

"No, I don't. My back was turned, and when I saw what was happening, I thought all three of us were goners. I just got down and tried to make myself as small a target as possible."

"If Olivia hadn't jammed the door on that booth that Stephanie got into, Stephanie would have snuck out the back, right?"

"Yes. Why?"

"She might have all but collided with the shooter as he or she came upstage."

"Huh. So you think it might have been Olivia, making sure Stephanie didn't get in her way?"

I shrugged. "That or she just wanted to embarrass Stephanie, like she claimed."

"It might have been magic, you know."

"*What* might have been?"

"Illusions are more powerful than you think. A master illusionist could have made it look like a clown did the shooting, when it was the illusionist himself."

I had to refrain from rolling my eyes. His need to be considered a suspect in a murder just so he could gain credibility as a magician had to be the most pathetic thing I'd ever seen. "Good night, Martin."

"What if he's telling the truth?" Jim asked as we headed toward our own car, where Karen and Nathan were already waiting. "What if he did this just because he wanted to make his career as pulling off the all-time best illusion?"

"You saw the show. He's not that good a magician. For the sake of his clients, I just hope he's a competent accountant."

As we got into the front seat I looked at Karen and Nathan. "So, guys, what did you think?"

Karen said, "I'd rather have stayed home and brushed the dog."

"What was your favorite part of the act, Nathan?"

"The levitating act," he replied without hesitation. He started laughing and elbowed his sister. "He was trying to hide the bar that was holding Mom up. So he was standing with the bar between his legs. Only he lost his balance and fell." At this last, Nathan was laughing so hard he had tears in his eyes.

"That was the only part I liked, too," Karen said, also laughing.

"Remember how funny his face looked? And he made this 'oof' noise. Like he was going to puke all over Mom."

The kids burst into hysterical laughter at that. Jim was trying hard not to laugh himself and made a game attempt at clearing his throat instead.

"I noticed you were nodding out during the act," I told him.

"He's no Houdini." He patted my knee. "Sure had a pretty assistant, though."

Betty Cocker was in a major state of anxiety when we arrived. She was always happy to see us, but this time she was frantic and kept barking.

She rushed ahead of me to the back door and barked to get out. When I slid it open to let her out, she didn't move, and I couldn't blame her. I stood there, frozen in a disbelief that was quickly mutating into shock and rage.

I glanced down at my husband, who was settling into the couch in the family room. "Honey? Could you come here for a minute?"

"Sure. What's up?"

"This is one way to distract me from worrying about the broken window-well cover." I waited till he was beside me, then stated the obvious. "The deck is gone."

Chapter 11

Hello, Mr. Rock.
Meet Mr. Hardplace.

In a reaction that was quite out of character, Jim stared out the back door and uttered a string of curse words. While I understood the sentiment, I had yet to see a situation change for the better as a result of having been cursed at. He tempered his language when Karen and Nathan joined us.

"Wow," Nathan said. "Maybe Martin is a magician after all and made our deck disappear."

"Or maybe Chester Walker would like the choice between rebuilding our deck and getting sued for all he's worth!" Jim retorted.

"How's Betty going to get out?" Karen asked. "She might hurt herself if she jumps down that far."

Nathan took a graceful leap out the door and said, "Come on, Karen. Let's get the slide!"

She hopped down and cried, "What a great idea!"

BC easily jumped down after them as they raced across the yard, despite the darkness, in search of the slide.

"At least the kids are happy," I said.

Jim reverted to unrepeatable language.

I grabbed the phone with the intention of dialing Chester. There was a message on the recorder, so I hit the playback button. In a cheerful voice a man said:

"Hello, Molly, Jim. This is Chester. It's a little after seven P.M. I promised you that I'd get my men out there working today, and I never break a promise to a customer. We got a bit backed up today, but I told my B crew you were personal friends and to put in some overtime. They reported that the preliminary work is done, at least. Hope you're pleased."

"Save that!" Jim said, pointing at the recorder. "That might prove useful if we have to take Chester to court. He said he never breaks a promise to his customers. I'll bet that's considered a legal contract."

"I don't think he ever promised not to hire idiots. All I know is, if this is the work of his B crew, I hope we never meet his C crew."

"This was the work of his F crew, and we both know what the F stands for."

The kids returned triumphant from having removed the stepladder and the slide from their swing set. They propped both into the opening of the door and set about trying to train BC to go down the slide by herself. Karen called to me, "This is *way* more fun than the deck, Mom. You should try it."

"No thanks. My rear end always sticks to the surface of the slide." I dialed Chester's house. His teenage son answered. At least I'm guessing that's who he was, because he kept saying "Yeah" and making a noise that sounded like the cracking of chewing gum. Chester wasn't home, and I had the feeling that his son was only pretending to write down my message, when all he really wanted was for me to get off the phone.

Despite yet another fitful night of sleep, I'd hoped to get some work done the next morning. Greeting card companies request samples in packs of ten, and I had only six that were ready to go. However, just when I'd settled into my big chair in the living room to doodle until an idea for a card emerged, a radio suddenly blared from the backyard. This set off Betty Cocker's furious barking, reminiscent of my husband's reaction the night before. The volume was so loud that I could feel the vibrations through my slippers, but the words were still the indistinguishable, "Ya diddy dah diddy diddy DAH." I slid open the back door and spotted four young men who looked barely old enough to shave, all wearing backward-facing baseball caps.

"Hello there," I called, but my words were swallowed by the diddy dahs of the rapper's actual words. I wished I had the vocal ability to belt out a stanza from *The Sound of Music* to get their attention. From a safe position just slightly behind my legs, BC continued to bark at them. I eased myself down to ground level between the slide and its stepladder, then promptly hit the power button on the radio.

They all froze and looked at me as if by turning off the radio I'd disconnected their own power sources. A nice-looking Hispanic man said, " 'Morning, ma'am. We're here to install your sunroom. Why'd you decide to have your whole deck removed?"

"We didn't. Your B crew did that all on their own, and we want it back. Are you guys the A crew?"

He glanced at his coworkers and said with a smile, "Sure."

BC had hopped down after me and took a post right next to my feet, where she resumed barking at the top of her lungs. The men glared at her. "Is Chester coming out to supervise?" I asked.

"Yeah. He should be out sometime today."

"When he gets here, I need to speak to him about the deck. And if you'll keep the volume down on the radio, I'll keep my dog in the house. Deal?"

He shrugged. "Sure."

* * *

Incredibly, by noon the crew had already passed a building-code inspection of the cement footers or sub-ground pillars—whatever those things are called—which, unbeknownst to me, had been installed at some point last night while the deck was being removed. They had also installed the plywood subflooring. This I learned when I entered my kitchen and discovered one of the men using the ledge of the former window as temporary storage for his soda cans. He also told me that they'd "have the walls up in no time." No mention was made of the roof, but I assumed that was implied.

I peered past him. It was awfully cold outside, and, with an enormous hole in place of the window, so was the kitchen. "What about the deck?"

"The deck?"

"The fact that it's missing, yes. When are you going to rebuild it?"

"We just remove people's decks. You'll have to talk to some deck builders about putting one on."

"Wait a minute. When you say 'we' remove decks, does that mean the four of you?"

I got my answer from their suddenly averted eyes.

"*You're* the B crew? You're the ones who removed my lower deck by mistake?"

The worker with the darkest backward baseball cap stepped beside the other man and set his own soda down. "Chester just told us to take the deck off, and that's what we did."

"I'm not paying anything until Chester convinces me that the deck is going to get rebuilt to our satisfaction."

"Suit yourself, lady. You might want to move."

"*Move?* You mean, I'm going to need a new house by the time you're done with it?"

"Nah. I just meant Billy's going to cut a hole for the door. It's gonna get real dusty where you're standing."

True to his word, a moment later a cloud of dust arose,

along with the considerable racket of an electric tool, and I left the room. A loud bang followed, which I took to be the Sheetrock falling from where the new door would be. Moments later came one of the worst four-letter words in the English language for circumstances such as this: "Oops."

"What just happened?" I asked as I returned to the kitchen and caught sight of the "oops" guy, a gangly young man now standing in the even larger gaping hole in the wall.

" 'Fraid I cut through a wire," he replied. "Good thing I had the circuit breaker off and was using our own generator or I might've electrocuted myself."

"That *is* lucky. How are you going to repair the wire?"

"We don't do electrical," a paunchy man behind him said. "You'll have to get an electrician out here."

"Just be careful to check their rates first, ma'am," said the Hispanic man, who appeared to be in charge of the crew. "Some of 'em will cost you an arm and a leg."

"You mean some of them will cost *you* an arm and a leg. This is your mistake."

"Says in your contract that you'll cover the electrical. You can take it up with Chester, though."

"Hope it don't get too cold tonight," the paunchy young man said. "We just got a piece of plywood to put in the door, but it's gonna leave some gaps, no matter how we do it." On that note, he and Mr. Oops put a huge piece of plywood up to block the irregularly shaped doorway—a fat cross where the would-be door crossed paths with the once-was-window. With the plywood in place, the kitchen was instantly dark and depressing.

To continue the argument, I had to either shout through the wood or go outside. I hopped down from the house and managed to slide the door shut before the ever-barking BC could join me. Opening the door again from this angle would be a bigger challenge. Oops and Pauncho were now fastening the plywood into place with long screws. The other two workers were packing up their tools.

"Why did you take out my window and cut the wall for the door before you had the roof and walls in place? Wouldn't it have made more sense to make the entranceway to the room the last thing you do?"

No one answered. I silently answered for myself: Only if you care about the people living in the house. Meanwhile, the crew chief brushed his hands in a gesture that was alarmingly reminiscent of someone who thought his work here was done. Indeed, he hopped down from the subflooring and said, "Have a good day, ma'am."

"You're leaving?"

His coworkers hopped down as well. Pauncho, the last to leave, started to round the house, carrying his toolbox in one hand and his boom box in the other. "We worked late last night," he said by way of explanation.

I trudged after them. "Oh, that's right. That was when you were removing our deck by mistake! You must be really tuckered out!"

"Have a nice weekend."

"It's Wednesday!" I shrieked. "You're not planning on leaving me with a hole in my wall for four days, are you?"

"We can only keep working if Chester tells us to." He was loading up his truck as he spoke.

I darted past them to stand in front of their vehicle, a truck with a king cab, and put both palms on their hood. "Now listen up. Before any of you leave my property, I want you to find Chester Walker. Until I see him face-to-face, I'm going to sit on the hood of your truck."

Oops glanced back at his coworkers, then stuck his hands in his pockets. "Gee, ma'am. I don't know if I can get him out here or not." I studied him, trying to memorize his features underneath his baseball cap in case I had to identify him in a lineup. Were the baseball caps there for a reason? Were the caps hiding their dodo logos?

I said evenly, "Then you're going to have an irate forty-year-old woman as a hood ornament."

Their Hispanic leader said soothingly, "I'll see if I can find him. Can I use your phone?"

I sized him up and decided that I was angry enough to take him in a fistfight, if it came to that. As long as he would stay inside my house as a hostage, it'd be more comfortable than sitting on his truck. I accompanied him inside.

He went to the phone and murmured something about putting a message on Chester's pager. In less than a minute the phone rang and he answered. He spoke in Spanish, but thanks to Ricky Martin, I recognized the word *loco*, and had the distinct feeling that I was being referred to as crazy. He hung up, grinned, and said, "He was already on his way over. Should be here any minute. Mind if I use your bathroom?"

I hesitated, calculating the odds of his escaping through the window, but decided to give my consent.

The doorbell rang just as my hostage returned. I opened the door and saw that it was Chester Walker, wearing a broad smile that I instantly desired to slap off his face. "Good afternoon, Molly. Did I tell you, or did I tell you?"

"Did you tell me *what*?"

"See ya later, Ches," my would-be hostage said to his boss as he left.

Chester gave him a slap on the back, then said to me, "See how fast my team works?"

"They're fast, all right. Right up there with hurricanes, tornadoes, and other natural disasters. I now have no electricity in my kitchen, a gaping hole in my wall, a broken window-well cover, and no deck!"

He, too, was now wearing a baseball cap over his bald head. "You're failing to look at the big picture, Molly. You also have a half-completed room in a mere twenty-four hours."

"But I no longer have a completed kitchen. And did I mention . . . Gee, now what was that concern I expressed to your son last night? Oh, yes. *Our deck is gone!*"

"I have good news on that front. After I got your phone message last night, I got right on it. I was able to find the dump truck and get your lumber back. We'll be able to put your deck on again, good as new."

"What about the screw holes?"

"Pardon?"

"Are you just going to screw everything back down the way it was or drill us new holes, or what?"

"Sure. It'll work fine. It might be a little creakier than it was." He gestured as he caught the fury in my eyes. "Looser boards, you know what I mean. But to compensate and so that there are no hard feelings, we'll pick up the entire tab for the electrical and get an electrician out here first thing in the morning. Your husband won't have to lift a finger."

"There wouldn't *be* a tab for the electrical if one of your workers hadn't carelessly cut a wire! I think I can speak for my husband when I assure you that he will be more than happy to lift a finger to you. His middle finger!"

"Look at the bright side. Dinner at a restaurant tonight is guaranteed. And I'll get someone out here in the morning. 'Fraid I'm going to need another check to cover the second third of the construction, as we agreed."

"Chester, you're swindling me!"

"I'm deeply hurt by that remark, Molly. All construction projects have their difficult periods. But once the room's complete, you're going to be so glad you agreed to this project you'll want to French-kiss me."

If memory served, he'd stolen that line from a TV commercial. "It would be difficult to put into words how very unlikely that is."

"Be that as it may, no check, no electrician tomorrow, and no deck." He gave me a shrug and a sheepish smile. "Sorry to play hardball, but a contract is a contract."

"If I don't pay, what happens?"

"Nothing, of course. We stop construction right this minute."

"That's tempting."

"You realize it would cost you two to three times our price if you were to hire somebody else at this point."

"As in somebody reputable? Somebody who knows what they're doing?"

"You're angry now. You won't be by the end of next week when you're sitting in your new sunroom."

I gritted my teeth, trying to think if I could use my predicament in a greeting card. At the moment all I could envision was me standing between two enormous ugly men who looked set to kill each other as I introduced them: Mr. Rock, meet Mr. Hardplace. But, hey, don't make me stand between you.

Feeling totally trapped, I got my checkbook and started writing.

"Thanks, Molly. This goes right into my savings for my son's tuition."

"That's something I've been meaning to ask you about. Why on earth is it so important that your son be the valedictorian? Isn't it enough that he's one of the top three or four students in his class?"

His jaw tightened and he narrowed his eyes. "I didn't ever go to college. Some people in this town have never let me forget it. I vowed to myself long ago that one fine day, my son would be valedictorian over their precious children. That's an honor we both deserve."

I was still fuming by the time my children got home from school, but my anger subsided somewhat when Lauren came over to ask about my shoulder. Just having my likable, sane friend there to commiserate with made me feel better, and it occurred to me that I hadn't even spoken with her about the bomb in my backseat. I asked how much Tommy had told her.

"Just about the pipe bomb and that you needed stitches. I was going to call you, but he said that your hearing had been affected. Nadine was curious about how you were doing, too, by the way."

"How did she know?"

"Tommy questioned her. The night it happened."

"Does he think she did it?"

"He isn't saying. He hasn't arrested her."

"My shoulder and ears are fine, but my house has seen better days." The children and dog were happily engaged in sliding out the back door as I showed her the damage.

"At least the house itself is still standing."

"They only started work last night. Give 'em time." I sighed. "All of this happened under the supervision of the man who built the contraption that protected my head while someone poked swords at me."

"Pardon?"

"I took Stephanie's place in Martin's act last night." Running my hands through my hair, I checked my skull for damage that might have escaped previous notice. As I did so it occurred to me that all of my life I've been under the *illusion* that I was a reasonably intelligent person. And yet I'd recently made some of the most blatantly stupid decisions I could imagine. I had erroneously assumed that the judge in the Garretts' case had made the wrong decision. I'd hired a contractor without checking his credentials. Not to mention that I'd failed to prevent a murder and had gotten bit by a bunny rabbit and a pair of doves.

"I honestly think that Chester Walker has decided to do me in by getting me so angry that my head explodes."

Later that evening Karen reminded me that she had a rescheduled piano lesson that day to make up for one that Elsbeth had been forced to cancel.

When we arrived at her house, Elsbeth's car was missing from its usual spot just outside of her garage, which didn't bode well. This usually meant that she wasn't home. But in its place was a different car, a minivan, which I didn't recognize, so maybe she'd changed vehicles recently.

Just as we reached her door she started to pull into the driveway. She gestured for us to let ourselves in. I opened the door and stood still, waiting for Elsbeth and not wanting to risk interrupting the beautiful music emanating from around the corner.

Elsbeth approached, and I smiled at her and walked in just as the music stopped. "Oh, my gosh, Elsbeth. I had no idea your daughter could play so—" I stopped abruptly at the sight of the pianist. It was Brian Underwood. Elsbeth's daughter was seated on the couch, next to Brian's mother.

"Hey, Mrs. Young. Mrs. Masters," Brian said. "I was just here doing some homework with Tamara, and she asked to hear some Chopin."

"Danielle? What are you doing here?" Elsbeth asked.

"I came over to pick up Brian, that's all. I had some errands to run, and they had a joint written report to complete this afternoon."

"Hello, Danielle," I said cautiously, wondering if I was about to get chewed out once again for being in the same room with her son.

"Molly," she said evenly.

Elsbeth had what had to be the phoniest-looking smile I'd ever seen plastered on her face. She looked at my daughter. "Karen, why don't you do some warm-up scales, dear. I'll be right in. I just want to walk my guests out."

Brian helped adjust the piano bench for Karen, then left the house without a word of goodbye. Tamara clicked her tongue at her mother and groaned, slumping farther down on the couch. Danielle walked up to Elsbeth in the foyer and said in a low voice, "I'm so sorry that Tamara's quit taking lessons, Elsbeth."

"She has simply decided to focus on her academics for a couple of months until school ends. When she's at Stanford next year she'll need all the practice she can get."

"I'm sure she will. Brian is going to Dartmouth. He chose that over Juilliard, despite his scholarship. Did he tell you?"

"Yes. I'm happy for him."

"As I am for Tamara," she replied, shutting the front door behind her.

"That bitch," Elsbeth murmured. "You know, my daughter is every bit as good a pianist as her son."

Tamara had made her way unnoticed into the foyer. "No, I'm not, Mom. Don't kid yourself. Brian's a musical genius."

"A genius? Please! He is not. The only person who thinks he's a genius is his mother."

"Corrinne used to call him that all the time, too. She'd have him play for our class."

Elsbeth set her dark features into a scowl. "She was hardly a judge. Everyone knows what the two of them were up to."

"That isn't even true, Mom. They were just friends. And he *is* a genius. I'm not. I'm only talented enough to be able to recognize the difference between good and great pianists. You can tell, too, Mom, and we both know it. Why can't you just accept the truth?" Tamara's voice had risen with every sentence. She stared at her mother, whose mouth was set in a thin line. Tamara stormed off toward her bedroom, slamming the door behind her. Elsbeth wrapped her arms around her chest and stared after her, but stood there frozen.

"Elsbeth, maybe we'd better reschedule today's lesson," I offered.

"That won't be necessary."

I glanced at Karen, her cheeks bright red as she pounded out the notes of her scales in an apparent attempt to drown out our voices. Then I looked Elsbeth directly in the eye and said firmly, "Yes, it is." I softened my tones and said, "Karen? We're going to reschedule. Let's go home."

"Have it your way," Elsbeth said, marching toward the piano. She was smoldering, largely because of my comment when I assumed Tamara was at the piano.

For Tamara's sake, I pleaded, "I'm sorry that I said anything about the quality of anyone's playing. Your daughter is a wonderful pianist and a really wonderful person. You must be really proud of her."

She turned toward me and nodded, but her eyes had a distant look, as though she hadn't heard a word. "Brian's overrated."

She sat down on the bench next to Karen and said, "Karen, before you go, let me share my idea for what I think you should begin working on for the next recital, all right? It's perfect for you."

She started playing some piece that I recognized and knew I should instantly identify, but I was too distracted by her hands. Three of her fingers had scabs from small abrasions. Come to think of it, she'd worn those long white gloves at the recital as if she'd been hiding her hands, and she'd worn gloves both when we were signing in for career day and in the teachers' lounge after our presentation.

I looked at my hands and verified the similar appearance of our respective injuries. Hers were further along in the healing process. A few days ago Elsbeth's hands had been bitten by birds.

Chapter 12

Inflated Attendance Figures

I drove Karen home, having made no mention to Elsbeth of the marks on her hands. What bothered me most was that I'd noticed no such marks on her hands while we were getting ready for the dress rehearsal. She could only have gotten them just as the birds were released—the distraction before the shooting took place.

The next morning, an electrician came and restored power to my kitchen. He took great delight in telling me how stupid this was of the builders. He got no argument from me, of course, but the difference was that he was earning a hundred bucks for a two-minute repair job, whereas I'd eaten too much ice cream the previous night. With no working freezer, Jim and I had agreed that "the bears" would eat our mint-chocolate-chip ice cream if we put it outside in the snow with the rest of our most perishable items. With all that sugar in our systems late at night, the bears had slept better than we had.

With electricity and refrigerator contents restored, I brainstormed card ideas by forcing myself to doodle and to write down words and phrases as they popped into my brain. No matter how often this method succeeds, I never believe that the process will work *this* time.

Soon my thoughts were focused on Martin's sparsely attended performance at the hospital, and how much better it would have felt if the chairs had been filled—even if the attendees had been asleep. There was a potential cartoon there. Now I just needed to find it.

Eventually, I settled on a drawing of a television reporter, microphone in hand, who says, "Organizers of tonight's rally are claiming a full house. However, this reporter has reason to believe that those attendance figures have been inflated." Behind him are the auditorium seats, almost all of which are occupied by silly-looking inflatable dolls.

Before I could complete the cartoon, my mother called to invite herself over, which was fine with me but unusual behavior on her part. During her visit, she was uncharacteristically chatty. She kept glancing at her watch, inspiring me to mention more than once that if she had someplace to be, I had plenty of work to keep me occupied. She ignored the hints.

Eventually, the doorbell rang, and Mom said, "I'll get it," then all but raced me to the door. She flung it open and, though I could see so for myself, announced, "It's your father, dear. Listen, Molly, I'd better run. I'll see you later, all right?"

"All right. Thanks for coming over, Mom," I replied, then looked at my father. He had stepped inside but was rotating his fishing hat in his hands and shifting his weight from foot to foot. My mother always insists that he wear a hat when he goes out, for he's bald and she is certain the hat prevents sunstroke.

He looked at me and said, "Er, we didn't get a paper this morning. I was wondering if I could read yours."

"Of course," I said, retrieving it from the kitchen counter where Jim had left it. "Go ahead and take it. We've already read it."

"I'd rather read it here."

"Dad, you don't mean that. Just take the paper with you."

"I, er, how 'bout a cup of tea?"

"Is there something specific you want to talk to me about, Dad?"

"No, just thought we could . . . shoot the breeze."

That suggestion was so uncharacteristic of my father that it cemented things for me. Someone had put my parents up to keeping me safe at home. "That's nice, but I have work to do. Tell Jim that I've absolved you of your personal duties to keep an eye on me, but that I'm already planning to stay home and work this afternoon."

"Will do." He returned the newspaper to me. "Already read it." He turned on a heel and left. At last I got back to my drawing. I had all of fifteen minutes to myself, when the phone rang.

When I recognized Lauren's voice, I had the immediate thought that Jim must be out of his mind if he honestly believed he could secretly join forces with my best friend to keep me in the house. Those thoughts were quickly laid to rest when she asked, "Do you have any interest in a short girls'-night-out kind of thing?"

"I don't know. This is just for short girls? I'm five-six, so I might not qualify."

Lauren ignored my joke and said, "It's Nadine's birthday. I told her I'd take her out for drinks at The Captain's Table after she gets off work. I can't find anyone at the high school who's free to join us. Or, more likely, willing to join us. Nadine is not exactly Miss Popularity. Will you come?"

My instincts were telling me not to go, but Lauren obviously didn't want to be the only one going, and as long as I was with her, my protective husband wouldn't object. "All right. Just as long as you and I don't wind up as her only friends in the world, if you know what I mean. There's something about Nadine—an edge to her personality—that's always bothered me."

"Tell me about it," Lauren moaned. "Thanks a bunch, Molly." She told me the time and place to meet them, then hung up quickly, as if afraid I might change my mind.

An hour later Jim came home for lunch. "Hi," he said, peering around the corner of the doorway to the living room as if looking for someone. "How's your morning been?"

"Fine. Uneventful."

"Oh. Good." He smiled and grabbed the makings of a turkey sandwich. "Did you get any work done today, then?"

"A little. Started on a new cartoon."

"Just started one? You usually work faster than that when you're not interrupted."

"Oh, I was interrupted plenty. Mom kept me occupied. You made a mistake when you sent my father over here to relieve her, though. He's totally guileless. I had him convinced to desert your plan not two minutes after he arrived."

Jim sighed. "I'm just trying to keep you out of trouble, Molly."

"And I appreciate that, but the thing is, I sincerely believe that if I try to stay home at this point, trouble will only find me." I decided to tell him something that I hadn't even wanted to admit aloud to myself. "Jim, every night since Corrinne was murdered, I've had this recurrent nightmare. I see the shooter in the clown costume, gun in hand. On the stage are you and Karen, Nathan, and Lauren, and the clown tries to hand me the gun, but I'm too scared to take it. So he shoots everybody—you, the kids, Lauren. And he laughs at me, puts the gun in my hand, and walks away. That's when I wake up."

"Oh, God." Jim pulled me into his arms. "I'm so sorry."

"I won't take any foolish chances, Jim. It's not like I'm going to risk getting myself killed."

He started to rub my back, then stopped when I

winced as he touched one of the injuries from the shards of porcelain. He dropped his arms and said bitterly, "No cause for me to worry. Just a pipe bomb in the backseat of my wife's car."

"I'm not saying that—" I stopped, distracted by the sight through the glass door. The dodo birds were returning to roost. They were entering the backyard. I pulled away from Jim and slid the glass door open.

Oops grinned at me. "Good news, Mrs. Masters. We misordered another customer's panels, so we're free to work this afternoon on your room."

Pauncho said, "We'll get the roof and walls up before we leave."

"Yippee," I said in a deadpan voice, glancing back at Jim.

Jim spread his hands. "They may as well keep going. It's not as if they can do a whole lot more damage."

By the time Karen and Nathan arrived home on their respective buses, we had the shell of a room—and no builders. I gave the kids my usual set of instructions and left, feeling a bit seedy to be leaving my children alone while I went to a bar, even if this was for a good cause.

The Captain's Table was located in what would have been considered Carlton's downtown, if only we had a downtown. Instead it was simply the busiest intersection in the area, with the shopping mall across the street and the edge of the school campus nearby.

I had my typical gag reaction from the air thick with cigarette smoke when I walked into the bar, which was depressingly crowded, considering that it was only a few minutes after four. Lauren had ordered a glass of chardonnay, and Nadine was gulping what looked like whiskey on the rocks. I'm such a lightweight when it comes to alcohol that even the smell of whiskey makes me shudder. Nadine, however, already looked more than a little looped, and stood up and gave me a hug when she spotted me.

"Why, 's Molly! Hey, I was just telling Lauren here that I realized something."

She shut her eyes and touched her nose as if giving herself a sobriety test. During the brief pause, Lauren clasped her hands together and mouthed "Thank you" to me, which I took to mean that she'd been having a miserable time with Nadine.

I expected Nadine to announce, "I'm drunk!" but, surprisingly, she centered her finger squarely on her button nose. Then, she opened her eyes and said, "I'm older than I can count while holding my breath."

"Fortunately, counting to your age while holding your breath is not one of the requirements in life."

She laughed and slapped a chair, indicating I should sit at the seat that I was already lowering myself into.

"Happy birthday."

"Thank you. It's been one hell of a past few days, but I'm sure the best is yet to come."

"True. Things can't get much worse," Lauren said.

"My point exactly. You two and our illustrious principal go way back, don't you?"

"Yes," Lauren replied. "We went to school here together."

"You don't have a thing to worry about then, Lauren. But *I* am going to have my neck out there when the ax falls over this stupid double-honors class business."

"Which business?" Lauren asked. As soon as she did, it clicked that Nadine was referring to classes such as Corrinne's. What those of us involved in the elementary school program called "TAG," the high school called "double honors."

"Take for example the fact that you have, what, four contenders for valedictorian, right? You've got four parents or sets of parents ready to murder one another just to give their child the edge. Then you've got a teacher murdered by one of those same four parents, one of whose sons had been sleeping with her."

"You think one of the parents killed her?" I asked.

"Of course. What do you think? That Dave Paxton did it? He's a mild-mannered, artsy-fartsy teacher type. He wouldn't know how to fire a gun if his life depended on it."

Nadine was also a suspect in my book, but I kept my mouth shut. I met Lauren's eyes; she gave me a sheepish smile. The waitress came over and I ordered a glass of tonic water. Nadine ordered another Rusty Nail, though she called it a "Russy Snail," which was no less appealing a name for a beverage, in my opinion.

"The way I see it," Nadine continued, "Jack's going to have to do something, sacrifice somebody, to gain the impression of control on the school." She held up her nearly empty glass. "So, this is to me, on my last days here at gold old Carlton. Good and old, I mean." She giggled at her verbal slip, then elbowed Lauren. "Good thing you're buying, Lauren. I won't be around to be taken out for drinks this time next year."

"Of course you will, Nadine," Lauren replied, furrowing her brow.

She shook her head emphatically. "Don't patronize me. I'm right. I am now what was once my favorite subject in school—history. Our Jack Vance is going to fire me. And good riddance to the whole of it."

I thanked the waitress and paid for the round before Lauren could get her money out. "Is that all you're drinking, Molly? *Tonic* water?" Nadine asked, as if appalled while watching me take a sip.

"Yes, but it has a fermented lime in it. Quite potent, actually."

She laughed. "I'm going to miss you, Molly. You were my favorite parent at Carlton High."

"Thanks, but neither of my children is even in high school yet."

"My point exactly."

"Well," Lauren said. "On a cheerier subject, Jasper has a new girlfriend."

"Does he?" I said, wondering if this could be Tiffany. Come to think of it, Lauren would not be thrilled that Stephanie, Lauren's least favorite person, was her stepson's girlfriend's mother. I was starting to reconsider my decision not to drink. "Who?"

"Believe it or not, I don't know yet. Of course, it's only a matter of time till I do. That's one of the benefits of working in the high school office. I learn about the high school romances pretty quickly. Not that they're all that interesting to me, mind you, except when we're talking about my own stepson."

"Now, which one is Jasper?" Nadine asked. "Maybe I can tell you who he's seeing."

Uh-oh. I really should have told Lauren that I'd inadvertently brought Jasper and Tiffany together. There was no way I could gracefully do so now, with Nadine present. And I certainly didn't want the news to come secondhand.

Nadine continued, "I'll bet he and this girl haven't been nearly as careful about holding hands, and so on, during your off days. Or days off, rather. Such as today."

"Tommy's boy," Lauren said. "Red hair. Nice looking. Tall. Kind of—"

"Speaking of Tommy, Nadine," I interrupted, "did he tell you that the shrapnel in the bomb in my car was fragments of porcelain dolls?"

"Yes, he did." Nadine reached over and laid her hand atop mine on the table. "I hope you don't think for a second that I had anything to do with it. Anyone could've gotten porcelain pieces from Corrinne. She was very generous with the dolls she made, and gave them away for almost every conceivable occasion. That was one of the reasons I knew our partnership could never work out. I mean, what kind of business sense is that? To give away the expensive product you're trying to sell?"

"Not very sensible, all right," I said.

"See, that's just it. Not smart. Here's this teacher in charge of the smartest students at Carlton, and she was a dummy herself."

Lauren and I exchanged glances again, and I knew she was equally disturbed by this posthumous put-down of Corrinne. We finished our drinks quickly and agreed that we had best be going. Lauren, thankfully, insisted on driving Nadine home, freeing me from having to do the dishonors.

I told Lauren to call me as soon as she had a few minutes. I wanted to tell her that I did have a very good guess as to who Jasper's mystery girlfriend might be.

The next day was Friday. There was no sign of Chester's crew. Every time I looked at the plywood blocking the doorway, I had this image of myself as Pinocchio, or perhaps more accurately, Geppetto—"Please, Fairy God-mother. If I'm good and tell no lies, turn this block of wood into a real door."

A little after eleven-thirty that morning, the doorbell rang. BC stopped barking when she recognized Tiffany, with Jenny a step behind her, as though she'd been dragged along as an unwilling passenger. I automatically glanced at my watch and said, "Shouldn't you still be in school?"

"Study hall," Tiffany said with a shrug. "We can't stay long."

"Come in."

Tiffany took a step back. "Actually, I'm gonna wait in the car. I just, like, wanted you to talk to Jenny."

While Tiffany trotted off, I looked at Jenny in surprise.

She frowned, then knelt down to pet the dog. "Everybody's telling me to do this or do that, and I don't know what to do, and Tiff got the idea that you'd be the best person to talk to because you know the least."

I laughed. "Apparently, Tiffany knows me better than I thought she did."

Jenny blushed and rose, stuffing her hands into the pockets of her faded jeans. "What I meant was, you don't know my mom, and Tiff says you and her mom are always butting heads. I just . . . don't know how to decide something like this. I thought I knew, but now I'm all confused."

The two of us sat and talked, and Jenny voiced a litany of complaints about her mother, every one of which was, sad to say, told in such graphic detail as to be both believable and depressing. I found myself not giving advice at all so much as being a sounding board for Jenny's complaints about a rough childhood. I told her that she might want to consider talking to a therapist, not because there was something wrong with her, but because so much wrong had been done to her.

At length, Tiffany let herself back inside to say that they had to get back. Jenny stood up and said, "Thanks, Molly. Tiff's right about you."

"That I don't know anything?"

"That you're easy to talk to." Both girls rushed out the door, and I sat there grinning from ear to ear, wishing I had a tape recorder to replay Jenny's compliment so my own children could hear. Of course, they would correctly point out that my being easy for Jenny to talk to was mostly due to my not being her mother.

The doorbell rang again and I answered immediately, expecting to discover that Tiffany and Jenny had forgotten to tell me something. To my surprise, it was Danielle Underwood, looking fit to be tied.

"You really can't keep your nose out of our business, can you?" she immediately snapped.

"What are you talking about?"

"You know perfectly well what I'm talking about. I saw my son's girlfriend leaving your front porch just now. How dare you butt in this way, after I already told you I forbid it!"

"For your information, though it's none of your business, I was talking to Jenny about a different matter entirely. Your son's name never even came up."

"I don't believe you."

"I don't care whether you do or not. And what are you doing here in the first place? Are you spying on me?"

"No. Didn't Chester tell you? I'm here to measure for your blinds. I'm a subcontractor. You ordered vertical blinds from Chester."

I dragged my hand through my hair and shut my eyes, unable to hide my frustration at this news. Apparently things weren't going quite badly enough with the sunroom. Time to get Danielle Underwood out here as a subcontractor. "The glass panels aren't even in place yet. All that's there is the roof and the aluminum framework. We're not ready for the blinds."

"Of course not. But I need to measure for them now so that they can be made."

Thinking I might just get a little pleasure out of watching her have to climb down from my house and hoist herself up into the sunroom, I said, "Okay. This way." I pointed through the glass doors to the room, such as it was. "This is the only access we've got. The kids use the slide."

She looked at me and said, "Molly, I hope you understand. I'm not some maniac where my son is concerned. I just can't survive his getting into another relationship with an older woman."

"I'm happily married. I have a teenager myself. There

is no possibility whatsoever that I'm going to develop a romantic attachment toward your teenage son."

"No, but your friend seems to have her eye on him, and I've decided in order to keep her away, it's best to keep you away, as well."

If she was making some kind of outrageous accusation toward Lauren, I was going to throw Danielle out on her keister. "What friend of mine are you talking about?" I asked, my hands fisted.

"Stephanie Saunders."

"Oh, for heaven's sake, Danielle! Stephanie would no more allow herself to be attracted to a teenage boy than she would to, well, to you or me. Status and image are everything to her. Imagine what it would do to her reputation if she were to take up with a high school student."

She paused, then said quietly, "Jeez. I never . . ." She met my eyes. "You're right. I never thought this through. Neither she nor you would—" She shook her head. "I was so crazed when this thing came up with Corrinne. I honestly thought she was a friend of mine, and I couldn't have been more shocked. Ever since then I've been paranoid toward all women."

"I can imagine how horrified you must have been. Again, though, *I* would never do what Corrinne did. Under any circumstances."

"I realize that now."

"Thank you."

She slid open the door and gracefully leaped down to the ground. "If it's all the same with you, I'm just going to get this over with really quick and get out of here."

Though I gave her a few token don't-be-embarrassed statements and truly did appreciate her apologizing, I, too, felt uncomfortable. She'd lashed out at me for merely speaking to her son. Maybe she was capable of murdering someone who'd had an inappropriate relationship with him.

* * *

The phone rang during dinner that evening. That was especially annoying, because I'd managed to actually get all four of us seated and eating while the food was still warm. I answered, and a young voice said, "Molly? It's Jenny Garrett."

"Hi, Jenny. How are you?"

"I'm fine. But I'm kind of worried about my mom. You haven't heard from her, have you?"

"No, why?"

"She was supposed to pick me up from Tiffany's house hours ago, and she never showed."

"Could she have gotten the time or date confused?"

"No, and I've been calling the house. There's no answer."

"Is there a neighbor you can call?"

"I tried that, but nobody's ever home when you want them to be. Tiffany's supposed to be baby-sitting but I told her I'd take care of it till my mom got here, so she's still on the other line, and Stephanie's someplace, too, and I just . . . Tiffany's gonna get off the phone any moment and I don't want to have to get into this. You know?"

I resisted the temptation to say, "Huh?" She wasn't making enough sense for me to grasp what she was hinting about between her and Tiffany, but I certainly understood that she was worried about her mother and wanted to check on her whereabouts. "Tell you what, Jenny. I have to go talk to your mom anyway about some PTA matters. I'll head out there just on the off chance that she's there and . . . has fallen asleep or something."

"Yeah, well, I guess that'd be okay. This just . . . I don't know. She used to do things like this a lot, but I can't believe she'd do this now. You know?"

"Don't worry. Something probably just came up that got her distracted."

"Yeah. Probably. Could you, like, call me as soon as you get there? I mean, even if she's not home?"

"Of course." I asked for the address, which she gave me, and muttered a few more reassuring phrases about how there was nothing to worry about, then hung up.

"What's up?" Jim asked. He'd already risen from the table.

"Jenny Garrett. I'm going to go see if her mom's all right. She—"

"I'm driving." He snatched up the slip of paper on which I'd written Olivia's address. "Karen, Nathan, we'll be back soon."

The fact of the matter was that I was worried, too. This was strange behavior on Olivia's part. I couldn't really see why she would choose to delay picking up her daughter, when reuniting with her had obviously become her number one goal.

We arrived at Olivia's house, and I breathed a sigh of relief that it was intact. During the course of the drive, I'd envisioned it as a pile of still-smoking cinders.

Jim pulled into the driveway, and I got out. "Wait here for a moment, Jim, while I ring the doorbell. Let me just make sure that if she's here, she's fully dressed."

I glanced at the garage door, wishing there were some windows to peer through to see if there were any cars inside.

No one answered the bell. I knocked as well, but there was still no answer. Telling myself I would check first and then decide what to do afterward, I turned the knob and discovered that the house was unlocked.

Now my heart was really thumping. I opened the door and looked inside. The room was a horrid mess, and the air smelled foul. Keeping my place on the front stoop, I called, "Olivia? It's Molly. Are you home?"

"She's not answering?" Jim asked, stepping onto the porch behind me.

"No. What's that smell?"

"Car exhaust," he said, shock registering on his face. He stepped inside the house. "The whole house reeks with it. Go see if you can open the garage door."

While Jim went into Olivia's house, I raced around to the garage door. I grabbed the handle, but one tug assured me that the only way we could open this door was from the inside.

"Oh, my God," I murmured. My car was not the only engine that was idling. The sounds were coming from the garage. A thin cloud of exhaust emanated from the cracks in the garage door.

Chapter 13

Help!

The garage door began to open. Jim must have found his way to the electric door opener from inside the house. I grabbed a gulp of air and dodged under the door while it was still rising.

"Molly?" Jim called.

"Here," I responded, still trying to preserve my breath. The cloud of exhaust was so thick, it was hard to see anything. My eyes were stinging and tearing up, compounding the problem.

Jim had found his way to the driver's door. "I'll carry her outside. Turn off the engine."

With the added lighting of the dome light, I found my way to the passenger door and opened it, steeling myself to shut off the engine no matter what happened. Meanwhile, Jim deserted the driver's door to open the door to the backseat, throwing me into a momentary confusion as I saw that Olivia wasn't in the front seat, but the back.

"Oh, my God," Jim muttered.

As I turned off the engine I looked into the backseat and caught sight of her. Jim was backing away, not removing her.

I couldn't continue to hold my breath. I staggered out of the garage and collapsed against the side of the house, struggling to regain my composure, to rid myself of the hideous vision of Olivia and the blood. And the gun in her hand.

Needing to collect himself as well, Jim stood on Olivia's driveway, bent over with his hands on his knees. He straightened and said, "We shouldn't go back in there. Let's see if a neighbor's home; use their phone to call the police."

"You go. I'll stay here."

He trotted toward the nearest house, cutting across the lawn, crusted over with the lingering remains of winter's snow. I sat down on a cement step, hoping that the feel of the cold, hard ground could keep me upright and lucid. "Poor Jenny," I said to myself.

Somebody was going to have to break the news to her. She would still be at Stephanie's house, awaiting my word on why her mother was late.

Corrinne's memorial service took place the following day. Though still hideously shaken by Olivia Garrett's death, Jim and I decided to go. It was well-attended, but I couldn't focus on the service itself. Two women I knew had died violently within a week of each other, and I couldn't fathom why.

After the service itself, there was a small reception in the church hall below. The furnishings were composed of folding chairs and six or seven round tables, augmented with flower arrangements and paper tablecloths. Set up on long tables against one wall was a buffet, which Jim went over to sample. I had no appetite, so I stood alone in a corner, numbly watching the sedate gathering of mourners.

Dave approached me. He looked horrible, his eyes red-rimmed and bloodshot, his features haggard. His dark suit looked rumpled, as though it had been hanging unused and cramped in a closet for a long time. "Rumor has it that you found Olivia's body last night," he said.

I nodded, tight-lipped, still desperately wanting to rid my brain of that hideous image.

"Olivia would never kill herself. She had to have been murdered." He ran a hand down the length of his face as if to relax his features, but it did no good. "My former girlfriend murdered. Now the gallery owner who sells my work. Everybody suspects me. I hear the murmurings in class. My own students think . . ." His voice faded.

"Try not to let all of this get to you," I muttered stupidly, wishing I could think of something better to say.

Dave didn't respond, but was swallowing hard, trying to keep his emotions at bay. "How's Jenny doing? I tried to call her this morning at the Saunders house, but was told she was sleeping."

"She's under sedation, from what I understand."

He nodded, his eyes vacant. "I keep thinking this can't possibly be happening, that things can't possibly have become this horrific. Then I think about poor Jenny, and I realize my pain is just a fraction of hers."

"Yes. This is hardest on her."

"I'm worried about her. She's such a sensitive girl. I was hoping to see her here, or at least Stephanie or Tiffany, to tell her how bad I feel."

"Next time I talk to them, I'll pass along your condolences."

"Thanks." He looked past my shoulder, but the vacant look in his eyes remained. "Well. Guess I'll go home. Thanks for talking to me. Not many people are willing to give me the time of day."

"Take care, Dave."

"You, too."

I watched him walk away. Some faces quickly turned away or averted eyes as he passed. Dave was under a cloud of suspicion, all right. Danielle, Chester, Nadine, and, lately, Elsbeth were equally deserving of suspicion in my opinion. Dave was either innocent or an excellent actor.

"Hey, Moll."

The words jarred me from my thoughts. I forced a smile. "Hi, Tommy."

He was in full uniform, but carrying his cap under one arm. His cap always left a band-sized dent in his thick red hair. "You'll read about this soon enough," Tommy said, "so I may as well tell you. The body was moved."

"Olivia's?"

He nodded. "The killer made a clumsy attempt at makin' it look like suicide."

I tried to decide if this made me feel any better for Jenny's sake. Was it more or less painful to lose one's parent to murder, as opposed to suicide? "Where was she killed?"

"Her kitchen. Near the door to the garage."

"Whoever did it knows her personal history, about how her husband killed himself." I searched Tommy's eyes, wondering if he'd answer my next question. "You must have looked into the records about his death. Was it definitely suicide?"

"Yep. And 'fore you ask, we checked into all the backgrounds, and none of the suspects in Corrinne's murder knew the Garretts before Olivia and Jenny moved to Carlton, so far as we can tell."

"Did you trace the gun Olivia . . . that was used on Olivia?"

"Knew you'd ask me that. You missed your calling, Molly. Should've entered the academy back when I did, 'stead of cartooning."

"One of us might have been the superior officer of the other." Odds were that we disagreed about which one of us that would be. He hadn't answered my previous question, so I tried again. "Was this gun also from the collector who supposedly died of natural causes?"

"From cancer. Yeah. Both guns were from the same collection."

"Weren't the missing guns ever reported?"

"Yeah, along with two more. Lot of good it does us."

"So the killer probably still has two more guns?" My voice had risen into something of a shriek.

Tommy didn't answer, but he didn't have to.

"Jeez, Tommy. There were only five other clowns who could have done this. Can't you get search warrants and go through their homes?"

He raised an eyebrow, and I clenched my teeth in frustration. "I know, I know," I said, answering my own question. "You'd be trampling on the rights of four innocent people. Never mind the fact that identifying the killer quickly could keep any of them from becoming the next victim."

Tommy laid a heavy hand on my shoulder. "Do us all a favor, Molly. I told you this info about Olivia because some reporter from the *Times Union* already ferreted it out. I got a hunch Olivia died because she got too close to the killer. Stay out of this. Don't make me have to look into a third murder. Please?"

"Okay."

Tommy rolled his eyes, knowing I didn't mean it, then moved off. I joined Jim and Lauren for a while, then spotted Brian Underwood, grim-faced as he stood beside his mother. Though it seemed inappropriate to notice such things at a funeral, Danielle looked especially attractive. Her black shift flattered her well-proportioned body, and her straight brown hair, recently cut short, emphasized her pretty features.

Now that Olivia, too, had been murdered, those contraband keys that Brian possessed last Friday seemed all the more important. Brian could have gotten those keys directly from Corrinne Buldock, or indirectly from Olivia Garrett through her daughter Jenny. Both of those women had been murdered.

Hoping that Danielle meant what she said about realizing that not all of us "mature" women lusted for her son, I said hello to them. She greeted me pleasantly for a change, so I took a chance and asked, "Could I speak to you in private for just a minute, Brian?"

"Sure. I guess."

We strolled to an unoccupied area of the large room. "Have you had a chance to see Jenny since last night?" I asked.

He shrugged. "Saw her this morning. She's just real wasted, though."

"I'm sure. Listen, Brian, I know this is a bad time for me to bring this up, but it's even more important now to know the truth about how you got those keys to Dave Paxton's room."

He furrowed his brow and shoved his hands deep in the pockets of his chinos. "From Jenny, like I said in my note."

"You said a lot of things . . . that you'd gotten them from Dave Paxton, that you'd—"

"The thing between me and Corrinne was blown way out of proportion. Why would she give me keys to the office she shared with another teacher at school? Why would I want them?"

"By the same logic, why would Dave have given them to Olivia?" Or, in a possibility with awful sexual implications that just occurred to me, to Jenny Garrett? I kept the last question to myself.

Brian frowned. "I don't think Dave *knew* Mrs. Garrett had his keys. Jenny says that caused one of the fights she had with her mom . . . that her mom thought it was hilarious to have stolen them out of Dave's desk."

"Do you mean that Jenny stole the keys, or Olivia stole them?"

"Olivia. She wanted to keep tabs on his paintings when he wasn't there."

"Why would she—"

Brian lifted his chin in a distant greeting to some other

teenager across the room. He said quietly, "Jenny's great, but her mom was a real witch. A couple weeks ago Jenny swiped the keys back from her mom and was going to return them to Paxton's desk, only she chickened out. That's what we were doing when you caught us . . . returning his keys."

I sighed, wondering if I could ever know for certain if this was the truth or not. Brian must have read the skepticism in my expression, for he said, "I'm telling you the truth, Molly. I wasn't gonna sit there in Vance's office and force Jenny to make excuses for her mother, like always."

By now Jim was heading toward me, and I knew we should get back home to the kids soon anyway. I believed Brian. "Okay. Thanks, Brian."

We had a quiet weekend for a change, though the plywood blocking the southern light in my kitchen was really getting to me. Bright and early Monday morning, Pauncho and Oops came over to complete the "finishing" work inside, which would presumably include a real door, while the other two workers installed the glass panels that formed the walls of the sunroom.

Mid-afternoon I was working away on a card when it finally hit me that a good half hour had passed with no pounding rap music or pounding nails. Sure enough, they were gone. I went out and inspected their work, which was—surprise!—not good. Partway through my formulating a mental list of complaints the doorbell rang.

It was Danielle Underwood. I braced myself as I opened the glass outer door, dreading another dressing-down for talking to her son yet again.

She smiled, her dark eyes meeting mine, but I remained guarded. "Good afternoon, Molly. I have your new vertical blinds in the trunk of my car."

"That's great that they're ready so soon, but there's no

sense in installing them just now. We don't have the carpeting yet."

"Suit yourself, of course, but I'll be leaving town during spring break next week and I'm heavily booked till then, so it's either now or three weeks from now."

"Eww," I muttered. This was going to be badly timed. Jim and I were going to put the carpeting in ourselves, but we hadn't purchased it yet and weren't planning to until Saturday, which meant two weeks with a room finished except for the blinds.

"Tell you what. I'll go ahead and install the runners and the valances. Those are the only hard parts of the installation. Then you can decide if you want me to go ahead and install the vanes, or put them in yourself once the flooring's complete. The vanes just snap into place. There's nothing to it."

"That sounds good. And I even have a door now, so you can get into the room without having to go outside." As I escorted her to my kitchen I continued, "Of course, the door was hung wrong, so it closes at an angle, but at least it opens and latches shut. I'm learning to lower my standards."

"You shouldn't do that, Molly. You should insist that the job be done right, or you'll withhold payment."

"Words to live by."

"My work is always perfect, Molly. So if you'll excuse me, I'll be done in two hours."

I went to my basement office to continue my work, and returned to the sunroom in just over two hours. She had installed the vanes, as well, and was snapping the last pair into place when I entered the room.

Hearing me approach, she stepped back to survey her work, hands on her hips, wearing a satisfied smile. "They look great, don't they?"

"Yes, but I thought you weren't—"

"I realized I wanted to make absolutely certain your

blinds were the correct length. If they're in your way, you give each one a slight twist like so—" She demonstrated. "—and they come right off."

Watching her, I thought to myself how flattering her recent haircut was and wondered who her stylist was, then realized I'd already missed the pertinent part of the demonstration—something about "a slight twist." Removing a strip did look easy when she did it, but then, this was her job, so she'd had lots of practice. She popped the vinyl strip back into place. Compared to the various troubles I'd had with Chester's men, having the vanes installed ahead of schedule wasn't something to complain about.

She led the way back into the kitchen and picked up the curtains that had once been over the window and were now atop the stack of papers on the desk. "You don't need these curtains anymore, do you?"

"No, I was just using them as a temporary dustcover while the room was being built. They're faded and dusty. I was just going to throw them out."

"I'll take them, in that case." She swept them up and began to fold them, setting free a great cloud of dust in the process, which she ignored, but which made me sneeze.

I grabbed a tissue and asked, "You collect fabric scraps?"

"No, but I know someone who does. Nadine Dahl. She makes them into dresses for her dolls."

"I doubt she'd want my curtains. The fabric's old and in poor condition." Not to mention filthy.

"That's how she likes it. It makes her doll dresses look antique, and she sells them for more money that way."

"That's dishonest. Why are you helping her defraud her customers?"

She gave me a nonchalant shrug. "I need to be on the woman's good side. It's a mutual thing, really. I help her out with this, she keeps me informed of the goings-on at Carlton High."

"Just like Chester, hey?"

She froze and searched my eyes. "Chester? What are you talking about?"

"I don't know if it's true, but the rumor is that Nadine's giving student transcripts to Chester, for some reason."

"Student transcripts?" she repeated, alarmed. "Oh, crap! She's got this program she runs on the computer to analyze grades for each teacher in the school. It lets her know which teacher gives the highest score for which class. That's what she's doing for me. Supposedly exclusively. That two-timing bitch!"

"How can you get mad at her for doing that for Chester when she's doing the same thing for you?"

"Because the agreement was *I* give her old cloth and keep my mouth shut about her so-called antique dolls. In exchange, she gives only me the information about which class to put my son in each year so he can get the highest possible GPA. That information is useless if she's giving it to all of the other parents as well."

"Maybe she's not. Maybe the rumor . . ." I let my voice fade. For all I knew, she could be peddling grade information to hundreds of parents. I was stunned to think that there were at least a few parents who would care so much more about their child's grade than their education that Nadine could actually find a use for her computer program. "Why are you and Chester dirtying your hands just to give your child the inside edge over the other?"

"Elsbeth's doing the same thing. Why do you think her daughter enrolled in Dave's art class? Because Elsbeth knew he gave out A's like candy, that's why. Hell, I've got my son taking art history from Dave, because Brian can't draw worth beans. But that boy can make angels weep with his piano playing."

I was so appalled that I couldn't stop myself from saying, "If the angels are paying any attention to the goings-on at Carlton High School, they're already weeping."

Danielle gave me a piercing look, then set her lips and headed toward the front door. As she opened the door, she looked at the curtains that were still in her hand, flung them onto the floor, and let herself out.

"That was unpleasant," I said to BC, who was barking in agreement. So much for getting the name of Danielle's hair stylist. More to my immediate concern, however, someone had to put a stop to Nadine.

I tried to call Lauren at the office, but Nadine answered. I held my nose to disguise my voice and asked if I could speak to Lauren.

"Molly? Is that you?" Nadine asked.

"Yes. I hab a cold."

"Must be going around. Lauren's home sick with one, too."

"Thanks. 'Bye." I hung up and called Lauren at home. "You've got a cold?" I asked her the moment she answered.

"Kind of. I had a sore throat when I got up this morning, but I don't feel too bad after all. I'm going to go in tomorrow on my usual day off to compensate. What's up?"

"Just wanted to warn you that if things go my way, you'll be minus one full-time secretary by then."

"What do you mean?"

"I already told Jack that I suspected Nadine was taking bribes from Chester to see the student transcripts. I didn't have any proof, and anyway, that wasn't such a big deal in the first place. Now I know that in exchange for cloth, she runs some program that allows her to advise Danielle Underwood which classes to put Brian in so he can get the best grade point average."

"Cloth?"

I didn't feel like explaining further, and said nothing. "I should tell Jack about this, too, don't you think? I can't stand the thought of someone selling information about grades."

"Absolutely. I don't know school policy on accepting bribes in exchange for information about grades, but it might be grounds for dismissal."

"Okay, then. I'm going to go down to Jack's office now and tell him about this face-to-face." I hesitated. "By the way, how are things with Jasper and his new girlfriend?"

"Great. But he says he doesn't want to jinx things by letting us know her name."

"That sounds reasonable. So I think I'll keep my mouth shut, too."

She laughed. "Molly, since when have you ever kept your mouth shut just because that was reasonable?"

"Now's a good time to start."

"I'd tell you if this were Nathan."

"Maybe I wouldn't want to know," I countered.

"But I do. So tell me."

"I'm not absolutely positive, but I think it's Tiffany Saunders."

There was dead silence on the line.

"Lauren?"

"Of all the girls at Carlton High, she's got to be the last one I would have . . . Who could have expected those two to get together? They're so different. I mean, it's just so . . . weird."

"I sort of got them talking to each other during their art class last week. So I'm somewhat responsible."

"Oh." There was another pause, then to my surprise, she chuckled. "Imagine what Stephanie's reaction is going to be . . . her daughter dating a future cop."

"My part in bringing the two of them together was

unintentional, but I have to say, they make a pretty cute couple. I'm glad you're not mad at me."

"You're about to march into Jack Vance's office and take on Nadine Dahl. You're going to need all the friends you can get."

A moment after I hung up, Karen and then Nathan arrived home from school, delaying my departure. I explained that I needed to get to the high school before everyone left for the day. Fifteen minutes later I arrived at the school office and let myself inside. Though the students had gone, Nadine was still there, and peered up at me from her seat at her desk. "I told you Lauren's home sick today."

"I know. I'm here to see Jack." His door was open, and I could see him at his desk.

"You seem to have gotten over your cold pretty fast," Nadine said snidely.

"The wonders of echinacea."

"Come in, Molly," Jack called, rising from his seat.

I took a step inside, then looked back at Nadine. "You know, Nadine, so many people have been doing things behind one another's back that it bugs me. Why don't you come with me and hear what I have to say about you to Jack?"

"About me?" she asked nervously. Then she stood up and assumed a confident air as she came into Jack's office with me. We took the two chairs that were situated right in front of his desk, while he reclaimed his seat.

"What's this about, Molly?" Jack asked, his eyes going from me to his secretary.

"Nadine has been accepting bribes in exchange for information about teachers' grading tendencies."

"Bribes? What are you talking about?" Nadine asked, her surprised reaction unconvincing.

"Aged fabric for your pseudoantique doll clothes from

Danielle Underwood. Twenty dollar bills from Chester Walker."

"Is this true, Nadine?" In my opinion, he was doing a better job of acting surprised than Nadine, and he'd known some of my accusation for several days now.

Nadine pursed her lips, then said, "The parents have a right to know which teachers are the easiest graders. Their taxes pay for the teachers' salaries!"

"Lots of people pay taxes, not just Carlton High parents," I fired back to her. "That doesn't give anyone a license to manipulate the system. Or *you* the right to sell the names of the easy graders. What's next? Hundred dollar bookmarks for you to tweak someone's transcript scores?"

"Could you excuse us, please, Molly?" Jack asked. His expression was inscrutable.

Nadine held up her hand. "No, there's no need for you to send her out of the room. I've had enough of working for you. I've been looking for an excuse to get fired for going on three years now. Hell, I've been coming into work tipsy for the last two months. Haven't you noticed the whiskey bottle in my bottom drawer?"

"I've told you before that you needed help," Jack replied.

She sprang to her feet. "I don't need help! I'm not an alcoholic. I might be by the time you take action, mind you, but I didn't start out that way. This is a high school, for God's sake!" Nadine leaned down and gripped Jack's desk, her cheeks flushed. "Why have you let me get away with bringing alcohol on school premises?"

"I confiscated the bottle every time, didn't I?"

"And I've all but rubbed this in your face. What more will it take? Fire me, Jackie boy!"

"I'll go wait outside," I muttered, slipped out of my chair and skirted out the door.

I sat in Lauren's chair. Jack's door was shut tight, so I

couldn't hear any of the conversation going on inside his office. Not five minutes later Nadine emerged, sporting a wide smile. She laid a hand on my shoulder. "Thank you, Molly. I'm finally free of this joint!" She walked around me, plopped into her desk chair, which was on wheels, and splayed her arms and legs as she pushed herself away from her desk and spun in a circle.

Apparently she was "a little tipsy" now, as well. "Why didn't you just quit?"

"A couple of reasons," she replied casually. "I was scared to leave a regular paycheck behind in order to pursue my dream—making a living with my doll business. I need unemployment compensation to tide me over till I can get my business on its feet." She released a big sigh. "You can't imagine what a relief this is."

"Great, Nadine. That's just what I want my tax dollars to be doing, too. Helping you to enjoy your unemployment."

"That's the way the system works, Molly. And it's finally working for me. When you see Lauren, tell her she's going to have to work full-time till they can get a replacement for me. And you'd better tell her to look very closely at the seniors' transcripts."

"Why?"

"You already answered that, back in Jack's office." She got up and started collecting some personal items from her desktop. "Thanks again. Like I said earlier, in spite of everything, Molly, you're my favorite parent."

I glanced behind me. Jack Vance was standing in the doorway of his office, listening to this.

"Jack, do you mind checking her keys before she goes?" I turned back toward Nadine. "As your 'favorite parent,' I'd just like to make sure you don't have the keys to the art room and to the building, for free use of the kiln."

She glowered at me for a moment, then lifted her

palms. "By all means. Check for yourself." She shoved her key ring toward Jack Vance and dumped the contents of her purse on her desk for extra measure. "You want to frisk me while you're at it?"

"That won't be necessary," Jack intoned as he studied each key. "I'm just going to double-check this set against Dave's door. I'll be right back."

We waited, the tension palpable and highly unpleasant. Nadine packed her belongings in silence, using a box that she'd apparently kept at the ready in the small corner closet. "I didn't kill either of those women, and I don't know who did. But you know what, Molly? You may have helped save my life in more ways than one. Not only am I finally free from this stressful, heart-attack-generating joint, but now I'm out of the killer's immediate circle. So if there's yet another victim, it's not going to be me."

Jack came back and returned Nadine's key ring, giving me a barely perceptible shake of the head. Nadine gathered up her purse and box of personal items and left without another word.

I turned to Jack, who was still somewhat red-faced. "My daughter will enter high school here in a few months. Is this the best we can do?"

"I thought Nadine was an alcoholic and needed help."

"When you hire her replacement, can you at least make sure whoever it is has a sense of ethics?" I left the building, swallowing the lump in my throat.

Chapter 14

Tooth and Nail

I came home feeling as though I'd been kicked in the stomach. Karen was doing homework on the dining room table. Nathan was in the kitchen, tossing soda crackers in the air and firing rubber bands at them, which made the cracker crumble in midair. BC was delighted with this cracker-skeet-shooting game, for she eagerly gobbled up the debris. I, however, had less cause for enthusiasm.

Somehow I'd believed that Carlton High could escape the violence and menace that had crept into other schools, as well as into society at large. It was ludicrous to think that one's own cherished places and people were somehow immune. But the knowledge that one's hopes were unrealistic makes their being dashed no less painful.

I took solace by entering my new sunroom and looking around. The room did look very pretty, as long as I squinted my eyes a little and blocked my view of the plywood flooring. And didn't look out the window that faced the rocky area where we'd once had a redwood deck. And didn't give any thought to how the door didn't close correctly.

I operated my new vertical blinds and immediately discovered something extremely frustrating. Danielle had installed the runners so they opened in the opposite direction as the sliding glass doors, which meant that, open

176

or shut, the blinds were always in the doorways. She'd put up all six blinds backward.

"I hate my life," I muttered as I returned to the kitchen.

Nathan looked at me, handed me a cracker, then went downstairs, no doubt to play computer games. BC, meanwhile, watched me with a hopeful expression on her canine features. The expression turned to disappointment when she watched me eat the cracker.

"Sorry, dog-face. I'm from the don't-fire-projectiles-at-your-food generation."

The doorbell rang while I was still weighing whether to call Danielle Underwood, reasoning that it might be less ulcer-inducing to simply reverse the vertical-blind tracks ourselves.

"Some man's out there," Karen reported, looking out the front window. "It's the sunroom guy you hired."

"Is he wearing a baseball cap?" I asked as I entered the room.

"Yeah."

I decided not to instruct BC to be quiet, but rather to vicariously enjoy her incessantly barking at him as I let him inside.

"Afternoon, Molly," Chester said with a big smile that I couldn't reciprocate. "I was just stopping by to see how things are going with your new room."

"Funny you should mention that. Have you used Danielle Underwood as a subcontractor for window treatments for quite a while now?"

"Yes. She does a wonderful job." He studied my face for what should have been longer than necessary, because it was obvious by my question and current demeanor that all was not well. He said hello to Karen, who'd returned to her homework, then asked me, "Why? Is there a problem?"

"Most of the time, don't people want their blinds to

open the same direction as their door, so they can actually *use* the door?"

"Of course. Let me take a look at your blinds." He headed into the room, followed by BC and me. As if it were going to be a big revelation to me, Chester announced, "These are backward." He stood with arms crossed and stared at the blinds. "Huh. She's never made a mistake like this before. You must have caught her on an off day."

"Apparently. Unless she did this intentionally just to annoy me."

"Why would she do that?"

"Oh, people can do all sorts of annoying things, intentionally or just because that's the way they are. Speaking of which, have you noticed that we still have no deck?"

"Yes, but you do have a sunroom and window coverings in record time."

"Which are installed backward. Plus the door is hung crooked. We're not making out our final payment until your crew rehangs the door, replaces the window-well cover, and rebuilds our deck to our satisfaction."

"Understood." Chester rocked on his heels for a moment, then said, "On another subject, the scuttlebutt is that you got Nadine Dahl fired. Is that true?"

"I don't know whose butt could have been scuttled this quickly, but the truth is she was looking for an excuse to get herself fired. Though, frankly, I'm surprised she wanted to walk away from her cash cow."

"What do you mean?"

I shut the door to the sunroom so my children wouldn't overhear, then replied, "Accepting bribes from you and other parents in exchange for helping their children's class ranking."

The muscles in his jaw tightened. He said under his breath, "Now I see how Danielle could have gotten so ticked off at you as to hook up your blinds backward."

"As a mother myself, it bothers me that you think it's okay to meddle in the school records. You're using underhanded methods to gain the advantage over eighteen-year-old schoolkids."

He jerked his palms upward in an angry gesture. "I have to do whatever I can to keep up! Look at what the other parents were doing. Danielle's been supplying Nadine with free materials for her moonlighting business. Elsbeth writes her daughter's music-theory essays. And did you really think that Olivia was fighting so hard to get her daughter back from Stephanie purely out of maternal love?"

"Of course she was fighting for Jenny out of love. And at least Olivia wasn't tampering with her daughter's ranking at Carlton High like the rest of you."

"Guess again."

"The woman's dead, for crying out loud. Exactly what are you suggesting?"

"Not to speak ill, but since you asked, she was the worst of all of us. She was trying to keep Jenny from shining too brightly, despite the perfect score she got on her SATs. Olivia didn't want to have to pay for her daughter to go to an Ivy League school."

"Oh, come on! I don't believe that for an instant, Chester!"

"We had the same lawyer. I happen to know about the provisions in the trust fund."

"The payouts from Jenny's trust fund were tied to her academics?"

He gave me a smug smile. "Indirectly. Olivia and Jenny have been living on a fixed income from the inheritance, and all of Jenny's college costs are to be fully covered, no matter how high they are. But after she graduates from college, she was supposed to receive half the inheritance in a lump sum, Olivia the other half. Thing is, though, that if Jenny were to enter an expensive college, Olivia's share would have been considerably less. And, if she lost custody of Jenny for those years, her fixed income would probably have vanished."

"None of this means . . ." I let my voice trail off. "How did you find out all of this, Chester? Did you bribe your lawyer's secretary as well?" He didn't answer, so I pointed out, "The terms of the will don't mean she was actually doing anything to undermine Jenny's standing in school."

"Maybe not, but that's exactly what she was doing. Get a look at Jenny's transcripts. The standings are based on the degree of difficulty of the course times the point system for the grade itself. Jenny would register for the classes she wanted, then Olivia would call the office with an excuse to switch her out of the higher credit courses. Your friend, Jack Vance, finally caught on and put a stop to it."

"How did you find *that* out? From Nadine? Or did Jenny tell you?"

"Nadine. Fortunately, Jenny never found out what her mom was doing. Even though it wasn't in my son's best interest to do so since Jenny's course ratings kept her below my son's grade-point, I . . . felt it was my duty to tell Stephanie. Figured it would be key evidence in the trial to show just what type of a parent Olivia really was."

"No wonder she lost custody."

"Except that information never came out. I went to the trial myself, so I know. Afterward, I asked Stephanie why she kept quiet. She said she decided not to reveal the information because it would have destroyed Jenny's connection to her mom forever."

"That's . . . awful. I mean, it's one thing to decide that you can't afford an expensive college for your child, re- gardless of how much money you have. But to try to keep your child's grade-point down to eliminate the option is just appalling."

"You got that right. So don't lecture me on my methods." He brushed past me, let himself out of the room, and started to trudge toward the front door. "If you'd've asked me just two years ago if I'd've ever used questionable ethics to help my son's grades, I'd've sworn up and down that there was no way. But just you wait." He looked at my daughter, still working at the dining room table, and said quietly, "Wait'll you find out *your* sweet little cubs are duking it out with the full-grown lions. Then we'll see just how fast *your* claws come out." He pivoted and said over his shoulder, "I'll get my foreman out here to rehang the door and put up your deck."

He marched out of the house without another word.

Was he telling the truth about Olivia Garrett? There was no way I was going to ask Jack about that now, under the circumstances. But I could check his story with someone else. I steeled myself, closed my bedroom door for privacy, and dialed Stephanie's house. She answered, and after I greeted her, said, "Well, Molly. I hoped this would be somebody else. I'll have to hook up my caller ID again. What can I do for you, my dear?"

I massaged my temples with my free hand and decided to simply plow forward with my questions about Olivia. Was it her use of "my dear" while she insulted me, or just her constant air of superiority that made me instantly want to do bodily harm to the woman? "Chester told me that Olivia had been sabotaging her daughter's grades, and I wondered if that was true."

"Yes. Chester told me about that at the beginning of the school year when this custody battle first erupted, and I immediately verified that in a private discussion with Jack." She paused. "You're not thinking that any of this had anything to do with Olivia's murder, are you?

After all, I know how you make these murder investigations into a hobby of yours."

"Yeah, well, I never learned how to knit." Wishing to avoid a discussion of the killer's motive with Stephanie, I asked, "How's Jenny doing? Dave Paxton asked me to express his condolences."

"She went to school today. She seems to just be going through the motions, but I have to believe that her decision to go on with her daily schedule is a good sign. I'd better get off and get some things done." She sighed heavily. "Take some advice from an old—" She paused. "Take my advice, Molly, and do us all a favor. It's high time you *did* take up knitting." She hung up.

In a demonstration of my level of maturity, I stuck my tongue out at the phone. Then I sat on the edge of my bed and pondered the situation. Chester had told me the truth. Were his predictions that I would be changing my tune in a few years also valid? What would I do if I learned that a parent was cheating to raise his child's grade-point so as to finish ahead of my child's?

I could see myself perhaps confronting the parent or school officials, but despite Chester's dire predictions, there was no way I would resort to cheating myself. Of course I would fight tooth and nail—be that with fingernails or with carpentry nails—for my children's sake. But that didn't mean I would ever resort to Chester's underhanded methods. Some simple truths remain in effect throughout all stages of child rearing. Parenting is largely done by example, and if you want your child to stay on the right side of any given line, you don't cross it yourself.

Chapter 15

For the Birds

Later that night, Karen and I drove to Elsbeth's house for her rescheduled piano lesson. My eyes were immediately drawn to Elsbeth's hands. Her wounds had healed, but my anxiety about how she'd gotten them in the first place still remained.

Karen's lesson went well, though I was a nervous wreck throughout. If the killer had scared off the doves that night as a diversion, Elsbeth was guilty. I couldn't bear to think of my precious daughter spending time every week with a murderer. After the lesson, I gave Karen my keys and asked her to wait in the car while I spoke to Elsbeth.

The moment Karen shut the door behind her, I said to Elsbeth, "Did you hear about my exploits as Martin's magician assistant the other day?"

She grinned. "No, what happened?"

"For one thing, the birds bit my hands several times."

"That must've hurt."

I waited, but she wasn't volunteering the information. I pressed on. "I noticed you had similar cuts on your hands after Corrinne's murder."

She stiffened. "I don't care for the implication, Molly. I got the scratches from the birds, yes, but it happened as I was trying to put them back into their cages after Nadine let them out. As I told you, she's the one who opened the cages."

"But Nadine didn't have any marks on her hands."

"Of course not. She was wearing those red gloves."

"So why weren't your gloves on then, too? You were wearing them when you came onstage after Corrinne was killed. All of the clowns had gloves on at that point, except for me."

Elsbeth sputtered, unable to come up with a response. Finally she uttered, "Molly, I didn't kill Corrinne. Or Olivia. I'm innocent. You have to believe me."

"I want to." Which was true—for heaven's sake, she was the only one of the suspects who came into frequent contact with one of my children.

She began to comb her hands through her wild, red hair then left them in place, her eyes wide open. "Okay. You're right. I was the one who let the stupid doves out of their cages, and the rabbits, too. I don't even know why I did it. It had nothing to do with the murder. I was just having a bit of fun. And I took my gloves off for a moment because I couldn't work the latch on the cage with them on. It was a stupid practical joke. We all looked so inane, dressed like clowns, Martin pretending to be a magician. I thought, Oh, why not let all hell break loose on stage? Next thing I knew, it did. Only it was someone with a gun, firing real bullets."

"Then why did you make up a bogus story about Nadine being the one to let the doves out of their cages?"

"That woman is destroying my life, that's why. I'm certain she's guilty." She set her lips into a thin line and said nothing more.

"I've got to get Karen home," I muttered, and let myself out, feeling numb.

I said nothing at first, my mind racing as I started the engine and pulled out of the driveway. "Do you like Elsbeth as much as you liked your former piano teacher?" I asked Karen.

"Why? Is she moving back to Carlton?" Karen asked, her enthusiasm at that possibility answering my question.

"No, I'm afraid not."

"Oh." A moment passed. "Tamara quit piano lessons completely."

"How did you know that?"

"The high school has been using our auditorium, and I ran into Tamara at a school assembly last week. I *do* have a life, you know, Mom."

"Oh, that's right. I keep forgetting."

She rolled her eyes and looked out the window. Either her hormones were running rampant or she was reflecting the strains from the tension of the adults and teens in her life. We remained silent the rest of the drive home.

When I walked in the door, Jim, transfixed by whatever show was on television, said, "Lauren called. She wants you to call her back."

"Okay. Thanks. How's Nathan doing on his homework?"

"I don't know."

"Is he in his room?"

I had surpassed the window of attention afforded to me, and he didn't hear the question. I located Nathan in my basement office, blowing up spaceships in some computer game of his. We went through our usual tiresome script for the daily homework argument, which we did in fast-forward, due to time constraints:

NATHAN: Why is there such a thing as homework? Why don't they just make the school day longer and call it schoolwork?

EXASPERATED MOM: That's not up to you or me to decide, so just do your work and get it over with.

NATHAN: But I just want to be able to relax and do what I want when I'm home.

EXASPERATED MOM: After your homework's done, you can relax all you want.

NATHAN: It'll be bedtime by the time I'm done!

EXASPERATED MOM: Then you'd best get started, hadn't you?

(Nathan grabs his school backpack and storms off. Exasperated Mom grabs the phone, half wishing that it were a vodka bottle.)

Lauren answered on the second ring and told me that she had a proposition for me. "We need some temporary help at the school office tomorrow. It's report-card day for the second trimester, and I'm there all by myself. I asked Jack if it was okay with him to have you fill in, and he said yes. Are you willing?"

"I suppose so. But couldn't you just borrow someone already trained from one of the other school offices?"

"Sure we could. But I figured you'd like to be on hand tomorrow. This reporting period determines the valedictorian. They waive the seniors' last trimester scores, because the grades won't be in until after graduation."

"That could prove interesting, all right," I replied, thinking about the parents who'd been so cutthroat in their attempts to influence their child's standing. "I'll be there."

The next morning, Lauren stiffened in her seat beside mine in the school office. I followed her gaze and spied Elsbeth storming up the sidewalk.

"Uh-oh," Lauren murmured, barely moving her lips and not looking at me. "We gave out the report cards during homeroom. Tamara must have called home and reported her grades to her mother between first and second periods."

While I watched her tight-fisted march toward us, I suddenly felt like a sitting duck. Elsbeth looked more angry than I'd ever seen her—or anyone else for that matter. "What do we do?" I asked Lauren through my teeth, forcing a smile for Elsbeth.

"Remain calm and seated."

Elsbeth threw the heavy front door aside as if it were nothing and stormed into the main lobby. With her clenched jaw, her hands fisted, and her arms pumping as she walked, she had the bearing of a freight train. She glanced at me in the office window, took a step toward me, then saw Dave Paxton, who was coming toward us down the hall, and spun around toward him.

"That does it!" she hollered at him over the general din of students chattering and lockers being opened and slammed shut. "I've had it! You lied to me, you bastard! You said you always give your students the grades they deserve, regardless of what you think of their parents."

"What are you talking about?"

"The report cards came out! You gave my daughter a C! She's a wonderful artist, and you know it!"

Dave furrowed his brow. "There must be some mistake. I gave your daughter the A that she deserved. On her own merits." He spread his hands and held them up in full surrender. He glanced over at Lauren, sitting beside me at the window to the office. "Bring up my grades for my fifth-period ceramics class, would you please, Lauren?"

She hit a few keys, then rotated the screen toward Dave so that he could read it. He leaned forward, scanned the screen, then pointed. "There. See, Elsbeth? She's got an A. Which is exactly what she deserved. Someone must have made a . . . bizarre error when the processing was done."

Both Dave and Elsbeth glared at Lauren, who also held up her palms in mock surrender. "Don't look at me, folks. I just printed out the report cards as stored in the computer and gave them to the teachers."

Elsbeth excused herself to find her daughter, and returned shortly with Tamara's report card, which we compared to the report in the computer file. The printed report card was all A's, except for one C in ceramics, which was clearly an A in the computer file. By now Jack Vance joined the three of us.

"I don't understand how this happened," Jack said once he'd been shown the cause of the trouble. "The report cards and the grades in the teachers' files should be identical. The computer is set up simply to sort by student name in order to print out the report cards."

"Unless someone went in and manipulated the grades after the computer had sorted them," I said. "Maybe someone whom the computer blocked from entering the teacher file, but not the individual report cards."

Jack said, "Nobody has the authority to do that on the computer. Except me, of course."

"And your former personal secretary?" I asked. An unnecessary question, evidently, for the color was already draining from Jack's face as he realized the same thing.

Jack grimaced and looked at Lauren. "Lauren, we're going to be working late tonight. I'm going to have to get on the intercom and tell the student body that a computer foul-up may have loused up their report cards."

"Since my children aren't even in high school yet, I have no vested interest in this," I offered. "I can help."

The second bell rang to signal the start of third period. "I'm sorry that this happened, Elsbeth. It's a good thing you brought it to my attention," Dave said, and left the office.

"I cannot believe this place," Elsbeth said under her breath as she started to head toward the door.

"Let me walk you to your car," I said.

She looked at me in surprise, but waited anyway, and we left the building together.

"What were you talking about earlier, Elsbeth?" I asked quietly. "You said that Dave and you had some sort of agreement about your daughter's grade."

She maintained her steady pace toward her car and didn't look at me. "That was . . . nothing. The point is that Tamara earned her A, as always."

"But you were afraid at one point that he wouldn't give her the A she earned?"

We'd reached her car, which, I noted, had been parked at a haphazard angle in the visitors' parking spaces. She shook her head, her brow furrowed as she fumbled with her keys. "You're reading things into it. All I said was that he promised to give her the grade she deserved."

"Then why were you accusing him of lying to you?"

She clicked her tongue and finally met my gaze with a blazing glare. "All right, Molly. You're right, once again. Congratulations." She let out a puff of air. "Dave caught me trying to sabotage the show and told me to quit it. I asked him point-blank if he was going to take things out on my Tamara, and he said no."

"You were sabotaging things by letting the animals out of their cages?"

"Yes, if you must know. Somebody had to teach that Corrinne a lesson. She was a teacher, for God's sake, and she was having an affair with a student. You saw how upset Danielle was because of what Corrinne was doing with her son."

"You and Danielle don't seem especially close. I have a feeling it was more personal than that."

Elsbeth flung her car door open with a vengeance. "Well, damn it, Corrinne Buldock refused to put my Tamara in her double-honors English literature class. Without those points, she didn't stand a chance of getting to be valedictorian." She averted her eyes. "Dave saw me open the cages at a rehearsal and confronted me. Said he'd raise a stink at the next PTA meeting if I kept that up."

"And yet you kept on releasing the birds from their cage."

She shrugged. "Like I care what the PTA thinks of me?

I just wanted to make sure he didn't hurt Tamara. No-body saw me open the cages that night, so I blamed Na-dine. She deserved to get into trouble. I'm certain that Chester paid her off to give his son an A and my daughter a C."

"You lied to the police and to me just to make someone else look guilty of a crime, because you *think* she tampered with your daughter's grades?"

Elsbeth set her jaw and got into her car without a reply.

I was so exasperated, I couldn't keep quiet. "Olivia sabotaged Martin's trick so as to embarrass Stephanie. You set animals loose on stage to make the director look bad. All the while, we had an inept magician and a stupid clown act, not to mention all of the insipid acts that pre-ceded us. Didn't you people ever stop to realize that we were lousing up the production just fine all on our own?"

Calmly now, Elsbeth replied, "My only concern was showing Corrinne to be the incompetent that she, in fact, was." She lifted her nose in the air. "It's hardly my fault that everyone else was a boob as well. That merely made it more difficult to make her look bad in comparison."

She shut her door, but I tapped on her window, and she rolled it down. "Elsbeth, I no longer care if you're the best piano teacher in the state of New York. I can't al-ways control who my daughter associates with, but in your case, I can. You're fired."

"You can't fire me. You've already paid through the end of the semester."

"Be that as it may, my daughter won't be coming to the lessons."

I returned to the office, but was already second-guessing my decision. Karen would be the one to suffer from lack of lessons, and it was impossible to get a teacher mid-semester. Without any teacher for the next three months, she would lose her enthusiasm and stop playing. It would be my fault. My only hope, then, would be to find a pianist who was willing to try his or her hand at giving lessons. Brian Underwood was the best young pianist I'd heard in quite a while. Maybe he could be convinced to teach Karen.

My piano-teacher situation was less pressing at the moment than the work of verifying student grades. Jack was chatting with Lauren, and they both looked discouraged at the task that lay ahead of them. "Jack, is it true that Olivia Garrett was all but sabotaging her daughter's ranking?" I asked.

He sighed. "That's nothing that I could prove, but it sure seemed that way. When she first transferred here, her mother kept coming in and swapping classes, always from the most demanding classes to the lower. She said it was because she didn't want her daughter to become overly stressed."

"Can parents do that? Change their child's schedule for them? Pick their teachers?"

"They're not supposed to, no. We try to explain to parents that part of being in high school is to have children develop the maturity to schedule their own classes, but if we take too hard a line on that, we get in trouble. Joe Junior won't have enough credits to graduate with his class, and Joe Senior comes in and bangs his fist on my desk and blames the school for not overseeing this, even though we mailed home ten warnings that were ignored."

"That's not really comparable to what Olivia had been doing with her daughter's course work, though."

"You're right. It isn't, but we tried to accommodate, because . . . well, frankly, she told us Jenny was in therapy. She implied that if the tough classes pushed her daughter over the edge, we'd have a lawsuit on our hands. So we'd make the change, then within days the teachers would be coming into my office, saying Jenny needed to be moved up, that her tests were off the charts and she wasn't challenged. I'd talk to Jenny, she'd say that, yes, she wanted to be switched into the more challenging classes. A day or two later I'd have Olivia back in my office, telling me that she was her daughter's guardian and to lay off. Miserable situation, let me tell you."

"Did it work? Is she out of the running for valedictorian?"

Jack frowned. "There are several solid A students. She'll finish third or fourth, most likely, behind Chester's, Elsbeth's, and Danielle's kids."

Someone opened the door to the office and we all froze and stared. It was Nadine Dahl, wearing sneakers, jeans, and a denim jacket.

"Hello, everybody," she said with a smile. "A certain irate mother, whom I won't identify—" She made a megaphone shape with her hands and whispered, "Elsbeth Young," then went on in normal tones, "left a message on my machine earlier today. Apparently someone uncovered my grade tampering. I came over to apologize."

"That's rather pointless, isn't it?" Jack asked through a tight jaw.

She smiled and shrugged. "Sure, but I figured, why not go in and 'fess up? What are you going to do? Fire me again?" She was the only one who laughed, apparently unfazed by the cold reception she was receiving from all of us. "I just did this because, like I said, I wanted to get fired. I only changed two students' grades—Paul Walker's and Tamara Young's. Both their parents were checking closely enough that I knew for certain I'd get caught."

"Even if that's true, we have to manually double-check all the students' grades to be sure." Jack sighed. "I've had the teachers go over each of their students' report cards and compare them to their master grade listing."

"For what it's worth," Nadine said, "I truly am sorry. I'd been hittin' the sauce a little too hard for a while there. Now that I've sobered up, I feel bad about what I did to the grades." She patted my shoulder. "I figured you'd be here, playing the Good Soldier after getting me fired right at one of the most hectic times." Nadine reached into her bag. "I've got some little gifts for the three of you. Please accept them. I gave a lot of thought to what would be most appropriate for each of you."

She gave Jack Vance a ceramic figure of a baseball player, Lauren a doll, and me a clown.

Lauren held the doll out for Nadine to take back. "I don't want a gift from you. It hardly makes up for the damage you've done to my children's school."

"Then give it to your daughter, or to a charity." She remained cheerful, our words having no effect on her. "Again, I wish you no ill feelings, and I hope that someday you'll be able to say the same for me."

With a little wave, she spun around and left the building. The three of us looked at one another. Jack said, "I, for one, am going to take this figurine out to the dump, along with my baseball bat, and smash it to pieces."

The three of us began the daunting and painstaking task of going over the records, beginning with the senior class. Hours later we verified that out of the 583 students in the Carlton senior class, only one grade besides Tamara's had been changed. As Nadine had indicated, Chester Walker's son was indeed the second student, but Nadine's motives had clearly been monetary, *not* to get that student's parent to catch her in the act; she'd *raised* the grade. He had been given a C and not an A in art history by Dave Paxton.

One thing was certain. With a half-dozen students having perfect scores throughout their four years of high school, and despite all of Chester Walker's efforts to influence things to the contrary, his son would not be the valedictorian.

Chapter 16

Play It Again, Sam . . . I Dozed Off

I spotted Brian Underwood during a break between classes and asked if he'd consider giving my daughter piano lessons. He said he'd think about it. At the end of the day he told me he'd like to meet my daughter and have a trial session. With Nathan already scheduled to go to a friend's house for a couple of hours after school, we decided today would work.

Somewhat to my surprise, when I told Karen that I'd "fired" Elsbeth, she said, "I thought you would. I already told Rachel that I'd probably had my last lesson with her."

She was enthusiastic about the possibility of Brian as her teacher, having remembered how well he played during our brief encounter at Elsbeth's house. Not at all surprisingly, his mother came to the trial lesson at our house as well.

Once Karen and Brian had settled at the piano in the living room, Danielle turned to me and said quietly, "Chester tells me there's a problem with your blinds."

"They open the wrong direction—into the doorway instead of away from it."

"I must have had my mind on other things when I installed them. Sorry. I'll take care of that now."

She had brought her toolbox with her, and I followed her into the room, closing the crooked door behind us. "Mind if I watch?"

"Not at all. Just don't talk to me, so I won't get distracted again, all right?"

"All you have to do is switch around the six runners, right?"

With her hands on her hips, she stared up at the runners for what seemed a long time, then said quietly, "This must have been my subconscious playing tricks on me, forcing me to come back here and talk to you."

How very flattering, I thought, but held my tongue.

She pursed her lips and shut her eyes for a moment. "Brian lied to you earlier. I overheard part of what he was saying."

"When?"

"At the funeral service. He was trying to protect me. He was afraid that I . . ." She met my eyes. "He didn't get those keys to Dave Paxton's office from Jenny, he got them from me."

Oh, for crying out loud! This was like some game of liar's poker, gone amok. "And how did *you* get them?"

"From Nadine." As she spoke she started to remove the blinds. "I was desperate to get information I could use against Corrinne that would force her to keep her claws away from my son. I thought that maybe she'd have something incriminating in her office, which I knew she shared with Dave. So I broke into her file cabinet, while I was supposedly changing into my clown costume. I was looking for love letters or diaries or anything, but there was nothing. Just her students' records."

She sighed and then spent a few moments in silence as she reversed the positioning of one of the runners. "Later that night, in all the commotion over Corrinne's death, I realized that I'd dropped something, probably in Dave's office, and since I'd jimmied the lock to Corrinne's file cabinet, it looked really incriminating. So I gave the keys to Brian to retrieve it."

"What?"

"The bulb to the stupid water-squirting flower. I was afraid the police would notice that it was missing from my costume. That if it showed up near Corrinne's file cabinet, they'd assume I had something to do with the murder."

The plastic bulb I'd found under Dave's couch! There was no way she could know that I'd seen that. At last I was confident that I was hearing the truth.

She began working on the next blind. "I told Sergeant Newton all about this yesterday, by the way. He just kept saying 'Uh-huh,' though." As if to herself, she added, "I hope he knows I didn't kill anybody."

"I see," I murmured, then gestured in the direction of the door. "I think I'll go listen to the piano lesson."

I returned to the living room, smiling at Karen and Brian whenever they looked in my direction, but my thoughts were elsewhere. Brian had concocted this elaborate, believable story about his girlfriend and the keys to protect his mother. What kind of a mother, though, would ask her son to break into a teacher's office to retrieve potentially incriminating evidence?

At a few minutes after eight that night, Stephanie called and sounded contrite, which immediately made me sit up and take notice. She made a couple of passing attempts at small talk, then said, "Molly, much as I hate to ask you this, I was wondering. Would you mind terribly coming over? I'd like you to talk to Jenny for a few minutes."

"About what?"

She sighed and said quietly, "Anything. I'd like your opinion about her emotional state. I'm worried about her."

"I'll be right there."

Jim, who'd been listening in, raised an eyebrow. I hung up and said, "That was Stephanie. She says she needs help with Jenny. For Stephanie to have resorted to asking help from me, the situation with Jenny must be truly dire."

He nodded. "I guess so. Should I come, too?"

"No, just stay home with the kids. I'll be back as soon as I can."

Nathan frowned at me from his post at the coffee table, where he was doing his homework. "Where are you going now?" he asked.

"Stephanie's house. I promise I won't be having as much fun as you are, doing your homework."

I headed out. It was all I could do to keep under the speed limit. I checked for external signs of trouble when I reached her upscale home and found none, although, really, what was I expecting—the grim reaper as a lawn ornament?

Tiffany opened the door, her little brother beside her. "Hey, Molly. What's up?" Tiffany asked.

"I got a new truck!" Mikey, her delightful, curly-haired little brother announced, holding out a plastic fire truck for my appraisal.

I opted for the easier response and bent down for a closer look. "Hey, that's really neat, Mike. Does it have a siren?"

"Sure it does!" He took a deep breath and then cried, "Wee-ohh, wee-ohh, wee-ooh."

"Good siren." I straightened and met Tiffany's eyes. "Is your mom here?"

"She's washing her hair. I can, like, tell her you're here, but you can forget seeing her for the next hour. You know how she is."

"Yes, I do know how she is." My ire had been instantly raised, but I quickly realized that this was the wrong reaction. Stephanie had not summoned me only to disappear in order to spite me, but because she felt that removing herself from the immediate scene was the best way to ease me into a conversation with Jenny. Whom I now needed to locate. "Please tell your mom I'm here and that I'll wait for her. Is Jenny around?"

"Um, yeah. Come on upstairs." She glanced at her brother, who was zooming around with his truck, making siren noises throughout the living room. "C'mon, little bro, let's get your toys put back in your room."

"You got *your* toys out," he retorted, and lifted a porcelain doll from a table in the corner.

"Be careful with that!" she snapped as she rushed to retrieve it. At her reaction, Mike immediately put the doll back down and grabbed his truck as if he intended to run over the doll. Tiffany got there first. "Play with your truck for fifteen minutes in the kitchen, then we'll put it away."

He charged off in the direction of the kitchen, making a siren noise all the way. "Where did you get the doll?" I asked Tiffany.

"Jenny gave it to me. I was going to see if she wanted it back, since her mom gave it to her. I guess it's supposed to be a pretty valuable antique."

"Really? Did Olivia get it from Nadine?"

"Actually, she got it from Corrinne Buldock. A couple years back, she and Nadine had a big blowup while I was in the room. Nadine said it was hers, or something like that, but Corrinne told me afterward that Nadine was confused. That this one was hers that she'd bought at some doll show."

I remember Nadine telling me about some disagreement they'd had, which had caused the end of their partnership and, I assumed, their friendship as well.

"If Jenny gave it to you, she probably wouldn't want you to give it back."

"Yeah, but I'm not sure *why* she gave it to me yesterday. She knows I'm not into dolls."

Alarm bells were ringing in my head. "How's she taking her mom's death?"

"Fine. You know. She's upset, but, like, she and her mom had so many problems. It's not like they were close or anything."

"Sometimes that makes it worse, Tiffany."

Tiffany shook her head and said with confidence, "You don't know Jenny. She's great at everything."

"Nobody is great at everything. And having others always think that you are makes it even harder."

"Jeez." Tiffany rolled her eyes. "Enough with the know-it-all-adult routine."

"Sorry. Good point. I was aiming at my usual know-nothing-of-any-value-adult routine, but forgot my lines. Do you think I could talk to Jenny for a bit, while I'm waiting for your mom?"

"Yeah, actually, that'll be good, since I've got to jam." She gave me a conspiratorial smile. "Jasper's picking me up any minute and we're getting a cone at Stewart's."

Not wanting to lose my temporary but hard-won standing as cool for a forty-year-old, I bit back my instantaneous you're-dating-on-a-school-night? reaction.

She escorted me to Jenny's room and knocked softly on the door. "Jen? Molly Masters is here to see Mom. Can you play hostess for a bit till Mom's free?"

"Uh . . . just a minute."

Tiffany turned, pounded on a second door, and yelled at the top of her lungs, "Hey, Mom! Molly's here, and I got stuff to do! Be back in an hour!"

A moment later the sounds of running water stopped and Stephanie called back, "Tiffany? Tiff? What did you say?"

"See ya, Molly," Tiffany said, placing the doll just inside the door of what I assumed was her bedroom, then racing down the stairs.

I turned and was about to suggest that Tiffany answer

her mother and inform her that her little brother was currently unsupervised in the kitchen. But Jenny opened her door just then, and her altered appearance distracted me. She had lost weight, her hair was dirty, her face callow and pale. As the sounds of Tiffany shutting the front door behind her emanated from below, Jenny said quietly, "I'm kind of busy with homework and stuff."

"Can you take a five-minute break? Show me where Stephanie keeps her tea?"

"I guess."

She lingered behind me as we descended the stairs. "I know I already told you this, Jenny, but I'm so terribly sorry about your mother."

"That's all I hear anymore. 'Sorry about your mother.' Thing is, though, she was a lousy mother."

"I didn't know her well, but I do know that no one *wants* to be a bad parent. And that it's never a reflection on the child. Children from even the worst of parents can grow up to be wonderful human beings."

Jenny was clearly letting my words sail past her, which was understandable. The last thing she needed now was a sermon from me. I hoped to turn the conversation to her college plans and the like as we shared a cup of tea. All thought of that was lost the moment we reached the kitchen. I managed an "Uh-oh," and Jenny sighed, "Oh, Mikey. What did you do?"

The answer was obvious. He had emptied the entire five-pound contents of a flour bag over himself and the fire truck.

"The firemen got a big mess!" he said proudly.

Jenny and I looked at each other. "A new meaning for the term 'flour arrangement,' hey?" I said.

"Yep," she said with a frown.

She and I cleaned the kitchen and kept the big mess contained by not allowing Mike to wander, spreading flour with each step. Stephanie, wearing a bathrobe and a towel around her head, entered the kitchen a minute later. She looked at her son, still caked with flour, then at me. "Baking something, are we?"

"The firemen made a mess, Mommy," Mike said.

"And so did you," she replied with a smile. Again she looked at me. "Did Tiffany leave the house?"

"She had a date," Jenny answered, "but she'll be back soon." She picked up Mike, who left a slight cloud of flour in his wake. "Come, white boy. Time to wash and change clothes."

"Thank you, Jenny," Stephanie said pleasantly. "And if you happen to see Tiffany before I do, could you please tell her that she's earned herself dishwashing duty for the rest of the week?"

"Okay."

Stephanie watched them leave, then smiled sadly. "That's encouraging, right? She joked about his having covered himself in white powder."

Our eyes met, and I knew I didn't have to mention that the flip side of this was that Jenny looked dreadfully withdrawn and depressed. I said quietly, "We only had the time to exchange a few words, and I'm no expert, but I'd get her in to see someone who is. Why take chances?"

She pursed her lips and nodded. "You're right. I'll get her into grief-counseling as soon as I can locate someone." She touched my shoulder. "Thanks for coming over, Molly. I'll finish cleaning up."

Though startled by her unexpected warmth, I said, "You're welcome. Please let me know if there's anything I can do for Jenny."

"Drive carefully," she said, as if completely distracted.

I let myself out and drove home, trying to assure myself that Jenny could have given Tiffany a cherished possession for numerous reasons. Other than the one possibility that scared me to the core.

* * *

Late the next morning the phone rang and my worst fears were realized. Before I could even finish saying hello, the frantic, young voice on the line said, "It's Tiffany. You've got to help. Jenny's . . . She says she's . . . I don't know what to do!"

"She's threatening to kill herself?" I asked, dreading the answer.

"Yes," Tiffany sobbed. "I can't find anyone to help! Our friends all left school for lunch."

"Where are you now? Can you get a teacher?"

"No! I can't do that! She'd flip! Besides, I'm on the cell phone. I don't want to leave her out of my sight long enough to go get someone. We're at this place behind school they call the Farmer's . . . uh . . . never mind. You won't know where I mean."

"Farmer's Make-out Grove?"

"Yeah. How'd you know?"

"I'll be right there. But if you can call the office, Lauren should be there and—"

"I'm not calling the school! Like I said, if a teacher or police officer comes—" She started crying too hard to continue, then said, "She told me if I told anyone what she was about to do, it would mean her last friend in the world will have betrayed her. I can see her from here, at least, but she goes all nuts when I come any closer."

"I'm on my way."

I dropped the phone, swept up my keys, and ran to the car. I could be at the school and the nearest parking lot in five minutes. Would that be fast enough? Should I have told Tiffany to call nine-one-one? Was she right that that would only have made things worse?

The elementary school was now the nearest building to Farmer's Make-out Grove. The school staff had been trying to keep lustful teenagers out of there ever since the first of the Carlton Central School buildings went in forty years ago. To my great annoyance, the moment I pulled into the lot, I realized that I should have asked which side of the grove they were on. I had entered one of the back parking lots for the elementary school, which was fenced off from the other lot, and I could see Tiffany in the distance of the second parking lot, standing alone and staring into the field.

Too harried to drive all the way around to the closer parking area, I deserted my car, stepped over the chain fence, and raced to Tiffany.

"Where is she?"

Tiffany's makeup was smeared from her tears and she was pacing in tight circles. She gestured with her chin, her arms wrapped tightly around her chest. "Up there. She told me she wants to be alone when she does it. You've got to stop her, Molly. She won't listen to anything I say."

"What happened, Tiffany?" I asked. I could see Jenny sitting in the distance, and much as I hated to risk leaving her alone in this condition for any longer than necessary, I had to know what I was about to face.

"Brian Underwood broke up with her this morning. She says she doesn't even care about that. I don't know what all else happened. Something about how she just found out her mom had been trying to block her admission to Harvard just 'cuz she wanted the money for herself."

I cursed under my breath. Someone might have told her this last bit. More likely she'd known all along but, in spite of everything, hadn't fully admitted the extent of her mother's betrayals to herself. And now her mother was dead, and there was no hope of reconciliation. What could I say in the face of so much pain—time heals all wounds? If I offered such a patronizing bromide to Jenny now, my presence would only make matters worse.

Tiffany went on, "She just asked to borrow my car after lunch and then she, like, was too upset to drive so, like, I did. You know? Then she had me take her into Albany to this pawnshop, and she tried to buy this gun, but, you know, the guy wouldn't sell it to her on the spot."

"Thank God," I murmured.

"I can't get through to her. I'm afraid what would happen if the police came, that she might lash out."

"She had you bring her here?"

"Yeah, only, like, she bought this incredibly sharp knife instead, from this knife shop, and said she's going to slit her wrists."

"She hasn't, though, right? Have you been able to see her well enough to know for certain?"

"Not for one-hundred-percent certain." She started to cry again. "I wanted to get the knife away from her. I just didn't know how."

"You did the right thing by calling an adult, Tiffany." Much as I wished it had been an adult with some background in counseling, or one that Jenny knew better and trusted. I glanced back up at Jenny, still rocking herself slightly. "Is she on anything? Drugs or alcohol?"

"I don't think so. Jenny won't touch the stuff. Says she doesn't like herself when—"

Tiffany's cell phone rang. She immediately answered with, "Mom?" After a pause she said, "Yeah. Molly's already here." Then Tiffany said, "Okay," and held out the phone to me. "She wants to talk to you."

I grabbed the phone. "It's me."

"How bad is it?" Stephanie asked, her voice as somber as I'd ever heard it.

"I just got here myself and I'm about to go try to talk to her. So far as I can tell, she's just sitting out there in the middle of the grove."

"Molly, I was clear across town when Tiffany first called me. I'm in my car and I'm almost there. You stop her from harming herself before I can arrive."

"Right." I returned the phone to Tiffany and started up the path. The moment she heard my footsteps, Jenny gasped and turned around to look at me. She had been sobbing. She got to her feet and held the knife out as if she intended to use it as a weapon.

"Stay away from me."

I stopped. "Jenny, don't do this."

"Who the hell are you, anyway? You've met me all of, what, two, three times? You don't care what happens to me any more than I care what happens to you."

Struggling to keep the urgency from playing itself out in my voice, I said, "You're right that we barely know each other, Jenny, though as an adult I care more about you than you do about me. Someday you'll understand why. But there's one thing that I do know about you. It's that you can't hold yourself accountable for your mother's failings. You've done a great job with your life so far, Jenny. Don't give up. Please."

She dropped back down onto the ground, but kept a firm grip on the knife. "You don't know how I feel! Nobody does!" She spat out the words with such venom and rage that what I really felt like doing was dropping to the ground as well and weeping on her behalf.

"True. I can't even imagine how much pain you're in now. My guess is that you've convinced yourself that the world would be better off without you. Only that isn't true, Jenny. You're eighteen. Give yourself a chance."

I hesitated. Should I tell her that my sense of humor had been born from my own need to keep my sadness and depression at bay? The risk was that she might think I was merely patronizing her and lose all willingness to talk with me.

"I've given myself plenty of chances," she shouted. "I screw up, every time. My own mother didn't love me."

"Even if that's true, it's not a reflection on you, Jenny.

Maybe she was incapable of letting herself be that vulnerable."

Beyond Jenny, I could see that Stephanie had arrived from the opposite side of the parking lot. She strode purposefully toward Jenny.

Jenny, too, saw Stephanie coming toward us. She broke into racking sobs.

Stephanie stopped in front of Jenny and said, "I hear you've had a really shitty day."

Still sobbing, Jenny nodded.

Stephanie bent down and took the knife from Jenny. Then, with her free hand, she helped her to her feet, put her arm around the girl's shoulders and said, "Let's go home."

The two of them walked off, Jenny struggling to regain her composure. After taking a couple of steps, Stephanie tossed the knife to the ground without breaking stride. Tiffany, still waiting from a respectful distance, joined them when they reached her, falling into step beside Jenny.

As I watched them leave, I knew that Jenny was in good hands.

Then I picked up the knife, which is what I knew Stephanie had intended for me to do. My hands were so sweaty now and I was shaking so badly that I wasn't sure I could carry the knife clear across the field and parking lot without dropping it. I set the knife back down and leaned against a tree and breathed deeply, trying to calm myself.

Past the newly budding tree branches, I could see several cars driving on the campus road toward the high school. Students and teachers returning from lunch, no doubt. The bell in the distance signaled that lunch period was ending for the high school.

I studied the knife, respectful of how close we might

have come to a very different outcome. The blade really was razor sharp, as Tiffany had described it.

I wondered about the wisdom of carrying a big, sharp knife back onto school property with classes still in session. Someone spotting me could easily get the wrong impression. I carried it carefully as I made my way back down the path to the car, with terrible visions of tripping on a rock and impaling myself.

My car was where I'd left it in the parking lot. It was strange, really, this drama playing out so close to the school and its hubbub of activity.

I took my keys from my pocket, but then remembered that I hadn't taken the time to lock the doors. I still needed to decide what to do with the knife, not wanting to put it anywhere my own kids could grab it. I could lock it in the glove box.

Resolved, I opened my car door and froze, though the muscles in my hand involuntarily tightened, so that I was now gripping the knife hilt as if for dear life.

Nadine's clown doll, the one that I'd tossed into my backseat and forgotten, had been moved. It was now propped upright in the front seat, its hands resting on the bottom of the steering wheel.

The clown's head had been tilted at an angle, its painted smile aimed directly at me.

Chapter 17

It Was Just a Joke!

My sense of terror and repulsion over the doll in my driver's seat eased slightly. Someone might have been playing an innocent anonymous prank. Perhaps some high school students walking by had seen the doll in my backseat. My doors were unlocked, and they might have gotten a laugh from propping the doll in the driver's seat.

Nevertheless, I got the willies at the mere thought of having to touch it. I put the knife in my glove box and locked it, but the doll needed to go to the police station to be dusted for fingerprints.

This was just the sort of thing that Tommy loved to tease me about, as he tried to beat me to the punch line. Odds were overwhelming that when I walked in with the doll to tell him it needed to be fingerprinted, he would say, in apparent seriousness, "Well, Molly, a doll doesn't *have* fingerprints."

Still, something was terrifying about that happy, motionless face. I felt a strong urge to throw the doll away, an urge immediately followed by a nightmarish vision of myself being chased by it. That quickly gave way to the thought of this tiny little clown doll running down the highway, waving its arms and yelling in a squeaky little voice, "Stop, Molly! I'm a clown! It was just a joke!"

This was what was simultaneously good and bad about my sense of humor: My ability to find a comedic side to almost any situation gave me the strength to survive. And yet that same humor hinted at a certain and undeniable absence of sanity.

Being careful not to touch the porcelain, which could smudge a telltale fingerprint, I snatched up the doll and listened for a bomblike ticking. Nothing. The doll's body was soft—stuffed cloth—with no telltale hard lumps. Just to be cautious, though, I stashed the doll in the far back compartment of my Jeep. At least if the thing exploded, the upholstery was already damaged. Meanwhile, the wounds in my back were throbbing in remembered pain.

I drove to the police station and carried the doll inside—a waste of time, I knew. It was either a child's prank or the work of a killer who knew enough about gunpowder residue to cover his or her clothing with a garbage bag and to steal my gloves. No way would this person now leave incriminating fingerprints behind.

Tommy was poring over some files in his office, his door open. I leaned in. "Sorry to interrupt, Tommy." I held up the doll. "I need you to get this doll tested for fingerprints."

He furrowed his brow and took the doll from me. "I dunno, Moll. This doll has awful tiny hands. You sure we're going to be able to make out its fingerprints?"

He laughed at his own joke with so much glee that I wasn't about to spoil it by admitting that I'd deliberately fed him the straight line. "Nadine Dahl made the doll and gave it to me yesterday, and it's been in my backseat. My car was parked at the school, by Farmer's Make-out Grove, and when I returned to my car, the doll was propped up in the driver's seat."

"What were you doin' there?"

"Reminiscing over things that never actually occurred."

"Boys in the lab should be able to get to it soon."

"Would you please tell me what they find out?"

He shrugged. "Maybe. Depends on what the results are."

I made no comment, reasoning that I was about to dispose of a knife, which I had no intention of telling *him* about.

The next morning, the doorbell rang. At this rate Betty Cocker was going to wear her tonsils out by barking at our unexpected guests. Provided dogs had tonsils. The visitor this time was Chester Walker, who again had on his baseball hat, covering his bald spot.

"Did you get your blinds fixed?" he asked by way of a greeting.

"Yes. Danielle fixed them yesterday."

"Good." Ignoring BC's barking, he walked through my house and stopped in front of the sunroom, glancing inside. "Satisfied with the job she did?"

"Overall, her work has been the smoothest part of the installation."

"Huh. I already called Danielle. I'm having her meet us over here."

"Over here? In my house, you mean?"

"Yes. Even if you're not, I'm very dissatisfied with the work she's done here."

"You didn't seem particularly dissatisfied when I told you about the problem. How can you be concerned now that she's fixed it?"

"It's a matter of principle."

"Um, not to be dense, but I'm not following your principles at all. How is it that they apply to my functional blinds and not to the door that doesn't quite close? Or to my nonexistent deck?"

The doorbell rang, and I left Chester to open and shut my blinds while Betty and I headed toward the front. "I keep telling you we'll handle the deck," Chester called after me.

"And I keep hearing you tell me that, with no results," I retorted. I opened the door to find Danielle Underwood. She had that grouchy look about her again, her brow furrowed and her lips set in a frown.

"Good morning, Molly. Chester said you had some sort of an emergency problem with your blinds and needed to see me right away."

"He's speaking for himself."

She rolled her eyes. "Is he here?"

"In the sunroom."

She marched ahead of me and entered the room, then stood with hands on hips, looking at Chester. "Something wrong with the blinds, Chester?"

"As a matter of fact," he fired back, hands on his own hips, "I don't think they'll do. You cut the valance wrong. They should have wrapped around. And the vanes are a bit too short. As you can see, they can get hung up on the runners for the doors."

"They look fine to me," I said.

"It's not the kind of quality product I want associated with a room that my company built."

"Is that so," Danielle said, more of a dare than a question.

"Yes."

"And this has nothing to do with your learning last night that my son, Brian, is valedictorian, hey?"

Chester pointed at her. "Your son should be run out of town on the next rail! He bags his own teacher, then he has the nerve to break up with Jenny Garrett, days after her mother dies!"

"You have no right to speak about my child like that! How dare you!"

"He's eighteen. He's not a child."

"And Jenny Garrett is an orphan at age eighteen, thanks to you! I've thought long and hard about this, and I'm sure you're the killer. You would stop at nothing to manipulate things so your son would finish on top!"

"What?"

"You thought killing Corrinne would upset my son badly enough that his grades would fall off." She was poking him in the chest as she shouted, she was so angry. She looked like a madwoman. "Then, when they didn't, you killed his girlfriend's mother!"

"That's nuts and you know it!"

"Do I? You were the only clown ruthless enough to commit murder, Chester. And you don't have to fire me over these perfectly good blinds. Because I quit! I won't have my work associated with your shoddy work!"

"My work isn't shoddy!"

"How can you say that when you're looking at the mess you've left poor Molly with?" She tossed her hair and nearly pushed me aside as she headed toward the door, as if she was too angry to see me.

In the doorway, she whirled around and pointed at Chester. "If you have an ounce of concern for your business, build Molly her damned deck!" She resumed her angry march through my house and slammed the door behind her.

Chester's cheeks were bright red, and I could feel my own cheeks warm at having witnessed this scene. I forced a smile and cleared my throat. When Chester remained silent and made no move to leave, I said quietly, "I must admit that a deck *would* be nice."

"I'll have someone out here this afternoon." He made his way to the front door, and it dawned on me then that he was dallying so as to avoid another confrontation with Danielle in the driveway. "By the way, Molly, she's wrong, of course. I didn't kill anybody. But it's a good thing that your blinds are finished. That woman is dangerous. You're well off without her."

* * *

Karen and Nathan arrived home after school that afternoon, along with Rachel, whose mom was neck-deep in office work these days. There were still no signs of this mythical deck builder Chester had promised. When Karen was settled into practicing piano and Nathan into complaining about homework, I heard a knock on my back door.

Because there was a three-foot drop next to my sliding glass doors, having someone stand there waiting for the door to be answered was comical-looking. I smiled at the sight of the young man standing there, primarily because his head was unfettered by a baseball cap. I slid open the door and said hello.

"Hi, Mrs. Masters. I'm Paul Walker."

Putting the last name and certain facial similarities together, I asked, "You're Chester's son?"

He nodded. "My father sent me to install your deck."

"By yourself?"

"I can do it. This is pretty much a one-person job anyway. 'Cept for carrying the boards, that is, but I can manage."

"Okay, great. How about I give you a hand with the boards?"

He shrugged. "If you want."

I climbed down on the slide steps, still unwilling to use the slide itself, and we rounded the house together. "I didn't realize you worked for your father."

"I don't. He said he didn't want to waste his men's time on such a simple task. And he, uh, says I better start earning some wages toward my tuition."

"I heard you missed out on being valedictorian. I'm sorry. That must have been a major disappointment for you."

"Not for me. I didn't want to make a speech in the first place. It was my dad, really, who was pushing for it. He kept saying it would show all those Carlton snobs when the son of a carpenter without a diploma got to finish on top."

"I see."

"No offense. I'm sure he doesn't mean you when he talks about the Carlton snobs."

A voice called to us from the head of the cul-de-sac. "Hey, Paul. Need some help?"

It was Jasper Newton. He must have been walking home from school past my cul-de-sac, as he sometimes did on nice days such as this one.

"Yeah, Jas. If you could just grab one end, Mrs. Masters won't have to do it."

Jasper said, "Hey, there, Mrs. Molly."

"Hi, Mr. Jasper." I returned my attention to Paul. "I'll just unload some of the smaller boards for you then."

"If you want," he said for the second time. As a gentleman, he clearly didn't want to deprive me of my desire to carry boards.

"Hope you're not bummed about the election results today," Jasper said to Paul.

"You kidding? I was just telling Mrs. Masters that I didn't want to make a speech in the first place."

"What election was this?" I asked.

"This morning, Jack Vance—that's our principal— asked the three students with the next-to-highest GPAs to be covaledictorians. Turns out Brian Underwood had the highest score but turned being valedictorian down, for some reason. The rest of our scores were, like, neck and neck. Anyways, none of us felt good about accepting the honor either, since we'd be getting it by default. So we decided to have a vote among the student body and let them decide."

"Who won?" I asked.

"Jenny Garrett."

"I'm so glad to hear that."

"She deserved it," Paul said.

"You gonna build this deck by yourself?" Jasper asked.

"Yeah, my ol' man's corked at me for getting a C in Paxton's art history class. Says I would've beat Brian out otherwise."

"How'd you manage to do that, anyway? I heard his class was a breeze."

"The guy hates me. He's been raggin' on me big-time, ever since I . . ." He let his voice fade and gave me a sheepish smile.

It was very typical behavior of a teenager to blame the teacher for assigning a bad grade. Nothing had indicated that this was anything other than an immature person looking for a scapegoat. Still, Brian had said the same thing, and I decided maybe I should drop in on Dave's class one more time. At this point Dave was probably going to conclude that I was either after his job, or after *him*.

Just as the boys were carrying a large load of lumber around the side of the house, I heard the squeal of brakes from the head of the cul-de-sac. I paused in my work of collecting smaller boards from Paul's truck bed to see what the commotion was. Tiffany Saunders, driving her mother's BMW, did a creative turn to get into my little street and, hitting her brakes again, pulled to a dramatic stop in front of the house. She was still rubbernecking in the direction of the boys as she got out of her car.

"Hello, Tiffany."

She was so focused on getting a better glimpse of Jasper that she acted startled by my voice. "Molly, hi. I was just . . . in the neighborhood and thought I'd see how Karen and Nathan are doing."

"Just fine. That's Paul Walker and Jasper Newton carrying the boards for my deck."

"Oh. Jasper's here?"

"You didn't recognize him when you were pulling a wheelie just now?"

She sighed. In conspiratorial tones she said, "It's . . . getting really close to the prom, and like, he still hasn't asked me."

"Maybe you should drop some hints."

"I already have. He doesn't seem to pick up on 'em, though. Could you help me?"

"Oh, Tiffany. This isn't really something I should get involved in."

"You don't need to do much. Just ask him if he's thinking of going. Please? If you do this for me I'll never ask another thing of you as long as I live."

"That really hasn't been a major problem anyway, Tiffany. But, we'll see."

"Oh, thank you!" She raced back toward her car and opened the door.

"You're leaving?"

"I have to go home so he can call me. I'm sure not going to wait around here and have him think I put you up to anything."

"You'd better hurry then, because they'll be back out front any minute."

She jumped back into her car and drove off, leaving a trail of car exhaust.

The boys reappeared. "Nice weather today," I said. "I guess spring is finally arriving. Which reminds me—who are you guys taking to the senior prom next month?"

Paul immediately said, "Jenny Garrett." He smiled broadly. "She asked me, today. You believe that?" he said to Jasper, shaking his head with disbelief at his good fortune. "Brian Underwood found out Karina likes him, so he went and dumped Jenny yesterday, after she'd already bought her dress . . . and her mom just died and everything. What a total lame-o."

Jasper said nothing, but colored deeply.

"Aren't you going, Jas?" Paul asked.

He shrugged. "I don't know. Those things are kind of lame."

I needed to talk to Jasper alone for a minute. "Would you guys like some lemonade or iced tea?"

"Sure. Lemonade."

"Me, too."

"Jasper, would you mind giving me a hand with something in the kitchen?"

"Sure, Mrs. Molly."

We entered through the front door. "I really hate that. It's going to have to be Molly or Mrs. Masters, but not a combination."

"Okay. What did you want help with?"

"Nothing. I just wanted to ask you something privately. But you can help get the frozen concentrate out of the can."

"Okay."

I got out a Tupperware pitcher and a can of concentrate, and handed them over to Jasper, along with a wooden spoon. "Tiffany used to baby-sit for my children. I know her pretty well. It's none of my business, of course, but if you ask her to the prom, I bet she'll say yes."

His face lit up. "You sure?"

"Positive."

He couldn't stop smiling the entire time he mixed the lemonade, then he did a leap complete with a war whoop out my back door, leaving me to serve them their drinks.

In an impressively short period of time the boys had set about reframing the deck. By the time Lauren arrived to get her daughter, the two of them even had the first several boards in place, and the kids were disappointed that this meant their slide would be passé.

Lauren looked and sounded tired. I told her about her stepson being out back, and she went out to chat with the two boys for a couple of minutes.

She came back inside. "Thanks for letting Rach come over. This supposed part-time job at the school office is turning into a major ordeal ever since Nadine left."

"Did you hear that Jasper is about to ask Tiffany to the prom?"

She looked at me blankly for a moment. "Well, Tommy's going to be less than thrilled. But it's nice that he's dating. This will be fine. Just so long as we don't have to actually see Stephanie. I mean, it's not like they're in love or anything."

"You should see their faces, though, when you even mention the other's name."

"Probably the same expression I get these days when someone mentions the word 'hot bath' to me."

"Of all of the low, miserable things to do to me!" Stephanie snarled to me on the phone that evening. "You had to get at me through my daughter, didn't you, Molly!"

"Are you referring to her date for the prom?"

"She told me all about how you brought the two of them together. My daughter! With the son of a cop! For her senior prom! She'll be lucky if he knows to rent a tux. He'll show up in some used, twenty-dollar plaid suit from the Salvation Army."

"He'll rent a tuxedo, and the two of them will make a perfectly handsome-looking couple."

"Easy for you to say. Why do you meddle so much? Tiffany tells me that none of this would have happened if you hadn't chatted with the two of them during art class. Must you always be so damned friendly?"

"I don't even know how to respond to that."

"Don't expect me to be warm and fuzzy toward you tomorrow."

"If you were warm and fuzzy I wouldn't recognize you, Stephanie. But what's happening tomorrow?"

"Didn't you get the flyer? I put it in the teachers' mailboxes. We've got a fund-raisers' meeting at school. We're discussing what to do regarding the variety show—scrap it entirely, reschedule, do a new fund-raiser."

"A reunion of clowns," I murmured. An idea occurred to me. Maybe I could flush out the killer tomorrow night by implying that I'd soon have access to a revealing clue. "All of the suspects are going to be there, right? Dave, Chester, Danielle, Nadine, Elsbeth . . ."

"Nadine won't be there. I wasn't even going to invite her."

"Oh, right. Of course. Can you do something to convince her to come? Tell her that one of the parents suggested she sell her dolls at the fund-raiser and donate a percentage of the proceeds. And then could you double-check and tell the others how important it is that they be present?"

There was a pause. She asked, "Why would you want all the suspects gathered together? You're not planning on doing something stupid as usual, are you?"

Her words rankled. "Could be. And would you call Tommy Newton and ask him to be there, too?"

"You're putting yourself in physical danger, am I to assume?"

"Of course not. I simply intend to stir things up a bit, see if one of the suspects takes the bait. Will you call everyone? It'll be too obvious to the killer that I'm up to something if I were to do it."

"Certainly. I'll call right now." She added cheerfully, "Thank you, Molly. It sounds as though this is *one* meeting that will be fun for me to preside over."

Chapter 18

Showing a Prophet

Olivia Garrett's funeral services were held the next day. With Jim entrenched in yet another meeting at work, Lauren and I drove together. Tommy joined us toward the end of the service, taking a seat on the other side of Lauren. The moment we found ourselves able to talk privately, I asked about the test results on the clown doll.

"No fingerprints whatsoever, Molly."

"Damn. I was afraid of that. I'd hoped it was just a kid's silly prank." I knew I didn't need to explain to him that if it had been a random prank, the doll would have been rife with fingerprints—mine and Nadine's, if not the prankster's.

He frowned. "At least we learned a couple of things. The suspect can recognize your car and doesn't like you a whole lot. Not that that narrows things down much."

"Thanks a lot, Tommy."

"Just meant you're stirrin' things up, as usual. Got an interesting call from Stephanie Saunders. 'Bout the meeting at school tonight, urging me to be there."

"Did she?" I asked as innocently as I could.

"She did indeed. Also suggested I find some bogus excuse to arrest you immediately and put you in jail for the next twenty-four hours, for your own protection."

"Stephanie suggested that?" I paused. That meant she was actually trying to prevent me from putting myself in the killer's path. "I'm touched."

"Listen to yourself, Molly. How many people do you know who would find it *touching* to learn that their friends are callin' up the police to ask that they be thrown in jail?"

"I'm flattered, Tommy. You realize how unique an individual I truly am."

"Thank the Lord for small favors," he grumbled. He glanced at Lauren, then rose. He stuck his finger in my face. "I'll be watching you like a hawk tonight. You give me the least little cause, I'll arrest you right in front of the whole PTA."

He would never do something like that to me, and we both knew it. "My. That would make me the talk of the town, now wouldn't it?"

"Sure would." He met his wife's eyes. "You know what Molly's got in mind for tonight's meeting?"

She glared at me and said, "No, she's kept me in the dark, too."

"I'm not necessarily planning anything tonight, Tommy. I merely asked Stephanie to make sure you were there, just in case there was trouble." I didn't add that it could be me who was causing the trouble, but then, I planned to play it by ear tonight.

"Uh-huh," Tommy said. He gave Lauren a quick peck on the cheek, said, "Like a hawk" to me with another finger wag, then left.

"I've got to get back to school," Lauren said. "I'll drop you off at home."

As we got into her car she asked, "What's the real scoop about tonight's meeting? Are you going to announce that you know who did it and see if anyone bolts for the door?"

"Not exactly. Unless I change my mind, I plan to claim that I'm going to be hypnotized by the police, and that I'm sure that will allow me to remember enough minor details to be able to identify the gunman or gunwoman in the clown costume."

"Molly, no! I don't think you should do that."

"Why not? It's not as if the current course of action—sitting around, while someone else gets shot—has been effective."

Lauren pursed her lips and said nothing more. We pulled up to my house.

"Don't tell Tommy my plan. Okay? If you do, he'll handcuff me to my kitchen chair, and this might really work."

"It's too dangerous!"

"No, it isn't. I'll have Tommy there to protect me. And who knows? If it doesn't work, maybe he'll decide to go ahead and have me hypnotized, and that *will* give the police an important clue."

"Except that Tommy once told me that hypnosis doesn't work as well in real life as it does in Hollywood, and it isn't admissible in a court of law, so even if you could pick the killer while under hypnosis, Tommy would still need corroborating evidence."

"I doubt the killer is going to realize any of that, though. Thanks for the ride." She drove off.

I tried hard to get some work done, but the friction between Lauren and me was too distracting. Maybe there was a safer means for me to help with the investigation. There had to be a clue someplace, something I'd forgotten.

I drove to the school and swung behind the elementary building. Puttering along at the back edge of the parking lot, I peered at the path into the farmer's property where we'd been the other day.

The center of the grove itself was well out of sight from any angle, which is why it had become such a popular make-out location in the first place. Someone, however, who happened to be driving between buildings at the right time could have glimpsed one of us on the path. Maybe if I went to the auditorium, something would ring a bell.

When I went to the office to sign in, Lauren was already looking frazzled, but she said hello to me. "Do you really think my plan for tonight is a stupid idea?" I asked.

She tilted her head, her personal version of a shrug. "Maybe since Tommy will be right with you, it won't be that dangerous. He'll probably insist on taking you straight to the station in the squad car and actually bringing in a hypnotist on the spot."

"Which would be fine by me."

All lines on both phones were now ringing, with every button illuminated. Exasperated, Lauren said, "Jack better hire somebody to replace Nadine soon. I had no idea how much that woman did in a day."

"You're not thinking of trying to get yourself fired, too, are you?"

She shook her head. "If I get too overburdened, I'll simply quit. But I'll tell you one thing—if I actively tried to get fired, it wouldn't take me more than a day or two. Jack barely glances at the reports he sends out before he signs them. It's practically a rubber stamp."

She answered the phone just as a couple of female students I didn't recognize called to her about needing access to the copy machine, their voices blending into an annoying high-pitched whine.

I left the office, and down the hall I tried the doors to the auditorium but discovered they were locked. Now what?

I still intended to drop into Dave Paxton's class again. I headed for the art room and found him in the midst of a rather noisy class that appeared to be freshmen or sophomores. The class was standing at easels circled around a model—a tall thin boy in a T-shirt and jeans, carrying a grocery bag. They were working in charcoal.

Dave had been at Olivia's service earlier, and was still wearing the same rumpled-looking slacks and royal-blue shirt, his tie and jacket now absent. He paused from working with a student and gave me a smile. "Ah, Molly, this is well-timed. Class, we have a professional artist who's just joined us. I'll have her take a look-see at your work. If she has any comments for you, you'd be wise to listen."

He gestured for me to go in a clockwise direction to view the students' work. I nodded and did so, not about to admit that charcoal had been my worst medium. Next to pottery. Never could "throw" a pot successfully, except out the window. Artists must be meticulous to work with charcoal. In no time I'd always have smudges and black fingerprints all over the drawing and would turn my sticky eraser solid black.

By and large, Dave's students suffered from the typical beginning artists' tendency to spend too much time focusing on their drawing instead of on the model. They would detail one small section far too early. I threw some catch phrases at a few of the students while being largely complimentary, and spent the most time with one girl who had charcoal smudges on her face and all over her drawing. She had real potential as a future cartoonist.

Having circled in opposite directions, Dave met me at the girl's easel and laid his hand on my shoulder. I was wearing an off-white, three-quarter-sleeve, knit blouse and hoped he hadn't been handling charcoal, but resisted the temptation to check. "Sorry to put you to work like this, Molly. I hope you weren't just here to deliver a message to me or something."

"No, no. I just wanted to drop in on your class again."

"Good. I appreciate—"

"Mr. Paxton, I feel dizzy," a girl whined. "I'd better go to the nurse."

"I'll go with her," a second girl immediately piped up. "Just in case she faints, she shouldn't go alone."

Dave shot me a quick glance, and I nodded. He turned back to our future fainter. "I'll have Mrs. Masters accompany you, Tara."

The "dizzy" girl's face fell. "I'll be all right. I think I should just lie down for a while."

After a couple of additional exchanges, Tara shuffled off with me to the nurse's office. She hadn't a thing to say to me as we walked along, obviously displeased that her escape with her girlfriend had been foiled.

En route I heard some lovely piano music emanating from the music room, and on my return trip I headed that way so I could hear better. The door was cracked open, and through the inner window I saw Elsbeth, playing to an empty room. Not being a sophisticated music connoisseur, I didn't know what she was playing—something with a lot of notes. I paused, listening, until she stopped. When she looked up and saw me, she frowned.

I pushed the door open. "I didn't mean to interrupt. It was a treat to listen to you, though."

"Thank you. Playing calms me. Helps me focus."

"I'm the same way with drawing."

"You're comparing cartooning to Johann Sebastian Bach?"

"Not exactly, no. Was he any good at caricatures?"

She glowered at me, not responding.

"I'm surprised to see you here."

"Substituting for the music teacher today. He's under the weather. This is his free period, which is about to end." She regarded me for a moment. "Did you find a new teacher for Karen?"

"Just till fall, then he goes out of town for college."

"Brian Underwood?" Without awaiting my answer, she shook her head as if at my foolishness. "Molly, what are you doing to your child? I'm the best piano teacher in the area. Don't you realize that?"

"It's nice that you're confident in your abilities. But I'm confident in my abilities to make good decisions regarding my own children."

She resumed her playing, simultaneously speaking in time to the metronome. "You made a mistake by firing me. But I suppose nobody gets every note perfect."

"Karen? Dinnertime," I called for the fourth time that evening. When there was still no acknowledgment, I pushed the "phone finder" button on the base of the portable phone, which emitted a shrill noise on the handset even when the phone was currently in use.

By the fifth time I pressed the button, Karen opened her door and yelled, "All right, already! I was on an important phone call! I'll be right there!"

"Wash up for dinner," Jim called back. "And be polite to your mother."

Nathan thought this last admonishment was hilarious, but we ignored him.

"Yikes," I said to Jim. "I feel like I'm the caretaker to a hibernating bear these days. I prod her with a stick upon occasion just to make sure she'll emerge from her cave and growl at me, and reassure myself that she's still alive."

"Don't worry. She still needs us to keep her supplied with nuts and berries."

"I hate nuts. And berries," Nathan grumbled.

Karen came frumping and slumping down the stairs just as I was rising from my chair, already having eaten. "You can use my seat, Karrie Bear," I told her. "I've got a mini PTA meeting tonight."

"You do?" Jim asked. "On a Friday?"

"The planning committee. For the variety show."

"Maybe I should come."

"No, why don't you stay home with the kids? Tommy and Lauren will watch over me."

"Just the same, I think—"

The phone rang, and I outraced Karen to answer it. The call was for Jim. "Your boss," I said. "See you guys later." After giving Jim a quick peck on the cheek and handing him the phone, I turned my attention to the children. "I'm not sure what time I'll be home tonight. It might be after your bedtime." Still angry at me, Karen shirked away, but Nathan let me kiss him goodbye on the cheek.

The group of people I'd requested were already there by the time I arrived. What struck me immediately was the contrast in appearance between Tommy, who looked utterly exhausted as he sat beside Lauren, and Nadine, who sparkled. I also couldn't help but notice that Nadine had three different dolls displayed on the table in front of her; we were clearly in for a sales pitch, but at least this had gotten her to show up. Dave Paxton, Chester Walker, and Elsbeth Young were sitting in different corners of the room, making a point, I felt, of distancing themselves from one another. Danielle Underwood and Martin were chatting amiably amid the group of twenty other parents and teachers present.

Though she never glanced at the clock on the wall, precisely as the minute hand reached the hour, Stephanie said in officious tones, "At the last meeting I presided over, for the PTA at large, the subject was brought up that a new PTA president should be found. No one has volunteered since then, but I thought it'd be best to begin this meeting by asking if anyone objects to my remaining in charge until the next regular meeting, when I'll insist we hold an election."

I generally found having Stephanie be "in charge" objectionable, but I doubted that was what she meant, and so I kept the comment to myself. She scanned the room and raised an eyebrow at me as if to dare me to speak up, but I resisted the obvious baiting.

"All right, then. We have a decision to make regarding the variety show. My original hope, as I'm sure would be echoed by most in this room, was that we would wait until such time as our—" She paused to gesture in Tommy's direction. "—illustrious police force made an arrest in the case. Unfortunately, no such happenstance appears to be forthcoming."

"You're not trying to put yourself in charge of the investigation, are you?" Tommy asked, his voice rife with sarcasm.

"My dear man, I wouldn't dream of such a thing. Though we would all sleep better if there was more progress."

I decided to leap on the opening. "I have a suggestion about how that might happen."

Tommy shot me the dirtiest look I'd ever seen.

I ignored him and said, "I came into personal contact with Corrinne's killer. He or she bumped right into me and I got a good look at the person. There were subtle differences in all of us that night. I really believe that if the police were to hypnotize me, I'd be able to recall the kind of minutiae that could identify Corrinne's killer once and for all."

"That sounds reasonable to me," Stephanie immediately chimed in.

I glanced at her, and she raised an eyebrow in haughty defiance. I now knew that she wasn't really anxious to see me put myself at risk but was only pretending to be. She was the only person I knew who was nice to me when my back was turned but insulting when we were face-to-face.

Tommy spread his hands and said through clenched teeth, "Far be it from me to stop you from giving this a try, Molly."

I scanned the room, hoping for some telltale change of demeanor on the part of the suspects, but the only person whose facial expression had changed noticeably was Lauren. She'd paled and was also surreptitiously studying the others' faces.

"I propose," Stephanie said, "that we go ahead and schedule the show for Friday, two weeks from today, and assume that Molly's strategy will work and someone will be under arrest by then."

"Wouldn't put that much stock in Molly, here," Tommy grumbled. "Hypnosis doesn't work every time. Might not work at all on Molly."

"Tommy's right," Lauren chimed in. "In fact, I think there's almost no chance Molly will remember anything significant."

"If that proves to be the case, we can always cancel the show for good next week," Stephanie said.

There were general nods and agreement from the group, and Stephanie took this as a done deal.

"Can we all agree that we need to ax the clowns?" Dave Paxton said. "The gag's been ruined anyway by the articles and pictures in the paper."

"I agree," Chester Walker said. "Let's just leave out the final number completely."

"All right," Stephanie said, "but we'll need a new final act."

"We have one," Martin said. "My magic act. It's the highlight of the show any way you look at it."

"I've got a better idea," Nadine said. "Porcelain marionettes." She rose and scanned all of our faces. "I'm sure most of you haven't heard Stephanie's brilliant idea for an additional fund-raiser. I'm going to set up a booth in the lobby for the event, and will donate a full half of my profits to the school."

"And just who do you think would buy anything from you, after what you did to the students of Carlton?" Elsbeth spat out.

The murmur of general agreement arose in the room.

Nadine's cheeks colored. An argument ensued among several in the room, some saying we shouldn't dismiss anyone's willingness to share half of their profits. But I tuned out, having thought up another silly card idea.

In my cartoon, a young man has entered a boardroom with an elderly, bearded man dressed in sandals and a white robe and sporting a Moses-like aura. The people in the boardroom are staring at them with jaws agape, as the smiling young man says, "You told me my division needed to 'show a prophet this quarter or else,' and here he is!"

The debate surrounding me was curtailed when Nadine lifted her chin and said, "Well, I don't need to give my hard-earned proceeds to your cause, if that's your attitude." She collected her dolls, stopped and glared at Stephanie, and said, "I hope you're satisfied, now that you've humiliated me this way."

"My mind must have been elsewhere when I made the inane suggestion to you," Stephanie said. "I apologize."

Nadine marched out of the room. I felt my own cheeks warming, but to Stephanie's credit, she did not look my way.

As if the incident with Nadine had never occurred, Elsbeth continued, "We should end with a tribute to Corrinne and Olivia. Maybe a medley of their favorite songs. I could create a piano arrangement in their honor. Better yet, we have that chamber orchestra as the second act. My musical arrangement could include them, too."

We'd come a long way from clowns to a chamber orchestra, but far be it from me to stand in the way of dignity.

"You know what would be even better?" Chester said, getting to his feet in his excitement. "If the whole cast got together to sing the medley. Like what they do in the Miss Universe Pageant. Elsbeth could make the arrangement and conduct the piece."

"So much for dignity," I murmured under my breath.

"Does anyone know what their favorite songs were?" Danielle asked.

" 'Love Can Build a Bridge' was Olivia's," Stephanie said quietly. "Jenny told me."

"The *Star Wars* theme song was Corrinne's," Dave said wistfully.

Elsbeth's eyes lost their sparkle. She looked across the room at Dave. "Are you absolutely certain 'Star Wars' was her favorite song?"

"By far," he said with confidence.

"Did she have a second favorite?" Elsbeth asked meekly.

Stephanie appeared nonplussed. After a pause, she gestured at Elsbeth and forced a smile. "There you have it, Elsbeth. 'Love Can Build a Bridge to Star Wars.' Are you up to the task?"

"Don't you need trumpets for 'Star Wars'?" Chester asked. "I used to play trumpet back in high school. Granted, it's been more than twenty years, but I could pick it up again well enough to do the one musical phrase."

Elsbeth squirmed in her chair. "I can't really envision a chamber orchestra *gettin' down* with 'Star Wars.' And it's a little lean on lyrics. Let's just say directly that this little medley would hardly be the pinnacle of my musical career.

"You know," Elsbeth continued with a sigh, "come to think of it, I wouldn't mind donning my clown costume again all that much."

Stephanie sighed and turned toward Martin. "You win, Martin. You're the final act."

"Yes!" he said, pumping the air with his fist.

A few minutes of debate continued, but then Stephanie called for an end of the meeting and everyone headed out. I kept my seat, however, lost in thought. Tommy and Lauren made their way toward me.

I looked around. The three of us were the last people left in the room. "Can you let me into the office, Lauren? I need to see a student directory."

"I've got one with me," Lauren said, reaching into her purse to retrieve it.

"Great. Let me see it and your cell phone for a minute."

"What now?" Tommy asked.

"I can't believe that Corrinne's favorite song was really 'Star Wars.' I think Dave Paxton lied. I'm going to call Brian Underwood and verify that."

"So what if he lied, Molly? Maybe he hates to sing and wanted to get out of it. So he named a song nobody would want to perform."

"Or maybe he lied because he hated her for purportedly going out with someone else. Remember, this is someone who's constantly professed his love for the woman. Now here he is, hatefully mocking her by suggesting that she liked the antithesis of her type of music."

I dialed as I spoke, and a male's voice answered. "Brian?"

"Yes?"

"This is Molly Masters. Do you happen to know what Corrinne Buldock's favorite song was?"

"Favorite song? No idea."

"Could it have been the theme song from *Star Wars*?"

"No way. She was into old folk songs. Joni Mitchell. Judy Collins. Like that."

"That's all I wanted to know. Thanks. 'Bye." I hung up. "I knew it! She was into female folk singers. It's Dave Paxton. He's the killer. I just know it."

"Great, Molly," Tommy said, making no attempt to disguise his anger. "I can arrest him on account've lying about someone's favorite song. That's a federal offense, right?"

"Let's do what we said we would. Hypnotize me. You still have the clown costumes as evidence, right? And you labeled who was wearing each costume?"

"Yeah, but—"

"There has to be something there. Some cologne scent on the costume that I could remember under hypnosis that will point at Dave."

"Listen to me carefully, Molly. Memories given while a witness is under hypnosis cannot be admitted into evidence in a trial. It's only helpful for finding the perpetrator, not for conviction. Even if under hypnosis you recall, say, a birthmark on the killer's neck which positively IDs the person, you can never testify in court about any of that. It'd be too easy for the hypnotist to plant memories. In fact, once you've been hypnotized, you can't testify in court at all. You'd no longer be considered a reliable witness."

"It would be enough for you to get a search warrant, though."

He spread his hands. "To search for what? Don't you think by now the killer's got any 'n' all incriminating evidence well buried?" He fisted his hands and seemed to focus on my neck, then turned to his wife. "Lauren, did you know this was what she was goin' to pull?"

"Yes, but—"

"You should've told me!" Tommy massaged his temples. "Now there's no time. I've gotta locate a signaling device." He looked at me again. "You wear it like a belt under your clothing and push the button on it when you're in danger. It'll immediately signal the station house that you're in trouble."

"Thanks, Tommy."

"I should be able to get it to you by midday tomorrow. Just stay out of trouble till then."

"We'll follow you home," Lauren said.

Just then Tommy's radio beeped. He responded, speaking mostly in numbers and acronyms.

"An emergency?" Lauren asked when he'd finished.

"Naw. Just gonna have to go check out things at the bowling alley after I drop you two off. Got a couple of overindulgers." He rocked on his heels and said, "Ready to go, Moll?"

We got into our cars. The lighting in the parking lot was enough to assure me that Tommy and Lauren were arguing. I had the impression whenever I glanced in my rearview mirror that the argument was continuing during the drive home. I pulled into my driveway and waved as Tommy and Lauren circled the cul-de-sac before driving off toward their own home a couple of blocks away.

Meanwhile, the garage door wouldn't open. The mechanism was old, and it often took two or three tries till the remote worked.

Having pressed the button five times already with no results, I yanked the controls off the visor and pressed again. The red button wasn't lighting. Plus its weight was abnormally light.

Someone had removed the batteries!

I needed to get the hell out of there!

A large figure was coming toward me from behind the bushes. I tried to throw the car into reverse while fumbling for the lock on the door, but it was too late. The person flung my door open.

"Get your hands away from the horn. You let out even so much as a peep, and I'll shoot you dead on the spot."

It was Dave Paxton. He had a gun pointed directly at my head.

Chapter 19

The Song Goes On

"Damn. It's a stick shift," he murmured. "Makes it a little harder to drive and keep a gun on you." He switched the gun to his left hand, which he rested on the steering wheel, and put the car in reverse. "Don't go getting any ideas, Molly. I'm ambidextrous. And a sharp shooter with either hand."

Your mother must be so proud, I thought, clenching my teeth. I had to battle the rage that enveloped me. If there was any chance of my getting out of this mess alive, it would likely require my calmly convincing him that he shouldn't kill me.

I eyed the gun in his hand. Now that he was holding it in his left hand, it was on the opposite side of his body. I had even less chance of grabbing it, if things came down to that.

My vision fell on the glove compartment, and I regretted that I'd already disposed of Jenny's knife. Maybe it was just as well. What good would a knife do me against his gun? An inferior weapon was worse than no weapon.

He struggled for a moment with the gears as he shifted into first and headed toward the main entrance to the Sherwood Forest subdivision. That was a mistake—he'd drive us right past Tommy Newton's house. He mustn't have known Tommy's address, and why would he?

If Tommy was still there, dropping Lauren off, maybe I could catch his eye somehow.

I had a brief but clear view of Tommy and Lauren's house between the trees, just before we reached the intersection with their cul-de-sac. Their garage door was open and their overhead light was on. They must have just pulled in. There was almost no chance that they'd see me, but this could be my only opportunity. He'd never recognize the car, let alone me, from this distance.

Just as we were even with the entrance to their cul-de-sac, I did the only thing I could think of that could signal Tommy—try to jump out. I opened my door and the dome light came on.

Dave grabbed me and hit the brakes. We came to a screeching stop, which was exactly what I'd wanted. I was certain that Tommy would turn and look at my car when he heard the tires squeal. Now if only he would recognize me in the dome light. Dave aimed his gun at me. "Get back in your seat! Shut the door and lock it! Now!"

Not wanting Tommy's signal to be my getting shot, I did as told.

"Damn it!" Dave snarled. "I need to think. I wasn't planning on having to do this, you know. I thought I was in the clear. You couldn't know what it's like, Molly, to love a woman like I loved Corrinne."

I couldn't imagine loving someone so much I needed to murder them. Though he apparently didn't discriminate against murdering those he *didn't* love either; he'd murdered Olivia and now intended to do the same with me.

"She was my life, my inspiration. All those drawings you saw that I did? They were for her, just her. I couldn't work after she dumped me for that . . . kid, Brian Underwood."

"You're a talented artist," I murmured, hoping a couple of compliments might convince him to let me go.

"I was."

"I got the impression that Olivia considered you the best-selling artist of her gallery."

Dave stiffened. "You should never have nosed through my stuff. She'd be alive if it weren't for you."

When had I nosed through his stuff? I'd flipped through his sketches that one time with Olivia. She'd said that the one sketch was from a work that was among the first paintings she'd sold. Only that sketch had been so out of balance visually, something an artist would have corrected in the final work. Suddenly, I knew.

"You killed Olivia because she remembered something incriminating she saw in that one sketch, didn't you? The one of the painting Olivia said she'd sold, where you show Corrinne standing in profile. You knew she remembered the original painting."

He chuckled, but without humor. "Very smart, Molly. I'd painted it with Corrinne aiming a gun. The sketch jarred her memory, about how I'd told her about my collection of guns back when she first accepted the painting for her gallery."

There was no sense in my pointing out to him that Olivia could have just as easily remembered about his gun collection when she witnessed Corrinne's shooting. "She threatened to tell the police?"

"Unless I paid her fifty thousand dollars. I don't have that kind of money, and anyway, it would never have been enough. She'd only have asked for more." He clenched his jaw. "Too bad you're not smart enough to keep your nose out of my business, Molly. I never wanted to do this to you. Didn't I give you enough warnings? The pipe bomb? That stupid clown doll of Nadine's?"

In retrospect, those were pretty clear "warnings," and I wished I'd spent the last week or two in bed. How did he get those porcelain shards? I wondered, then the answer immediately occurred to me. He was likely to have access to Corrinne's dolls and to have taken vengeance by smashing them.

We were at a stoplight. It was too dark outside for me to signal anyone. If I jumped out of the car, he'd stop the car and shoot me. I felt sick to my stomach. That was going to be my last act on this Earth—vomiting.

Dave ran his free hand through his curly hair and shook his head with disgust. "It was a stupid mistake, forgetting about that damned sketch. I should have destroyed it, but I never took any slides of the painting. That sketch was the only thing I had left of Corrinne."

The poor, lonely, homicidal maniac. "You could just drop me someplace and keep going, drive into Canada or someplace. You don't have to . . . keep this up, you know."

He chuckled. "You got part of that right, anyway. And I am really sorry I have to kill you, Molly. You haven't done anything to deserve it. Except being in the wrong place at the wrong time, and getting in my way on stage that night. If only you'd been all the way backstage, like you were supposed to be."

I put my trembling hands on the dash as if afraid of his driving speed—the last of my worries now. *Please, God. Get me out of this!* "If I could change the past, I wouldn't have been on the stage at all, believe me. But, you know, they were never going to hypnotize me. They'd have lost me as a prospective witness."

"Ironic, isn't it? You tried to set up a stupid trap for me, and I fell for it." He laughed. "Too bad for you I acted so quick. And that no one was watching your backside." He grinned, enjoying this immensely. "That's the one good thing in all of this. We've got that idiot Tommy Newton in charge of the police force."

If I somehow lived through this, Tommy would hear no end to how little I appreciated the fact that he'd left me at my driveway instead of making sure I was safely inside my home. This was my doing, though. I'd been foolish and reckless, and my soon-to-be-motherless children were going to suffer for it. Why hadn't I thought this through before I blabbed about hypnosis? I *deserved* to be shot for my stupidity!

"He's not an idiot, Dave. He's right behind us. So there's no point in your killing me. He'll just witness the whole thing."

I was bluffing, of course, but it made him look into the rearview mirror.

"Shit!" Dave cried. "You're right!"

I am? I looked back then, too, and tears of gratitude filled my eyes as I saw that Tommy was indeed directly behind us. Though it was dark, I could tell it was him by his familiar silhouette and that of the telltale lights on top of his squad car.

Dave wedged the barrel of the gun into the gap between the armrest and the driver-side door. "Shit! I've got to lose him!"

With both hands on the steering wheel now, he floored the gas pedal. I slipped my seat belt on and sent up an emphatic prayer.

We nearly tipped over as we squealed around a corner. I pressed back into my seat as hard as I could. "This is a ten-year-old Jeep Cherokee! You're not going to outspeed Tommy's V-8, or whatever his motor's called. We'll both get killed this way!"

"Shut up!"

He kept glancing in the rearview mirror. When Dave accelerated, Tommy had turned on his siren.

This whole area had grown so much lately. We were outside the town limits, probably someplace around Route 146, but Dave had apparently had it in his mind to take me to some remote field and shoot me.

A police car sped around a corner in front of us. "Look out!" I hollered. We swerved. Yet another police car was in front of us, which we quickly caught up with. Tommy must have put out an all-points bulletin for this car.

"Shit!" Dave cried. He had to slow down to get around this first car. A second one was parked diagonally across the road, blocking the pavement entirely.

Dave swerved and hit the brakes, and we skidded toward a tree. I shielded my face with my arms, feeling the car swerve yet again. Luckily, there was only the sound of a minor impact as the side of the car swiped against something relatively small.

We were still moving, being jarred up and down on a rough surface at teeth-breaking speed. I lowered my arms and saw that we were in a field my car would never be able to cross. We were being jostled far too violently in our seats for me to say anything to Dave, not that he would have listened anyway.

The tires began to spin in what must have been the mud of the recently irrigated field. Dave stopped the car and snatched up his gun again. "Take your seat belt off!" he demanded.

I unlatched it, and he threw open his door. He grabbed a fistful of my jacket and said, "Come out my side. Now!" I had time only to get my feet up on the seat before he started dragging me by the fabric of my jacket out of the car, toward him.

I grabbed his arm, trying to wrench myself free, but he was too strong. I fell onto the muddy soil, but with one arm he pulled me to my feet and got a hammerlock around my neck, squeezing my body against his to use as a shield.

A couple of the police cars had followed us into the field. They now pulled to a stop, the high beams of their headlights shining on us.

A third car pulled up then. The driver rolled down the window and spoke into a bullhorn. "This is Sergeant

Newton, Mr. Paxton. Release Mrs. Masters and throw down your weapon immediately."

The other officers, two to a car, had gotten out of their vehicles and trained their guns on us as well.

Dave was completely outnumbered. With my back pressed tightly against his chest, I could feel his panic-striken breathing. I thought I could feel his heart beating as well, but that might have been my own.

His forearm was putting so much force against my neck that I could hardly breathe. With both hands I tried to pry his arm farther away from me, but he was so strong I felt like a rag doll. He continued to back away slowly from the police, dragging me with him.

"Drop your weapon and put your hands up!" Tommy again ordered.

"You can't shoot me through her!" Dave called back, his voice high-pitched and maniacal.

"Can't breathe!" I said, though I wasn't really choking. My only hope was that he would realize my value to him would be lost if he did succeed in strangling me.

He lowered his hold on my neck to my collarbone instead. As he did so, I finally regained my footing and remembered a defensive move from my son's karate classes called "a Superman."

Giving it my best effort, I thrust both arms and my upper body forward with all of my might, suddenly and forcefully bending forward at the waist.

Dave, caught off guard, immediately lost his grip on me. I flopped on my stomach onto the hard earth, my arms absorbing much of the impact.

"Don't shoot!" Dave immediately screamed. "Don't shoot! I give up!" Behind me I heard a soft thud that I assumed was Dave's gun dropping to the ground.

Two police officers came forward, shouting instructions to Dave. Another officer helped me to my feet and got between me and Dave.

Tommy called, "I'll take care of her." He came forward, grabbed my arm at the elbow, and half carried me to his patrol car. He all but stuffed me into the backseat and got into the front seat, slamming his door shut. "Molly, you are personally responsible for every white hair on my head!"

I leaned forward and sank my face into my hands. "I made a bit of a tactical error back at the meeting," I murmured. "I never should have taken such a stupid risk. I don't know what I was thinking. It will never happen again, I swear."

"If only I could believe you."

"I got in over my head, Tommy, and nearly got myself killed. You saved my life. Thank you."

"Shut your door."

I did as ordered, and watched as a pair of officers escorted Dave in handcuffs to another vehicle.

"See if we can get out of here," he said under his breath. He put the car in reverse and backed all the way to the road. As soon as the other patrol cars made it back onto the asphalt, Tommy got on his radio and said that he was "taking the hostage home," and that he'd "get her statement there."

We drove in silence. I was shaking horribly by the time we reached my driveway, where a familiar BMW was parked. Stephanie and Lauren were talking to Jim on the front porch. Lauren and Jim raced toward us. Stephanie remained on the porch, watching.

"Honey, are you all right?" Jim asked as Tommy and I got out of the patrol car. In the lighting from our motion detector, Jim's face looked pale. So did Lauren's. "Stephanie called us to see if you'd gotten home all right. None of us knew where you were!"

Jim pulled me into a hug before I could respond.

"What happened?" Lauren asked, her eyes darting between mine and her husband's.

"I got taken hostage, but I'm fine now," I answered as Jim released me from our embrace. I glanced toward Stephanie, who was still standing on my front porch. She was making a big show out of fidgeting with the fabric of her skirt, as if trying to remove a particularly persnickety piece of lint. "Can I tell you what happened in a minute? I'd like to speak to Stephanie first."

At the mention of her name, Stephanie strode toward us.

Lauren and Jim exchanged glances, then Lauren said, "Tommy? Can we go on inside and have you fill us in?" The three of them went inside the house.

"Well, Molly," Stephanie said with a toss of her head, "as you've gathered, I called your house and Jim said you hadn't gotten home yet. Knowing you and your sense of direction, I figured you'd gotten lost."

"Lost? Between Carlton Central and my house?"

"I put nothing past you." She averted her eyes. "And anyway, I owe you one for helping Jenny. Not that you are all that deserving, after your ridiculous and ill-thought-out matchmaking efforts regarding Tiffany."

"I'm fine, Stephanie, and it's all over. Dave Paxton is under arrest for both murders."

She nodded. "I'm glad to hear that justice has been served. It's about time."

"Would you like to come in? Jim's probably already offering everyone a glass of wine. Can you join us?"

"I can't. I need to get back home to Tiffany. She got a little worried about you when she overheard my phone conversations with your husband and Lauren."

"Stephanie, I really appreciate your driving out here to check up on me. Thank you for caring."

"Please." She gave her head another haughty toss and muttered, "You've pushed your luck far enough for one day, Molly."

She got back into her BMW and backed out of my driveway. Halfway down my cul-de-sac she stopped and honked the horn. I obliged and came toward her. She rolled down her window, gave me a chilly look of appraisal, then said, "You're welcome."

My eyes misting, I smiled at her, but she merely shut her window and drove off.

If you enjoyed *When The Fax Lady Sings*,
try another Molly Masters mystery . . .

THE COLD
HARD FAX

by Leslie O'Kane

Published by Fawcett Books.
Available at your local bookstore.

More mirth and mayhem from
Molly Masters. . .

THE FAX OF LIFE

by Leslie O'Kane

"Molly Masters is a sleuth with an
irrepressible sense of humor and a
deft artist's pen."

—Carolyn Hart

Published by Fawcett Books.
Available at your local bookstore.

Molly Masters returns in

—◆—

THE SCHOOL BOARD MURDERS

by Leslie O'Kane

"O'Kane is certainly on her way to making her Molly Masters series the *I Love Lucy* of amateur sleuths."

—Ft. Lauderdale Sun-Sentinel

Meet Allie Babcock

Dog therapist Allie Babcock
of Boulder, Colorado, is drawn into chilling
cases of murder in . . .

PLAY DEAD

The first Allie Babcock mystery

and

RUFF WAY TO GO

by Leslie O'Kane

Published by Fawcett Books.
Available at your local bookstore.

7/06   7